Suddenly there was a [barcode] *in her dresse* Y0-CDJ-703
Valerie bolted upright, her heart
pounding . . .

Trembling, she got off the bed and slowly approached the dresser. No one but herself appeared in the mirror. She was all alone, except for Gavin, but something was definitely making noise in that dresser drawer. Valerie jerked it open and jumped back.

Her underthings were moving, rising. Valerie blinked and stared hard. Nothing changed, the pile was still growing, something beneath it was pushing it up. Valerie held her breath as a half-slip fell away and unveiled the duchess. She was sitting up, staring at her with her china-blue eyes.

"You didn't think I would give up, did you? After what you did to me?"

A high-pitched squeal escaped Valerie's throat as she backed farther away, eyes round with terror. "I'm not seeing this! I'm not! You're not real!"

The duchess stood up. "I'm real enough to kill you."

"You can't. You can't really move. You're just a doll! If Jade was here she would tell me I'm not seeing any doll standing up in my dresser drawer, talking to me. You're not really there. I'll just relax, lie back down and take a nap. Nothing here can hurt me."

"That's right, Valerie," the duchess said, smiling. "She would tell you that, and you should . . . you should lie back down and take your nap . . . so I can cut open your throat with a razor blade . . ."

What's Wrong with Valerie?

D. A. FOWLER

POCKET BOOKS

New York   London   Toronto   Sydney   Tokyo   Singapore

An *Original* Publication of POCKET BOOKS

POCKET BOOKS, a division of Simon & Schuster Inc.
1230 Avenue of the Americas, New York, NY 10020

ISBN: 0-671-72658-7

First Pocket Books printing August 1991

10 9 8 7 6 5 4 3 2 1

POCKET and colophon are registered trademarks of Simon & Schuster Inc.

Printed in the U.S.A.

This book is dedicated to my cherished grand-mother, Juanita Durham, who is forbidden to read beyond this page.

I would like to thank my agent, Perry Browne, for the much-needed support and encouragement he supplied along the way; and also my editor, John Scognamiglio, for his considerable contribution in the refining of this work and his devotion to making it a success.

I would also like to thank KMD, M.D., for the memories of '79, which inspired the fictional albeit felicitous kitchen scene with Valerie and Doug, by far my personal favorite.

She was dreaming about the strange man living with her, who was paying her twenty dollars a week for a downstairs room with kitchen privileges. It was the end of the first week now, and she still didn't know much about him at all, other than that he was dark and brooding, which she had known from the start. He would have been handsome but for a wide, jagged scar on his left cheek. She wanted to ask him about it, but couldn't get up the nerve. Maybe it was something he was sensitive about. He had a look sometimes that warned if she did ever ask, he would probably tell her it was none of her business. And it wasn't.

She was dreaming that he was standing at the bottom of the staircase, contemplating her bedroom and what it might look like—where she was in it and whether or not she was sleeping. The dream made her uneasy; she didn't know this man or what he might be capable of doing. She should have hired a private detective to check his background. Maybe she would, if the cost was reasonable. The money she had inherited from her grandmother, along with the house, was probably going to have to last a long while, unless she got lucky. But Valerie Scott had never gotten lucky except this once, getting the house and the money. It would probably never happen again. The inheritance hadn't been luck anyway; it had been damn hard work on her part, for almost three years. She'd gotten what she deserved, along with a chance to write, which was something that she had always wanted to do. She was thirty-three; about time she did what she wanted.

He was massaging the curved end of the banister, staring at the worn carpet of the staircase. Maybe he was thinking of raping her. But it would be her word against his, and what would the court think anyway, her renting a room to a total stranger without even asking for references. She should have taken in another woman, but no one else had responded to the ad. No one at all. Only this Gavin Sheffield. For all she knew, the name was an alias. For all she knew, he was one of "America's Most Wanted." Maybe she should watch it next Sunday and find out.

In her dream, she was getting more and more nervous about Gavin standing there in the dark, rubbing the polished oak banister, thinking evil thoughts, as indicated by the look on his face. He was up to no good. He had no business being out of his room, what used to be the dining room, at this hour of the night in the first place. His room had two entrances: one door leading to the kitchen, and double doors opening onto the living room. There was a bathroom off the kitchen, exclusively for his use, and a back screened porch through which he was expected to come and go. So there was no good reason for Gavin to ever be in that part of the house where he was, by the staircase. That area was exclusively hers, along with the living room, the three bedrooms upstairs and the bathroom on the right end of the hallway.

The bathroom off the kitchen had a shower stall large enough for a wheelchair with an open seat, with additional working room for her to wield the long shower hose—a duty no longer performed. The dining room had been converted into her grandmother's room some time ago, after she had broken her hip, making it impossible

2

to get her up and down the stairs. Gavin didn't know she had died on the bed in which he slept.

Valerie got out of bed then, still in the dream, and put on her robe. She was going to go out and lean over the railing, harshly asking Gavin what he was doing, something she would never do in real life. In real life she would very quietly lock the door and then lodge a chair under the doorknob for good measure. She would slip back into bed, the covers clutched up under her chin while part of her wished he would come on up.

She left the robe open. Her blue polyester nightgown was moist with sweat. It clung to her shape, outlining her breasts and caving in at the navel. There was no air-conditioning in the house. They'd made do with fans, but she had turned off the one in her bedroom window because it was only making her feel hotter. Trembling slightly, she opened the door and walked into the dim hallway. She approached the oak railing, curling her fingers around it. Cool, smooth. It was as if she were really touching it, and the carpet was prickly beneath her bare feet.

Drawing in a breath of courage, Valerie leaned over to look down at Gavin. Only she had changed her mind about what she was going to say. She wasn't going to ask what he was doing in her part of the house in the middle of the night. She was simply going to tell him to get back where he belonged and to stay there or she would throw him out. Still, she knew her voice would not be strong. It would lack assertiveness, which might give it all away. Gavin wouldn't go back to his room. He would start up the stairs, slowly, his features erased in shadow, only his intent clear.

Valerie stared at the bottom of the staircase. Gavin wasn't there anymore. Probably he had heard her bedroom door open, and he had quickly vanished through the foyer into the kitchen. Then the sound came, and Valerie felt tingles at the back of her skull. It was a strange, wet sound, like a foot pulling out of a bucket of mud. What was Gavin doing? She closed the robe and tied the belt, walking to the head of the stairs. Again, the same sound, like a release of suction. Strange.

She started down the stairs, becoming submerged in the darker shadows away from the mid-landing window, listening for the sound to be repeated so she could figure out what it was, not quite like anything she had ever heard before. It didn't come again. Standing by the front door, she could see the ghostly shapes of the living room furniture. All of it was much older than she was, and looked it, but new furniture was expensive.

Nothing stirred but the lacy drapes over the picture window. She thought that was odd, since that window couldn't open. So where was the breeze coming from? But in dreams the unexplainable always happened, so Valerie ignored it after a while, turning her attention to the floor, looking for whatever it was that Gavin had apparently stepped in. It would have been easier to inspect the floor with the light on, and if she were really doing this, she would have gone for the light switch next to the front door. But the dream compelled her to stay planted where she was, looking in the dark for some sort of mess.

Perhaps it had been a trick of her imagination, but a few moments later she thought she noticed a glint of something on the mantel. Yes, there up on the mantel, a gleaming pair of yellow eyes. A cat. Damn that Gavin! She'd told him no pets. There was little question now as to what he had stepped in, and now that she thought about it, there did seem to be an odor.

Valerie began moving toward the eyes, and they blinked. The arrogant animal probably thought she was coming to pet it. The eyes grew larger as she got nearer, too fast, actually, to account for the distance she had crossed. And suddenly, though she was still a good five feet from the mantel, there were those yellow eyes right in front of her face. A little lower, actually. But right there, round and large as golf balls. No cat had eyes that big, and anyway, it couldn't possibly be perched on thin air; who would dream a thing like that? Just to make sure, Valerie put out her hand to investigate, and something closed around it—something hot and slimy. She screamed.

A strip of light then appeared through the double

doors of Gavin's room, and one of them opened. There he stood, Gavin Sheffield—if the name was true—in the doorway. "What the hell—"

Valerie was hit by another shock wave, a dose of reality she wasn't prepared for. She was actually standing in the living room, approximately five feet from the fireplace mantel. Her mouth opened but nothing came out. Had she really screamed? She must have, or Gavin wouldn't be asking her, "What the hell?" But the rest, no—the eyes, the thing that had closed around her hand, the billowing curtain—all that had been a dream. Now she could see the floor, and there was nothing on it, and the smell was gone too. She'd been sleepwalking. Strange, she had never done it before, not even as a child. Still, despite her reasoning, her eyes were drawn to her hand, and she half expected it to be wet, with something slimy sticking to it. But there was nothing on it—no sign of wetness. Rubbing her fingertips together, she was even slightly amazed at how dry they were.

Gavin was still waiting for an explanation. "It's nothing, I—oh, never mind, sorry I disturbed you," Valerie said, not looking directly at him. From the corner of her eye she could tell he was clad only in his briefs, so of course she couldn't look directly at him. That would be worse than what he was doing, standing there in front of her like that, so indecent.

Gavin said nothing further, that she could understand anyway, but he did mutter something under his breath as he closed the door.

Valerie had just started her fifth novel, novels one through four lying unfinished in a stack behind her typewriter. Number four had actually swelled to a full seventeen pages before she decided it was no good, but she couldn't bring herself to throw these aborted attempts away. Maybe later she would decide their beginnings were all right after all and get them finished.

The late morning sun streamed in through the front bedroom windows, making the room bright but not cheery; it smelled too much of age, of rotten wood, of death. Her great-uncle Herb had died in this room of a stroke three years ago; it was hard not to remember that. Maybe that was why she wasn't getting anywhere with the writing.

At the time of Great-Uncle Herb's death, Valerie was living in Savannah with Doug Chambers. Their relationship had lasted two long, dreary years. She told him, after receiving the letter from Herb's wife, Vonda, that she was going to move to Huntington, West Virginia, to take care of her grandmother for a while. Vonda was tired, having cared for Herb so many years. She was getting on in years herself and wanted to see a little of the world before she passed on, as she and Herb had planned to do together.

But Vonda didn't want to stick her senile sister-in-law Amanda, Valerie's grandmother, in a nursing home.

Doug had looked up from the book he was reading and asked Valerie, "Why would you want to live in a crummy town like that? I'd go nuts." And Valerie had surprised herself by saying, "I wasn't asking you to come with me." She'd wanted to end it with Doug for a long time, but never could get up the nerve to come out and say so. The relationship was dead, had barely been alive to begin with, and the smell of its decay was getting stronger by the month. He was just something she picked up after, empty beer cans, socks, damp towels, brown-streaked underwear. Sex, when they bothered to have it, was hardly worth staying awake for.

"So," he said. "That's the way you want it."

"That's the way it has to be," she had answered, already feeling the weight lifting from her shoulders. The weight that would replace it would be ten times worse, but she didn't know that yet. All she knew was that Vonda had power of attorney over Amanda's estate and would sign it all over if Valerie would come. But even if Valerie had known what she was in for, it probably wouldn't have made any difference. This was a great excuse for escape. For some reason Valerie always needed a great excuse. Simply wanting her way was never sufficient.

Gavin had left half an hour ago. She'd heard the back porch door slam against its frame, then his battered old Chevy puttering backward along the narrow driveway, passing below the room in which she sat. He worked at the library, he said, putting back the books people had checked out or left on the tables. Valerie hadn't checked with the library people, so she didn't know if that was true or not, but surely he wouldn't lie about anything as easy to check out.

She had leaned over her desk to watch him leave, wondering what else he did besides work at the library. It closed at nine o'clock, and often Gavin didn't get home until after midnight. Perhaps he went to a bar. Or to see his girlfriend, if he had one.

Valerie reread the few pages she had written the day

before and tore them up. It was to have been a humorous story, about a girl who was constantly inviting disaster, but funny disaster. Maybe not funny to her, but what other people would laugh about. It seemed like an utterly stupid idea now.

She rolled in a fresh sheet and stared at the blank page for several minutes, waiting, circuits open. What about a woman who was married for a long time to a guy she really hated, and started to go a little crazy? Maybe she started (for entertainment) to think up ways to kill him, because he refused to give her a divorce. Let me count the ways . . .

And then, when he did die, unexplainably, she became convinced her thoughts had killed him, and since he was in the spirit world now, he knew about her secret lover, so he stayed around to haunt her. So she was no better off, in fact she was much worse off, and there was nothing left to do but kill herself. Only it had all been her imagination, a trick of her guilt, and she found nothing beyond, only darkness and silence, her consciousness winked out like a light. The delight of irony.

Her thoughts started wandering, and she recalled Steve Whitman, at her first high school reunion: "I thought you hated me, Valerie. If only I'd known . . ."

She'd had four gin and tonics, so she could say then what she never could say to Steve before. "Are you kidding? I had a crush on you since the seventh grade." Steve's fat wife had gone to use the ladies' room. Of course she hadn't been fat when Steve married her right out of high school, ex–head cheerleader and prom queen, with the figure of a Barbie doll. Three kids had done her in. And the kids, Steve explained, were the reason he couldn't ask for a divorce. Thinking about it, Valerie shook her head. He'd thought she hated him! "Let's sneak out to the parking lot," he said. "I've got some grass."

"You go first," she said, "so people won't think we're up to something." Steve thought that was funny. She thought it was funny too, right up to the point when Steve ejaculated into her over the trunk of a '73 Thunderbird and said, "Thanks, I needed that. I can hardly stand to touch my wife anymore." The rest of that night was a blur.

Valerie came back to the room that smelled of age and rotting wood and death, and looked at the blank sheet of paper in her typewriter. Only it wasn't blank anymore. It had three words on it. She read them and felt a shiver go up her spine.

they are here

Valerie's eyes, disbelieving, skimmed the message again. She looked at her fingers on the keyboard. Had they typed this? Of course they had—those words hadn't appeared by magic. But she could swear she hadn't moved a muscle. Yet she had, obviously.

they are here

What the hell? Suddenly she had to get out of the room. Out of this house.

Valerie had never been close to her cousin Elisabeth, but she didn't know where else to go. There was no one else to talk to, except for old Mrs. Rothford next door, but at Mrs. Rothford's you didn't talk, you just listened. Couldn't get a word in edgewise. Everything the late Mr. Rothford had ever done or thought about doing, Valerie knew. She also knew every detail of every operation Mrs. Rothford had had. She knew all about the Rothfords' two sons too, and their wives and their children and the fact that none of them ever came to see her anymore.

All Valerie had wanted to do on these occasions was take a walk, or sit on the front porch swing for some air, or trim the rosebushes in the backyard. *Just shut the hell up, Mrs. Rothford,* she would scream at the top of her lungs. *Leave me alone! Can't you see I don't care?*

But actually she only screamed in her mind. The words had no voice, and Mrs. Rothford was almost deaf even with her hearing aid, so she probably wouldn't have heard if Valerie had said it out loud. She would have had to repeat it three times.

Elisabeth was saying, "So how is that roomer working out? Is he nice?"

"I guess so," Valerie said. "I still don't know him very well. Keeps to himself, mostly."

Elisabeth made sort of a face, an expression that meant she thought something other than what she was about to say. "Well, that's nice. I don't suppose you would want him underfoot, with your writing and all."

That was it, Valerie decided. The way Elisabeth mentioned the writing, like it was something Valerie should be ashamed of. Who did she think she was, anyway? Hemingway?

"Actually, it would be nice to have someone to talk to now and then," Valerie said.

Elisabeth's finely sculpted eyebrows arched. What about me? she seemed to be thinking. What do I look like, a stone wall? Valerie knew very well her cousin couldn't really care for her all that much, because she never invited her over.

"Well," Elisabeth finally said, "so what did you come over to talk to me about? I can tell you've got something on your mind." She glanced at her watch. "Davie should be waking up any minute now."

This meant, You'd better quit beating around the bush. Elisabeth was living in the real world. She had laundry to do, a young toddler to feed and bathe, a house to clean, dishes to wash, beds to make, a life to live. They were sitting in Elisabeth's living room, on a couch that bore the stains of three older children and a husband who worked in the coal mine. She undoubtedly thought that caring for Grandmother had been nothing. A free ticket to a house and more money than her husband made in two years.

Valerie tested her voice by clearing her throat. This was going to sound crazy. Nutso. It was going to sound like she was cracking up, and Elisabeth would snort; what did Valerie have to crack up about? She didn't have the worry of four kids, and a husband who any day could die in a collapsed mine.

They are here, Elisabeth.

Who?

I don't know. Whoever told me they were here didn't

say. I was wondering if they came with him, with Gavin. Nothing like this ever happened before he came.

Nothing like what, Valerie? You're not making any sense. Just spit it out.

"I'd better be going," Valerie said. "It was nothing. Just missed you, I guess."

Valerie tore the sheet out of the typewriter, wadded it up into a tight ball and threw it in the trash. Then she sat in Uncle Herb's favorite chair and began gently rocking herself.

They are here.

Grandmother and Herb? Vonda hadn't died here, but she was dead now too. She'd seen a few sights in London, where she took her last breaths, in a hurry to cram all the living she'd never done into a few short years she didn't have. Did "they" mean the three of them? Maybe. Who else? But if so, who had told her they were here? Herself? How did she know? No one else had ever lived in this house, except Amanda's husband Elwood, but he went out long ago, when Valerie's father was just a few months old, for the proverbial loaf of bread, and never returned. Seemed unlikely he would come back, if he was even dead, though no one knew. So Valerie could have a few ghosts in the house. Maybe she was a natural medium or something, some kind of clairvoyant. Or not.

But all right, suppose "they" really were ghosts. Valerie had no problem believing such things did exist; there were too many accounts from very unweird people who had encountered such phenomena. So that shouldn't be too terrible, if in fact they were ghosts Valerie knew. Grandmother had been harmless as a lamb except for her mouth. She too suffered from strokes, a series of small ones, and with them had acquired a sailor's tongue, which got considerably worse after she fell down the stairs and broke her hip. Valerie would never have dreamed Grandmother even knew such words, but out they had come. Endlessly.

So, what did they want? Valerie stopped rocking. This was crazy. Amanda, Herb, and Vonda were dead and gone. Rotting in their graves, nothing more. She had written the message subconsciously. They are here. Maybe she meant herself and Gavin. They were there. Strangers living under the same roof. Perhaps that was bothering her.

A few minutes later she found herself downstairs in the former dining room, where Gavin now lived. The furniture was all hers. He'd only brought his clothes and a few boxes of books. The room was a mess and smelled of stale cigarette smoke. Old oil prints hung on the walls. The prints were of flowers in vases, fruit in bowls, and pictures of dead relatives captured in their youth.

Feeling like a trespasser, Valerie walked over to the far wall and studied the faces in black and white, some blushed with artificial color on the cheeks and lips. Her great-grandparents and Amanda's brothers and sisters, nine of them, posed stiffly in the group photo, their eyes haunted with secrets of the past. Great-Grandfather Willy had died of black lung disease; he'd been a miner too. It suddenly occurred to Valerie that she should have taken these pictures out; why would Gavin care to look at old pictures of people he never knew? These pictures had always been there on the wall, ever since she was a little girl. Maybe she felt she had no right to remove them. But they were her pictures now; she could burn them if she liked. Aunt Sadie, Elisabeth's mother, had gazed over the collection wistfully after Amanda's funeral, but Sadie wasn't shy. If she had wanted them, she would have said so. All Sadie had gotten was her mother's mink stole.

Valerie's dad, Charles, had gotten the locket Amanda had always worn around her neck, encasing a small picture of herself and the grandfather Valerie never knew.

This wall was a shrine. Some of these people had walked these floors, had dinners in this very room, perished with their memories of this house. Valerie started taking them down. What did she care?

They are here.

All of them? No, they had their own houses to haunt, if that was what they wanted to do. No, these people weren't here. Not anymore. Never again.

Gavin came home early that night, shortly after nine. Valerie was in the kitchen fixing a glass of iced tea. The house was oppressively hot and humid, and now that it was safe to go sit on the front porch (Mrs. Rothford went to bed at eight), Valerie was going to drink a glass of iced tea on the swing and try to cool off. She had finished pouring her tea when she heard Gavin's car drive up, but she stayed in the kitchen, stirring the sugar in her tea, waiting.

When he came in, she acted surprised to see him. "Oh, hi. Would you care for some tea? I was just about to take mine out on the front porch. You're welcome to join me."

She expected him to decline, as he had the one other time she'd been bold enough to make a similar offer, but he thought it over for a second and nodded. "That sounds okay."

Valerie poured him a glass and put in some ice cubes, adding no sugar, per Gavin's request, and preceded him through the front door to the porch. She sat on the hard swing, he across from her atop the low, wide cement wall around the porch, which gaped in the center where the steps were formed. Fireflies flickered over the yard, their lime-green fluorescent tails illuminating the darkness briefly, like falling stars.

"It feels halfway decent out here," Valerie commented.

Gavin drank some of his tea and nodded. "Quiet street."

"Mostly old people. They're all tucked in by now."

"So what was that scream about last night?"

Valerie knew she was going to end up telling him. There was no way to stop herself. He was the only one. She had no idea what he would think. Perhaps he would quietly move out during the night. What was this, the Bates Motel?

She told him, even about the message on her typewriter. And then she laughed, as if it had all been a joke. Or that she was worried about beating him to it. But Gavin didn't laugh. He didn't do anything. He just sat there looking at her, a still photo in grays and blacks, his eyes especially dark. Gavin had very dark eyes, even in daylight. For all she knew, they were closed.

"Maybe I need a vacation. Do you suppose?" she asked him, still laughing it off.

He put his glass down next to one of the pillars that supported the eave. "Never know about the imagination, it can play some strange tricks on you, all right. But that's all it was. You were only dreaming, I'm sure, and you already know how that message got there. I mean, you were sitting at the typewriter with your fingers on the keys. If you'd been nowhere near it and that had happened, well, then, that would be another matter. I thought I heard a strange noise myself a few nights ago, in my room. A wet sound, like you described. There must be a slow water leak under the house and it made some mud. Cats like to get under houses. That's probably all it is, a cat or something getting stuck in some mud."

Valerie began nervously rocking the swing. "You really think so? You don't think we're being haunted?"

He shrugged. "Who knows? That what you think?"

Well, at least it wasn't just her, hearing things. But she couldn't forget the feel of that thing, as real as the railing under her hand, the carpet under her feet, which had both turned out to be real experiences. Those big round yellow eyes, glowing in the dark, in midair. Not cat eyes, not human either, for that matter. Couldn't have been Grandmother's or Herb's or any of the people's whose pictures had hung on the dining room wall. So she supposed they had to have been cooked up by her imagination, along with what had happened when she reached out her hand in the living room.

Cats under the house, getting stuck in mud. She would be able to hear that from upstairs? Maybe what Gavin heard wasn't what she had heard.

Gavin picked up his glass again and finished his tea while wiping his forehead with a shirtsleeve. "Well, I don't think it's anything to worry about."

It didn't seem he had much to say to her, as if he wanted to keep distance between them. He hadn't asked anything about her the first day he'd come, only the price of the room. But she had offered some personal information anyway, a little, such as where she was from, how long she'd lived in Huntington, how she'd come by the house, and about her desire to be a writer, expecting him to then give her some information about himself. He worked at the library, that was all she got in return. Not even a reason for why he worked at the library.

"Would you like some more tea?" she asked.

"If you don't mind."

Valerie took his empty glass and went back in the house. It felt ten degrees hotter inside. She wanted to put her hair up, but she was afraid if she took too long, she'd lose him. The pitcher of tea was in the refrigerator. She took it out and began to pour into Gavin's glass. Something black plopped out, a coagulated mass of some sort.

At first she thought it was the tea bag. She put the pitcher down on the counter, then held the glass up to the light to make sure. The thing floating in the amber fluid looked like a tangle of entrails. The glass slipped from her hand, shattering on the floor. Valerie shrieked and ran out of the kitchen.

Gavin met her at the front door. "What happened?"

She couldn't speak, only point toward the kitchen. Gavin left her standing there and went to see.

She'd done it again, spat a mouthful of meat back onto her plate, half chewed. It looked disgusting.

This tastes like shit. You're feeding me shit.

That's not shit, Grandmother, it's the best steak money can buy. Now open your mouth.

Another piece was waiting for her on the end of the fork. Valerie was getting impatient. She was hungry, but couldn't get to her own dinner until Grandmother had been fed.

Come on, open. You're going to eat this.

You sonofabitch, dirty stinking bitch. I want my straw-berries.

The first time her grandmother had called her a bitch, Valerie felt she'd been knocked in the face with a two-by-four. By this time she was used to it. At other times, Amanda would be her sweet old self, calling her "Precious," like when Valerie was a little girl, even smiling. But not very often.

The strawberries are for dessert. You can't have them until you've eaten the rest of your dinner. Now open your mouth or I'll put you to bed hungry.

Then the struggle, forcing Grandmother's jaw open, shoving down the piece of meat. She gagged and threw up, green-black spinach, blood-red beets, yellow bile, all down the front of her flower-print house dress. It looked like she'd thrown up her guts.

"What was it? I don't see anything now, except the broken glass."

Valerie jumped, startled. "You didn't see that . . . that thing on the floor?"

"Thing?"

Valerie clutched her stomach, suddenly feeling sick. "Something was in the tea pitcher. It came out into your glass. It looked horrible."

Gavin stared at her blankly, as if confused.

So she had imagined it, even though she'd even heard it plop into the glass. There was nothing on the kitchen floor but broken glass, tea, and ice cubes. But maybe it crawled away, Valerie thought.

They went back to the kitchen together. The thing was indeed gone. Had it been a mouse? Half drowned, but still able to move, get away, hide? How it could possibly have gotten into the refrigerator or up the slick side of the pitcher was beyond her, but that's what it had been, a mouse, surely. Not her imagination. Her imagination didn't play tricks like that. What the hell was happening in this house?

"Where do you keep your mop and broom?" Gavin asked. "I'll get this cleaned up for you."

"I'll do it," Valerie said with a shake of her head, trying to rid herself of doubts about the mouse theory; that's what she preferred to believe it had been. The mop and broom were kept in the pantry. She stepped through the poinsettia-print curtain to get them, came out a second later and started gathering the scattered shards of glass with the broom. Gavin watched her silently.

"I think it must have been a mouse," she said, not looking at him. "Its tail . . . could have looked like . . . what it looked like."

"Guess that's possible," Gavin agreed, having no idea what she had seen. "Well, I think I'll take a shower now. Excuse me."

Carefully avoiding the broken glass, he entered his private bathroom and closed the door. His expression suddenly grim, he engaged the lock and hoped the sound conveyed a message to Valerie: stay away from me.

Stripped of his clothes, he turned on the shower and stepped under the cool spray, thinking about the bizarre things she had told him out on the front porch. She actually believed her typewriter had clacked out its own message.

Right. Happened all the time, didn't it? In the Twilight Zone?

But that was nothing compared to her description of what had happened in the living room the night before. Christ! Yellow eyes the size of golf balls floating in midair. Something like a hot slimy mouth closing around her hand . . .

Now she was seeing things in the tea. No question about it, the lady was getting squirrelly. He wondered if she was messing around with some heavy-duty chemicals, like LSD or PCP. That would explain things. Or maybe she was just wacko.

As he lathered, he began to consider the wisdom of looking for another place to live. He'd just about have to, if he expected to get any sleep. There was no way to lock the dining room doors, and if Valerie was in fact flying around on angel dust or something, she could damn well be dangerous.

He remembered meeting her for the first time, how the initial contact with her ice-blue eyes had sent a quiet shudder through him. He'd almost decided to look elsewhere for a room, but she'd sounded okay.

Then.

Now she was starting to sound the way she looked, and that was downright scary.

Gavin was standing at the bottom of the staircase again, but this time things were clustered around him, wet, slimy things with big yellow eyes. *They are here.* She needed to get out of bed and put the chair up under the doorknob, but Valerie knew that wouldn't keep them out, not these things. They could go anywhere. Doors and walls were no barriers to them. Except for him, Gavin, their keeper. They were waiting for her, though, to come down, and that she didn't understand. To join them willingly? Never.

We are here. Come to us.

"No," Valerie whispered in her sleep. "No . . ."

4

The library smelled stale. Gavin was in the nonfiction section next to a metal cart piled with books. He saw her and acknowledged her presence with an impersonal nod. Valerie timidly approached him. So he really did work here. "I thought maybe I should check out some books on the supernatural."

Gavin continued with his task of carefully replacing the books on the shelves. Valerie's eyes were drawn to the scar on his face. She hoped he couldn't tell she was looking at it.

He said in a low voice, "Don't guess it would hurt, but I don't really think anything supernatural is going on at your house."

"Where should I look?"

He told her which aisle. After a lengthy scan, Valerie picked out *Ghosts and Other Phenomena* by George L. Goode, *Beyond the Dark Veil* by Arthur Lewis, and *The Tibetan Book of the Dead,* then took her selections to Gavin to see what he thought. He barely glanced at them and shrugged. "Won't know till you read them."

"Do you like to read?" she asked.

"Sometimes."

She wanted to ask what sort of books drew his interest,

but she could tell she was disturbing him. Now was the time to thank him for his help and tell him she'd see him later.

Before she could, however, he said, "Why did you take all those pictures out of my room?"

She laughed. "Why, did you like them?"

"Guess I'd just gotten used to them. That wall looks naked now."

Valerie's gaze briefly swept Gavin's tall, sinuous body, imagining it naked. Imagining both of them naked, writhing on the bed in the dining room. But not alone, not alone . . .

"There's some other pictures in the attic. I'll get a few of them down for you. Or maybe you'd like to pick out your own."

He turned and grabbed another volume off the cart. "I'll have a look, I guess." He was afraid to tip her off that he was planning to move out. If she didn't want him to leave, she might do something really crazy. Maybe he was being overly paranoid, but there was certainly no harm in playing it safe.

"All right, this evening, then." Valerie smiled. "I'll bring them all down. There must be a dozen or so."

"Don't bother," Gavin said. "Be easier for me to go up."

The attic smelled like mothballs, and the air in it was heavy and hot. Oppressive. Gavin wasn't home yet, it was only eight o'clock, and sunlight still filtered through the attic fan. Dim yellow light glowed from a single bulb next to the top of the ladder. On either side objects recessed into shadow. Valerie still didn't know what was up here. Not many of her things, mostly Grandmother's and Herb's and Vonda's clothes and personal effects, mementoes, trinkets. Moth-eaten quilts, dusty still lifes in gilded frames. An antique full-length mirror upheld by a center bar in the brass frame, so you could tilt the mirror back and forth. There was a crack running down the center of the glass. Valerie stared at her disjointed reflection. Two half-people stared back at her, both familiar. Once this mirror had been in Grandmother's upstairs bedroom, before her fall and subsequent transfer to the dining room. She would sit in front of it while Valerie combed her hair.

You're pulling my hair, you bitch. Leave me alone.

But we're having company today. Don't you want to look nice?

I'm eighty years old, doesn't make a goddamn how I look. Stop pulling my hair.

Valerie yanked the comb through the matted yellow-white locks, which came out stuck in the comb's teeth. Of course it matters how you look. I don't want people thinking I don't take care of you.

Wheels whined by on the brick street out front. Not Gavin. Too early yet.

Later that night in the attic he seemed more interested in the small cedar chest than in any of the pictures. "Mind if I look inside?"

Valerie didn't mind; it had been Aunt Vonda's. He opened the lid and pulled out a folded tapestry which was on top, spreading it out to see the picture. "This would look good on that wall," he said, admiring the work with his dark, dark eyes. Valerie looked and blanched. What in Christ's name had Vonda been doing with that? The tapestry was of a man and woman naked, the woman tied to a post.

"I used to ride horses a lot," Gavin said.

Valerie blinked and refocused, now seeing two white horses on a field of green, one reared on its hind legs near a tree. She was either losing her sanity, she thought, or there were outside influences at work she couldn't begin to comprehend.

"I did too, when I was a teenager. The last time I got thrown, though, and got knocked unconscious. It took me about three months to even remember going to the stables. Haven't been on one since."

Gavin refolded the tapestry and put it aside, looking to see what else was in the chest, frowning at what he saw. "Dolls. Guess I can do without those."

They were Vonda's beloved antique dolls, which she used to have displayed on a shelf in her room. Valerie had never been allowed to play with them. "Well, we ready to go back downstairs?"

"Suppose so," Gavin said, picking up the tapestry. Valerie hoped he would stay with her and talk for a while, but after they got downstairs, he went on to his room without saying another word.

Elisabeth put the last child to bed and joined her husband in the living room. "Forgot to tell you, Valerie came to see me yesterday. Didn't say what she wanted, but she sure was acting strange. Or should I say stranger than usual."

Jonathan grunted, keeping his eyes glued to the nightly news broadcast.

"She's probably feeling guilty about not having put Grandma Mandy in the hospital, like she should have," Elisabeth continued, knowing that was all the response he would give. "Should have known how sick she was. The doctors had expected her to live another five years at least, unless she had a massive stroke, which she didn't. I talked to the funeral director. He said Grandma's body was covered with bed sores. I think we should have contested the will."

Down the hall she heard one of the kids crying. It sounded like Tamara.

"Better go see what's the matter," Jonathan said.

As if she needed to be told, Elisabeth thought angrily as she rose from the couch. "I still think we should have contested that will," she repeated, and went to check on her seven-year-old daughter.

Elisabeth was dismayed to find Tamara had wet the bed. "Tamara, how could you do this? Couldn't you get down and go to the bathroom? Damn, look at this. I'll have to change your whole bed. Get down."

Tamara was still crying. Her body trembled, eyes glued to the closet doors.

"What is it?" Elisabeth asked impatiently. This was her time to relax, and now she had to change the linens on the top bunk, then wash the soiled ones before the stains set in. "Let's move it, I want to get this over with."

"I saw eyes looking at me," the girl said in a loud,

quivering voice. "In the closet." The closet doors were closed. Tamara's younger sister, Jennifer, asleep on the lower bunk, stirred slightly and murmured something unintelligible.

"Lower your voice," Elisabeth hissed, "before you wake Jennifer. Now look, Tamara, the doors are shut, and there's nothing in front of them. You were only dreaming. Are you sick? Let me feel your forehead."

Tamara leaned over the railing, sniffling, so her mother could check for fever. Elisabeth decided she was a little warm, but not warm enough to excuse what she'd done, or to qualify for any pity. "You're not that sick, now get down from there so I can change your sheets and pad. Go put on some clean pajamas."

"But I saw it," Tamara insisted as Elisabeth dragged her forcibly over the railing. "It opened the door, and I saw its eyes, looking at me. Big yellow eyes."

Elisabeth jerked the sheets and pad off the upper mattress. "You do this again and you're going to get a spanking." She paused to study the closet doors again, and this time realized what Tamara had seen, what she thought had been big yellow eyes. Elisabeth stalked over and pointed them out. "See these knobs, Tamara, that you pull the closet doors open with? There's your eyes for you. A car passing by probably shined on them for a few seconds."

"Are you sure?"

Elisabeth sighed. "Damn it, Tamara, I'm running out of patience with you. Get out of those wet pajamas right now. No more of this monster business."

Valerie couldn't find the books she had checked out at the library anywhere. She was certain she'd left them on the coffee table in the living room. Had Gavin borrowed them without asking? That was the only explanation. She went to the double doors and knocked. There was no answer. Surely he wasn't asleep already? It had only been fifteen minutes or so since he'd followed her out of the attic. Valerie wondered if he'd had any dinner. It didn't seem he would have had time to grab anything between the time the library closed and when he'd gotten home.

He kept no food in the kitchen, though she had cleared a shelf in the refrigerator for him, and one of the kitchen cabinets. She thought of offering him some leftover meat loaf, then changed her mind. If she started that, he might expect to be fed all the time. He'd turn into Doug, who more often than not was out of a job and into her pocketbook, her paycheck, her tips. No more of that.

Valerie knocked again, a little louder. Still no answer from him.

Grandmother, are you awake?

Who are you? I don't know you. Get out of my house.

It's me, Grandmother, Valerie. I thought maybe you would like me to read to you awhile.

Read what?

This novel about the Old West. You like Westerns, don't you? I remember you used to watch Gunsmoke.

You bitch, how would you know what I like? I don't know you. Get out of my house. Where's Vonda? Did she go to the store with Herb?

The door suddenly opened. Gavin was standing there with a shirt wrapped around his waist. "It's hot," he explained, as if she might not have noticed. Then, when she didn't speak, "You need something?"

"The—the books," Valerie stammered, looking over his shoulder at the tapestry hanging on the wall. A big improvement over the black and white photographs of dead people. No more spies. You could do anything in this room and no one would know. No one would see. "You know, the ones I checked out of the library. I'm sure I left them on the coffee table out here, but now I can't find them anywhere. I thought maybe you borrowed them?"

Gavin shook his head. "I didn't touch them. Didn't see them either. Have you checked your car? Maybe you left them in the front seat."

Valerie knew good and well she'd carried them in, but she nodded anyway. "Maybe so. All right, well, sorry I disturbed you." He kept standing there with the door open, staring at her.

"The tapestry looks nice there. I like it."

"Anything else?" he asked.

25

Yes, everything. "No, I guess not. Good night."

" 'Night," Gavin mumbled, and closed the door. He plopped down on the edge of his bed and took a Marlboro from the pack on the nightstand.

Were books disappearing now? What next? He didn't want to stick around long enough to find out.

He lit the cigarette and inhaled deeply. He'd looked at a couple of other places during his lunch break, but neither had been suitable to his needs. He had to find something soon, though. Valerie Scott was giving him a chronic case of the jeebs.

Valerie went upstairs to take a cool bath. The books were gone, somehow. Maybe the house had eaten them, and she would probably end up having to pay for them. Unless Gavin had lied about taking them, planning to turn them back in to the library so she wouldn't read them for some reason.

The tepid bathwater felt good. She'd put in foamy bubble bath, quite a lot of it, which had belonged to Grandmother. Valerie didn't particularly care for the scent, but there was no use in letting it go to waste. This was how she pampered herself, soaking in the big claw-foot tub with the water up to her neck, her head rested against the curved porcelain opposite the spigot, with a scented candle burning on the back of the toilet for light. Most relaxing. The strange things that had been happening lately seemed unreal now, like scenes from long-ago dreams. Ghosts, yellow eyes glowing in the dark, big yellow eyes with a mouth below it, entrails in the tea. *We are here. We wait for you at the bottom of the stairs. Come down, Valerie. Come down.*

A gust of hot wind blew in through the open bathroom window and the candle went out. Valerie tensed in the darkness, her eyes wide, pulse racing. Only the wind. Nothing to panic about. She was still alone, the door was shut and locked. But something was breathing, she could barely hear the sound, between the sink and the toilet, in the corner, breathing. Watching her. The shadows seemed to deepen. Valerie covered what she could of herself with the washcloth, afraid to get out. If she did, it

26

might touch her, maybe envelop her completely in hot slime. Then she heard the voice, like a strangled whisper, barely audible, coming from the same corner.

Kill him, Valerie. Before it's too late. Kill him before they kill you.

"Uncle Herb?"

Kill him.

"Is that you?"

Silence. Another gust of wind, surprisingly cold, blew in.

5

The next morning, after breakfast, Valerie sat at the typewriter thinking she ought to go to the library, just to check. If the books were back there, then she would know for sure Gavin was a liar, and so what else might he be? What were *they*? He didn't want her to know.

Her mind refused to work on a story. It was too busy worrying about what was going on with Gavin. Valerie switched off the typewriter and turned toward Uncle Herb's favorite chair, with its sagging seat and tattered arms. It was a comforting sight. Uncle Herb had always been nice to her.

"Was that you in the bathroom last night, Uncle Herb? You that gave me the message on my typewriter? Are there really things in this house that want to kill me?"

The chair was empty, and here she was asking it if things were in the house planning to kill her.

Who were you talking to, Grandmother?

There was no one else in the dining room.

It's Elvis, what, are you blind? He came to offer me fifty thousand dollars for my Elvis records. Give them to him.

Grandmother, Elvis is dead.

You stupid bitch, he's standing right there, can't you

28

see? Give him the records. I want my fifty thousand dollars.

All right, Elvis, come on. They're in the living room.

The doorbell rang. Valerie was still staring at Uncle Herb's empty chair. Who on earth could that be? She went downstairs and peeked through the gathered lace curtains covering the window in the door. It was a young man inappropriately dressed for the weather, if not the decade; he wore a heavy tweed jacket over a linen shirt, dark baggy pants, black lace-up shoes. A salesman, probably, only he wasn't carrying anything. His face looked vaguely familiar. Valerie opened the door. "Yes?"

"I was wondering if you could spare a glass of water, ma'am. I'm terribly thirsty."

Valerie felt imposed upon; why should he come to her house for a glass of water? And why should she give him one? But she couldn't say no. "All right," she said stiffly, aware of the chance she was taking. He could be an escapee from a mental institution, a madman. She stepped aside and he walked past her.

"Wait here. I'll go get it."

She ran water from the tap in the kitchen, not bothering to put ice in it. He hadn't asked for cold water anyway, just water. When she went back out, he was gone. "Hello?"

Where the devil had he gone? Had he hidden himself somewhere in her house, or had he left, deciding he wasn't so thirsty after all? Valerie stepped out on the porch and looked both ways up the street, seeing no sign of him. Mrs. Rothford was sitting in her porch swing, fanning herself. She looked over and waved at Valerie.

"Good morning, hot though, isn't it? Care to come over and sit? Made some oatmeal cookies early this morning, my mother's recipe."

"Did you see that man leave?" Valerie shouted.

"What's that, dearie?"

Valerie repeated the question louder.

This time Mrs. Rothford called back, "What man was that?"

It was ridiculous trying to communicate with Mrs.

Rothford from this distance, but Valerie had no wish to go over and explain; she would be trapped until the cookies were gone. Mrs. Rothford obviously hadn't seen him, anyway. That man was in her house, somewhere. "Never mind," she bellowed Mrs. Rothford's way, and ducked back through the doorway before the old woman could protest.

He wasn't in Gavin's room, or the shower, or the pantry or the back porch, so he must have gone upstairs. This made Valerie furious, at herself mostly, for letting him in in the first place. She should have made him wait outside the front door, with the screen locked. Maybe she should call the police. But what if he'd slipped away after all? Then they might be angry at her for wasting their time. The stranger was a small, slightly built man, even skinny, pale and weak-looking—someone she should be able to handle by herself. Leaving his glass of water on the telephone table, Valerie started up the stairs.

I saw the way you were looking at Dennis. You want him, don't you? Admit it.

Don't be ridiculous, Doug, I think he's a creep. I can't stand him.

Well, you were looking at him like you could stand him, all right. You licked your lips about every two minutes.

For God's sake, they're chapped. And that was totally subconscious. I don't even remember doing it.

Pucker your lips, Grandmother, so I can get your lipstick on.

You trying to make me look like a common street-walker? A whore like you, you little bitch? I want to see my lawyer. I'm going to cut you off, you worthless tramp.

He wasn't in the three upstairs bedrooms or their closets, or under the beds. He wasn't hiding in her bathroom, or behind her desk or Uncle Herb's chair. That only left the attic. But the hinges creaked loudly whenever the ladder was pulled down. Surely she would have heard, even from the front porch. Still, she wouldn't be satisfied until she had checked.

How stupid of her to be doing this without a weapon of some sort—to protect herself with should he jump out from a dark corner and grab her. If indeed he was hiding in the attic, something was definitely wrong with him, she thought as she climbed the ladder, creak, creak. At the top she pulled the chain for the light, but nothing happened.

The hell with it, she decided. He'd gone away, probably through Gavin's room and out the back, knowing the paces through which she'd be put, the time she would waste wondering. And she had work to do, a story to write. Grandmother's money wouldn't last forever, and she didn't want to go back to waitressing. The supplement from Gavin only half covered her car payment, due for another twenty-two months. Then there were the property taxes, utility bills, groceries, the lawn that had to be mowed—but not by her, not in this heat. She didn't own a lawn mower anyway.

Valerie returned to her typewriter and rolled in a clean sheet of paper. She began her new story:

The woman heard voices whispering in the dead of night, "We are here." Wet voices, lips oozing slime. "Give us your flesh to eat." The woman shivered though the room was hot.

Never, never.

The school nurse had called, asking Elisabeth to pick up Tamara from school; she was running a fever of 102 and she'd thrown up her lunch. Elisabeth sighed; it was always something. She hoped it didn't get any worse, requiring a trip to the doctor, forty dollars down the drain by the time the prescription was filled. And today it was her house for the weekly afternoon Scrabble games she played with her friends from the block, Amy, Vicky, and Lynn. They were coming over at one—Amy with her three-year-old and Lynn with her infant daughter, Lisa. With Tamara sick, Elisabeth thought it might be best to beg off. But she didn't want to miss out; the Scrabble games were the highlight of her week. She packed Davie into the car seat and went to get her daughter from the neighborhood grade school.

"I threw up my lunch," Tamara announced on the way back home.

"So I heard," Elisabeth sighed. "As soon as we get home, into bed you go."

"Can't I lay down on the couch and watch TV?"

"No, because the girls are coming over for Scrabble. Jeremy and Lisa will be there, and I don't want you getting them sick."

"But what if I see the eyes again?"

Elisabeth gritted her teeth. "You won't, it's daytime. You can see it's only the knobs. You'll be just fine."

"Do you like cousin Valerie?"

"Why do you ask?" Though Elisabeth knew, Tamara must have heard what she said to Jonathan in the living room last night. She stole a glance at her daughter. Tamara's cheeks were flushed, her eyes a little glazed.

In answer to her mother's question, she just shrugged. "I dunno, I just wondered."

"Of course I like her," Elisabeth lied. "She's my cousin."

Tamara fiddled with the zipper of her backpack, back and forth, back and forth. The sound was getting on Elisabeth's nerves. "Stop doing that, you're driving me crazy."

"I had a dream about her last night," Tamara mumbled, pulling the zipper closed one last time. "I dreamed something bad happened to her, but I can't remember what."

Good, Elisabeth thought. Would serve her right, as long as it was bad.

"I think I'm going to throw up again," Tamara said weakly.

Elisabeth uttered a mild curse under her breath and pulled the station wagon off the road.

There had been a few times in the past that Tamara had displayed what Elisabeth could only describe as psychic revelations. The morning Uncle Herb died, she came shuffling into their bedroom, still clad in her pajamas, and told them Unkie was in a box and couldn't breathe. A week before the stair accident a year ago, Tamara asked why Grandma Mandy stayed in bed all the time. The first time she was only four, she asked why Nathan Simms, the little boy next door, had metal legs.

Two days later he was diagnosed as having muscular dystrophy.

Now she'd dreamed "something bad" had happened to cousin Valerie. Another premonition? Or just a dream? Elisabeth frankly hoped it wasn't the latter.

"So is that guy still living over there?" Lynn asked, adding AST under the P in *perfect* to make *past,* the T landing on a double-score square. She clucked with satisfaction; they were not professionals.

Elisabeth had convinced her friends of her oldest daughter's powers, and now having told them about Tamara's dream the night before, Lynn was apparently trying to guess from what source the calamity might come. The man living with Valerie was a good possibility, Elisabeth supposed.

"Maybe you should warn her," Amy added, frowning at her letter tray. "He might be dangerous, maybe a psychopathic killer. A grown man renting a room like that, he's got to be some kind of loser."

"Maybe fate can't be tampered with," Vicky Street said, using Lynn's T to spell *tusk.*

"I suppose I should at least mention it," Elisabeth muttered, knowing she wouldn't.

By two o'clock Valerie was surrounded by crumpled paper. She felt lobotomized. She wasn't making any progress. It took five minutes to write a single sentence, and it came out wrong anyway.

"We are here."

"So what?" the woman asked, tossing back her raven hair and laughing. "So am I."

They were doing this to her, Valerie finally decided. They didn't want her to write about them. If she wrote about them, she'd be exposing them. She went downstairs to eat a late lunch, and while she ate at the tiny kitchen table, metal with folding sides, which were down, the top covered with a red-and-white-checked plastic tablecloth, she tried to think how she might get rid of them. Uncle Herb said that killing Gavin would do it.

So then, she would just have to kill Gavin.

You're not my grandmother anymore. I ought to get rid of you. Stick you in a nursing home and forget about you. How would you like that? They'd give you sedatives. That might keep your hateful mouth shut.

Don't send me to a nursing home, please . . .

Won't help to be nice to me now, after calling me a bitch all this time. I'm going to put you in a nursing home, a dirty one, that hires women convicts as nurses' aides. What do you think an ex-convict will do if you call her a bitch? She'll slap your horrible old face, that's what. Slap it hard. I ought to slap you myself, I've had about enough of you.

Poison. That would be quiet, wouldn't be messy. Cyanide. She had some under the kitchen sink, as a matter of fact, that she'd bought for the mice.

Valerie finished her lettuce and tomato sandwich and smiled.

Gavin didn't get home that night until almost one. Valerie was in the living room. She'd just fallen asleep on the sofa. When she heard Gavin come in through the kitchen door, she bolted upright and looked at her watch. It would look suspicious, wouldn't it, to offer him some tapioca pudding at this hour? So tonight they would have another chance at her. Maybe they wouldn't stay downstairs this time, if they knew what she was planning to do. They were getting hungry.

She laughed softly. Wasn't this crazy? She was fighting things, invisible things that wanted to eat her flesh. She was sure that's what they were after. If she told that to Elisabeth, her cousin would have her committed. Only it was true. Gavin knew it too. That's why he'd taken her books and hidden them, telling her the noise she heard was cats in mud under the house, nothing to worry about. Oh, sure. He was part of it. He was their apostate. He led them to their victims. One rooming house after another.

Gavin was in his room now, probably getting undressed. Valerie turned out the light and hurried upstairs as silently as she could. In her bedroom she locked the door and put the chair against the door, then pushed the heavy dresser up against the chair. By the time she was finished, sweat was pouring down her face and her blouse was soaked. Too damn hot. She turned toward the window to turn on the fan. She was going to strip and stand in front of it naked, but there he was, bigger than life, perched on the vanity that once belonged to Vonda. Valerie barely stifled a scream. "What the hell are you doing here?"

"I'm still waiting for my glass of water." He smiled. "I'm still thirsty."

So he'd been in the attic after all. Did something to the bulb so it wouldn't work. Valerie wanted to run, but she had no strength left to move the dresser again. She was trapped, unless she wanted to dive out the window, in which case she'd probably break her neck below. All she could do was wait and see what he planned to do.

"Actually," he admitted after a long pause, moving away from the vanity to stand before the window, "I didn't come for a glass of water. I came to warn you, you've got this all wrong. I'm your great-great-uncle Armand. Don't you remember me from the pictures?"

And that's my uncle Armand, Precious, who died in World War One. Wasn't very handsome, but such a kind man, always gave me presents, told me I was his favorite niece. Everyone said he was odd, I heard them talking about him once at Thanksgiving. But I thought he was nice, very nice.

He looks nice, Granny.

Well, Precious, shall we go to the park? I'll swing you, way up high.

"What do you mean, I've got it all wrong?" Valerie asked, suspicious. If the man before her was really the ghost of her great-great-uncle Armand, he should be transparent, not solid-looking as a rock. He looked no different than Gavin or anyone else on the street, except for his clothes. This was some sort of trick.

"I mean," the pale man said, moving toward her now, "that I know what you're planning to do, and it's wrong. You're just crazy, can't you see that? Been getting that way for a long time. I went crazy too. I didn't die in World War One. That's just what they told people to save the family's pride. I died in an insane asylum."

Valerie was pressed against the dresser, trembling. "Did Gavin put you up to this? Are you a friend of Gavin's?"

"That fellow you're planning to kill?"

How did he know? Had he seen her put the cyanide in the tapioca? Perhaps he had been shadowing her all day. Yes, of course. He didn't go upstairs, or into the attic; he could have been cornered up there. Downstairs you could go around and around forever, through the kitchen, into Gavin's room, out to the living room, across the foyer, down the hall and back to the kitchen again. So he had seen. "Are you going to tell him?"

Valerie stared, unable to believe what she was seeing. The room was empty now. He had somehow vanished. Could he have possibly slipped out the window without her noticing? Sweat trickled between her breasts. She heard the ticking of the windup clock on the dresser and nothing more but her own ragged breathing. Hallucination. That was all. She'd just had an hallucination, because her subconscious had continued to gnaw on the fact she'd never found him, so he still had to be somewhere in the house, right? No, that wasn't quite it. They were trying to use her mind now, using hallucinations against her, visions of a great-great-uncle, thinking she would trust him. What he'd said, about her being crazy, that it was wrong to kill Gavin, that had been their words. But Uncle Herb had already told her the truth. She had to kill Gavin before it was too late.

At three-thirty A.M. she heard them coming up the staircase. Valerie sat up, her eyes open wide, heart thrashing in her chest. This was no dream. She pinched herself to make sure, and it hurt. So she was definitely not asleep. And they were definitely coming up the stairs, with Gavin leading the way. By the sound, the creatures' bodies squished along the walls, taking the steps as if they were mud puddles. Only Gavin moved silently, his hand sliding along the banister. Now they were on the first landing, only five more steps to the second floor. They could see her bedroom door. They couldn't see through it, but they could smell her through it, smell her living flesh, her fear, and they hungered. Valerie wondered if they would eat all of her, even the bones, not leaving so much as a strand of hair. It would appear she had simply vanished from the face of the earth. Gavin wouldn't be accused of anything; there would be no evidence. He would quietly move on, looking in the newspaper for another room to rent. Those ads almost always led to lonely women—women who wanted things done to them they would never admit, even to themselves. Gavin's appearance suggested dark pleasures. They would let him in, and the creatures would come with him.

There was a light knock on the door. Valerie held her breath, blood pounding in her ears. From the hallway she could hear slurping sounds, lips smacking, drool oozing from toothless mouths. They didn't have teeth, didn't need them. Their saliva worked like an acid, like a housefly's. Their victims melted in their mouths like Jell-o, bones and all.

The knock came again, a little louder, then Gavin's voice whispered through the wood, "Valerie, are you awake?"

Of course she wouldn't answer him, nor would she move a muscle. If she responded to him at all, she would be in his power. The lamp next to her bed was on. She could see the room clearly, her own reflection in the dresser which kept the chair in place. As long as she kept Gavin out, she would be safe.

But suddenly there was someone else in the mirror with her. It was Great-Aunt Vonda with her dyed brown beehive hairdo, pruney lips smeared with deep red lipstick, dots of pink blush on her wrinkled, sagging cheeks. Valerie knew if she took her eyes off the mirror and looked beside her, the space would be empty and when she turned back to the mirror the image would be gone. So she kept staring at it, and Vonda smiled. "There's a young man here to see you, Valerie. Aren't you going to invite him in?"

"No," Valerie hissed, aware at once that this was another trick, determined not to fall for it.

"You're not being polite, Valerie. When someone comes to see you, you should let them in."

Then suddenly Herb was on the other side of Valerie in the mirror, scowling. "Don't listen to her. She doesn't know what she's talking about. Never did. You have to kill him, Valerie, that's the only way. And don't fall asleep tonight."

"Stop talking nonsense," Vonda snapped. "You never said a word that made sense after your stroke. You thought we were still in World War Two."

"Valerie, it's Gavin. Can I come in?"

Valerie jumped. Herb and Vonda had disappeared, only her face remained in the mirror. She shivered though the room was hot. Her skin looked blotched with dark circles under her eyes, her mouth hanging slack, black hair limp, strands clinging to her hollow cheeks. She could smell them, their fetid breath, or maybe it was the slime oozing through the cracks around the door, tinged with yellow, like snot. "Go away," she croaked.

"Valerie? Did you say something? Speak up, I can't hear you."

"Go away!" she screamed.

On the other side of the door Gavin cringed. Christ, did she have to scream at him? Did she think he'd come up to rape her or something? Sex was the furthest thing from his mind. Teri had taken care of that earlier with her usual proficiency.

Teri had also turned him on to some rather exotic weed, and he now had a bad case of the munchies, with nothing to munch. All he'd wanted to ask Valerie was if she'd mind if he borrowed a snack.

As he trudged back down the staircase, he decided to go ahead and help himself to whatever he could find. If she got mad about it, so what? He was moving out anyway. His new room would be ready tomorrow, and it was scarcely a block from the library. He'd save a lot of money on gas.

He stepped through the kitchen drape rubbing his stomach. Maybe Valerie had some ice cream.

6

It was morning and the alarm clock was jangling. Valerie had gone to sleep only an hour before. She'd set the alarm for seven o'clock so she would be sure to catch Gavin before he left for work. So she could offer him the tapioca pudding for breakfast. She couldn't go through another night like last night.

· The alarm finally expired, leaving her in peace. It was tempting to go back to sleep. She had lain awake the whole night, listening, after she heard Gavin go back downstairs, the hungry mob following, angry, pieces of them sticking to the carpet and walls. But she'd feared they might return.

This was madness. Maybe if she just got out of the house for a while, all this would stop. She'd been a prisoner here for three years because of Grandmother, but now she could go anywhere she liked, stay out as long as she wanted. She ought to go to the mall and buy some new clothes. It had been a long time since she'd bought new clothes. Maybe Elisabeth would care to go with her. They could really get to know each other, get close like cousins should. It would be nice to have another woman to talk to, nice to have a real friend.

God, I'd give anything for someone else to talk to. All you do is cuss. But after you're put away in that awful nursing home, I'm going to throw parties. We'll have orgies in your old room. Won't that be nice?

Get out of my house. I want to see my lawyer. You're not my real granddaughter! Your mother was a whore, tricked my son into thinking you were his because he was the better catch. Where's Vonda? Tell Vonda to get my lawyer on the phone. I'm going to tell him a thing or two about you.

Valerie got out of bed and put on her robe, then pushed the dresser back to its place against the wall. After putting the chair back under the vanity table, she went downstairs to call Elisabeth.

The phone rang and rang but no one answered. Valerie let it continue to ring. She had to talk to someone . . . anyone. She needed to hear a voice. Finally, after twenty rings, the phone was picked up.

"Elisabeth? This is Valerie. I was wondering if you'd like to go shopping with me today. We could have lunch at the mall."

The voice on the other end was curt. "I can't. Tamara's got a stomach virus. Maybe some other time." Hesitation. "Is everything all right?"

"Sure, fine. Well, I'm sorry Tamara isn't feeling well."

"How's the book coming?"

Valerie sighed. "I'm afraid I've got a bad case of writer's block. Thought getting out of the house for a while would help. I'll go alone, I guess."

"How's Gavin?"

"Oh, okay. Don't see much of him. Well, I'm sure you have things to do. Talk to you later."

"Sorry I couldn't go."

"No problem."

Valerie put the phone down and looked at the heavy dark blue drape covering the kitchen doorway. She could picture the refrigerator and the dish of tapioca pudding sitting alone on Gavin's shelf. She'd better throw it out. A shopping trip, some new clothes, some fresh air and sunshine was all it would take. Then these horrible things would stop happening. She had become too detached from the outside world. Things like this happened to people when they lost contact.

She was still wearing her nightgown and robe. What would Gavin think if he came into the kitchen while she was putting the tapioca down the garbage disposal? But it would take too long to get dressed; he could wake up any minute now. Overlapping the robe to completely cover the gown, and tightening the belt until it was uncomfortable, she stepped through the drape. A vague stench like putrid garbage ripened by heat assaulted her nostrils. Time to take it out, but not in her robe. The neighbors might think it was improper. All she had to do now was dump the pudding, then afterward she would go back upstairs and get dressed. The garbage could wait. After she took it out, maybe she would cook up a big breakfast of bacon and eggs and ask Gavin to join her. Just this once.

She opened the refrigerator door and gasped. The pudding was gone. After coming back downstairs, Gavin must have been looking for something to eat, to pilfer from her, and had taken it.

Valerie closed the refrigerator door and took a deep breath. She never imagined he would look in there, since he never brought groceries home. But he had looked, and he'd felt free to take the pudding because it had been sitting alone on his shelf, like a gift. He must have eaten it. So he must be dead, in the dining room. She didn't want to look, but she knew she had to.

She realized something else. How much better she felt this morning, even with so little sleep. She felt clearheaded. Normal. She had planned to dump the pudding out, hadn't she? Yes. And go shopping, have a good time. That meant the creatures were gone, because Gavin was dead. They weren't messing with her mind anymore.

With a sigh of immense relief, Valerie headed for Gavin's bedroom.

Gavin was sprawled out on the floor next to the bed, his eyes wide open in horror, features twisted in a grimace of pain. His dark skin had a bluish cast to it. Gavin's got the blues, Valerie noted. Permanently.

Dried pearly vomit covered the bedsheets. That's what she'd smelled, besides what Gavin had done in his briefs after he'd lost all muscle control. He was dead all right, dead as a doornail. One thing for sure, she couldn't call the police. They'd arrest her for murder as soon as the autopsy was done. She had to get rid of the body.

How would you like it if I put you up in the attic, Grandmother? With all the spiders and mice, they'd crawl all over you, and I'd leave it dark, so you couldn't see them. Call me a bitch and whore all you like. Maybe I'll just let you rot up there.

Of course, the attic. She wouldn't have to mess with digging a grave in some creepy woods.

"Come on, Gavin," Valerie muttered, tugging on a stiffened arm. "I'm moving you up to the penthouse suite."

It was a good thing Gavin wasn't a big man, or she would never have gotten him up the ladder. She tied a rope around his neck, looped her end around one of the support beams in the attic, and slowly hoisted him up. She'd hosed him off first, in the shower downstairs, and he was still nude. His clothes and other belongings she could hide up here with him. Tonight she would drive his car to Charleston and take a bus back.

Finally she had him laid out behind the cedar chest. She'd tried to close his eyes, but they wouldn't stay shut. Didn't matter, they saw nothing. They couldn't see her looking at him, at the dark scar on his face or his shriveled-up penis. Might have been an interesting experience, she thought, if things had been different.

The hot air up here was good. He wouldn't smell for long, and he'd soon dry up, like a husk of corn. People might come around, asking questions, but what did she know? He had hardly ever said a word to her. You never knew about those silent types. He tried to get in her bedroom the last night he was there, she thought to rape her. What else? Fearing for her safety, she'd told him to get out. Now did they mind dropping the subject? She had work to do.

* * *

Elisabeth checked Tamara's temperature; it was 103 now. She hadn't been able to keep anything down; it all came out one end or the other, like a freight train. Elisabeth poured some more water into the Donald Duck cup and ordered her daughter to sit up and drink. She couldn't have her getting dehydrated. A hospital bill was the last thing they needed.

Tamara forced the liquid down her throat after chewing two more baby aspirin. One minute she was burning up, the next she was freezing. She felt dizzy, as if she'd spent too much time on the carousel at the school playground, exactly like that. She kept thinking of her second cousin Valerie, trying to remember what it was that had happened to her in the dream, but it remained just outside of her mind's reach. Maybe it was too terrible to remember.

"Can I call cousin Valerie?"

"What for?" Elisabeth snapped, taking the cup and refilling it. She wasn't taking any chances; two cupfuls an hour, minimum. "You're too sick to talk to anybody."

"But I need to tell her something."

"You tell me, and I'll pass on the message. You're not getting out of bed unless you have to go to the bathroom." She'd put Tamara in the lower bunk for convenience; any more accidents and Elisabeth would hit the ceiling. "So what is it? What do you have to tell her?"

Tamara shivered violently. "I think I'm going to be sick again, Mama."

Elisabeth let out an aggravated sigh and held up the plastic bucket. Tamara took it and held her face over it.

When she spoke, her voice had a slight echo effect. "Just tell her—" Tamara didn't get to finish. The water came up with yellow mucus.

Elisabeth called the family physician and explained Tamara's symptoms to his nurse, Wanda.

"There's a lot of that going around," Wanda told her. "It's a nasty virus. Just let it run its course. Give Tamara Kaopectate and that electrolyte formula for babies. Fortunately it only lasts about forty-eight hours, so by tomorrow morning there should be an improvement."

The Kaopectate Elisabeth had already been giving, but

not the formula. She'd have to run to the store. But Tamara was too sick to be left alone. What if she strangled on her own vomit? One of the girls could come over to sit with her, but Elisabeth would feel terrible if they caught the bug and passed it on to their families. As it was, her other kids were sure to come down with it, maybe one at a time. She'd be going through this forever, it would seem, all the extra laundry, the cleaning up, the worrying about complications that could lead to big medical bills. God forbid Jonathan would get it and not be able to work for two or three days, even though he had a lot of sick pay saved up. Only thing was, half of what he didn't use was paid as a bonus at the end of the year, and that was what they used for Christmas. It would cost them. Cost the kids, anyway.

Then Elisabeth thought of Valerie. What did she care if Valerie came down with the virus?

Valerie arrived fifteen minutes later. Elisabeth let her in, Davie saddled on her hip. Valerie tickled him under the chin. "How are you, Davie? Getting to be a big boy, aren't you?"

Elisabeth turned to get her purse and car keys off the foyer stand. And also to get Davie away from Valerie. Elisabeth didn't want him to grow up liking her, or even knowing her, for that matter. In her opinion, the less anyone had to do with Valerie, the better off they would be. "I shouldn't be longer than half an hour. I might as well get some other things I need while I'm out. Tamara's asleep now, best not to disturb her."

"I'll just park myself on the couch and read one of your *Reader's Digest*s," Valerie said, somewhat miffed at the instruction. What did Elisabeth think she was going to do? Jump up and down on the child's bed?

"Help yourself to anything in the kitchen," Elisabeth offered as she opened the screen door to let herself out. "Just made some fresh coffee." In other words, please keep your hands off the pop, it's expensive.

Valerie got the message. "Thanks," she said, waving good-bye to Davie. He giggled and hid his face against his mother's bosom.

As soon as Valerie heard the station wagon roar down the street, she tiptoed down the hallway to peek in Tamara and Jennifer's room. Tamara lay on the bottom bunk, the covers kicked off, her eyes open.

"Hi, cousin Valerie."

Valerie stepped into the room though it smelled of sickness, her smile sympathetic. "I hear you've got a terrible virus. Sorry you're so sick."

"I wanted to call you, but Mama wouldn't let me."

"She wouldn't? Well, she knows you're weak. She didn't want you to fall down and hurt yourself."

The girl shook her head. Her skin was flushed by the fever, Valerie could see how miserable she was.

You're dying, Grandmother. Your pulse is so weak I can barely feel it. I doubt you'll live through the night.

Tears. Take me to the hospital, please. I've got to go to the hospital. Where's Vonda? She'll take me. Where's Vonda? Tell Vonda to come here.

Vonda's dead.

You lying bitch! You just don't want me to go. You want me to die so you can get all my money. Vonda!

"I don't think she wants me to tell you about the dream I had."

"What dream was that, Tamara?" Valerie stepped closer to the bed. "You had a dream about me?"

Tamara nodded weakly and shivered, groping for the blankets. Valerie helped her pull them up, tucked them around her, then sat on the edge of the bed.

"Was it a bad dream?"

"Yes, only I don't know what happened. I can't remember."

Valerie smoothed back the girl's damp bangs. "Your mother doesn't like me very much, does she?"

"She says she does, but I don't think so. I heard her tell Daddy once she thought you were being mean to Grandma Mandy. Did you be mean to her?"

Valerie shook her head. "Of course not. Why should I do that? She just said things because she was senile. Her brain wasn't right anymore. It was wearing out. She kept having strokes, little ones. That's when blood vessels collapse in the brain, which made her say things she really didn't mean, so I didn't get mad at her for saying them."

Tamara closed her eyes, not really understanding, only knowing if that's how it was when you got old, she never wanted to. "Oh."

"You sleep now," Valerie said, patting Tamara through the blanket. "That's the best thing."

"Don't let the monster get me, okay?"

Valerie stiffened. "What do you mean, monster? What monster?"

Tamara's eyes fluttered open and she nodded toward the closet, then they rolled back into her head, the lids closing again on white. "In the closet, it has big round yellow eyes. Mama said I just saw the knobs, but I think it was really a monster."

So, one of those things had followed Valerie over here when she had come to talk to Elisabeth the other day. Maybe it had gotten tired of waiting on Gavin to feed it. Maybe it liked children's flesh better.

Valerie patted Tamara's hand. "Don't worry honey, I won't let the monster get you."

A woman called shortly after Valerie got home and identified herself as Sara Hensley with the Huntington Public Library. She asked if she could speak to Gavin Sheffield. Valerie told her he had moved out and she didn't know where he went. Sara Hensley thanked her and hung up, her voice trailing off in confusion.

This was bad, Valerie realized. Gavin's car was still parked in the driveway. What if someone from the library—Sara Hensley, for instance—drove by to check? If they saw the car was still there, would they think Gavin had put Valerie up to telling them a lie, maybe because he didn't have the nerve to tell them he'd quit his job? Or would they wonder if something had happened to him and call the police? Valerie had to get rid of the car now, and since it was daylight, she would have to look like Gavin as much as possible.

His clothes were up in the attic now. She would put on one of his shirts and pairs of pants, and put her hair up under one of Uncle Herb's old hats. So maybe Gavin had never worn a hat before, what was the big deal? Valerie had given it to him as a present, before she found out what he was really like. Giving him the hat was probably what had made him think he could come up to her bedroom for sex. Only she couldn't say that she'd thrown him out that night; Mrs. Rothford might remember the car being there the next morning. Details, details.

Gavin seemed to be staring at her as she put his clothes on over her own. She would ditch them at the bus station in Charleston, in the rest room, where she would put on Aunt Vonda's blond wig and a pair of sunglasses, just in case.

Though Valerie felt she would have passed for Gavin at a glance, fortunately Mrs. Rothford wasn't out on her porch when Valerie backed Gavin's Chevy out of the driveway. It was good she was getting this taken care of today. She had something else to do tonight.

Just after two A.M. Valerie pulled up to the curb in front of Elisabeth's house. She doused her headlights and switched off the Datsun's engine, listening for several moments to the song of crickets and the distant rumbling of a train. Overhead, the moon bloomed full and yellow.

Quietly as possible, she opened her car door and stepped out, closing it back just far enough to put out the interior light. After taking a few deep breaths, she sprinted for the left side of the house.

Through the slightly parted curtain over Tamara and Jennifer's bedroom window, which she had unlocked earlier, she could see the soft orange glow of a night-light. She wouldn't need the penlight she'd brought.

But like the Boy Scouts say: Be Prepared.

Valerie patted the bulging pockets of her windbreaker. She was prepared for just about anything, she supposed.

A few minutes later she was inside the room and all was quiet. Her eyes had adjusted to the darkness, and in the night-light's pale glow she could make out the features of Tamara's face on the lower bunk's pillow. She'd kicked off her blankets. Still feverish, Valerie guessed.

Jennifer's still form lay behind the upper bunk's safety rail, one arm wrapped tightly around a stuffed giraffe.

Valerie sniffed. Traces of a foul odor hung in the air. Shuddering, she hurried to kneel beside Tamara's bed. That creature had just been here. She hadn't arrived a moment too soon.

"Tamara?" she whispered, stroking the girl's face. "Tamara, wake up."

Tamara made a face but didn't open her eyes.

A little louder: "Tamara, wake up. You're supposed to come with me."

Tamara uttered a little whine, kicked the covers bunched at her feet and groped blindly for Valerie's face. She was confused by the voice she was hearing in her dream. She was alone with Davie in the playpen, and Davie couldn't talk yet.

"You're just a baby," she mumbled, unconsciously batting at Valerie's nose.

Losing patience, Valerie grabbed Tamara's hand and gave it a rough squeeze. "Tamara, wake up. You have to come with me *now.*"

The girl's eyes suddenly flew open, then widened in fear. Valerie's shadow loomed over her. Shrinking back, she cried out, "Mama . . . ?"

Valerie quickly covered her mouth. In another room bedsprings creaked, then fell silent. Valerie waited, tense, until she was certain no one had gotten up.

"Be quiet now, we don't want to wake up the whole house," she said, keeping her voice low. "It's me, Valerie. Come with me now. I have a surprise for you."

She tried to pull Tamara out of bed, but the child resisted.

"What kind of surprise?"

"If I told you now, it wouldn't be a surprise anymore, would it? I don't have time to argue with you, Tamara. You'll see. Come on."

Tamara thought there was something terribly wrong about all this. It wasn't even morning yet, and the curtains were blowing in. That meant Valerie had come through the window like a burglar. She was even dressed like a burglar, wearing all black clothes.

Tamara backed against the wall, trembling. "I'm gonna yell for my mama if you don't go away. You're not supposed to be here now."

With a sigh of disgust, Valerie turned so Tamara couldn't see what she was doing. "Of course I'm supposed to be here now. Didn't your mama tell you I was coming? She must have forgotten. You must trust me, Tamara. I'm doing this for you."

"Doing what for me?"

In the upper bunk Jennifer moaned softly and rolled over.

Tamara wrinkled her nose. What was that smell? It reminded her of Doctors General Hospital, where Davie had been born. It was a scary smell now, and it made her feel sick again. What was cousin Valerie going to do?

Suddenly Valerie lunged at her, clamping a moist rag down over her face. Tamara struggled to push Valerie's hand away, to get the rag away from her face so she could scream for help, but she grew weaker every second.

Everything was getting fuzzy. Valerie's voice drifted to her from the other end of a long tunnel.

"I'm saving you from the monster, of course, just like I promised."

Tamara's terror melted into unconsciousness.

7

The phone rang early the next morning, just after sunrise. Valerie listened to the shrill ringing downstairs and knew who it would be. It would be Elisabeth, hysterical because Tamara was gone. Valerie already knew that; Tamara was sleeping safely in the next room.

Humming softly to herself, Valerie went down the stairs, her fingers playing along the banister. Maybe she would just keep Tamara for good. No one would ever know. Tamara was a sweet little girl, and smart too. She'd make perfect company.

Valerie picked up the receiver. "Hello?"

It was Elisabeth all right, and she was crying. "Tamara's gone," she wailed. "Someone kidnapped her last night. The screen was cut on the girls' window."

Valerie knew that too. "Have you called the police?"

"Of course I called the police! They're searching the neighborhood right now. I need you to come over and answer the telephone if it rings. There wasn't a ransom note, but whoever took her might call, and I'm afraid to let the police answer, in case that scares them and makes them do something to Tamara. Everyone else I know is helping us look. I can't sit around here waiting. I've got to look too."

"Well, I really needed to get some writing done today. Don't you have an answering machine?"

A gasp. "How can you think of writing at a time like this? Don't you care?"

"Of course I do, but—"

"God, never mind." Click.

Valerie dropped the receiver back in its cradle. Of course she cared, that's why she'd done it.

You never cared about me, you bitch. Never! Now I'm dying, and all you do is sit there and watch me die.

That's right, and I'm enjoying it too. I think I'll make some popcorn.

Herb, thank God you're here. Take me to the hospital, save me. Don't let me die . . .

"Cousin Valerie?"

The small voice came from above. Tamara was awake. Probably hungry too. For breakfast they'd have pancakes and Log Cabin syrup. Tamara would like that.

But Tamara was still a little sick. Valerie knew the moment she touched the girl's forehead. It was still too warm. "Let's get you in the tub," she said, pulling back the blankets. "Some nice cool water will bring the fever down."

Tamara frowned, her eyes darting furtively around the room. "Why am I here? Where's Mama?"

"She asked me to take care of you. She's not here. Be quiet now and come with me. We need to get that fever down."

"I wanna go home."

Valerie smiled patiently. "What's the matter? Don't you like me? I'm going to fix pancakes for breakfast, which we'll have with syrup and orange juice. Doesn't that sound good? Then we'll play checkers, or I'll read you a story, whatever you want."

"I want my mama," Tamara sniffled. A vague memory surfaced, of Valerie lunging toward her in the dark and pressing something over her face. Or had that just been a dream?

Valerie's smile faded. "Listen to me, Tamara. It's dangerous for you to go home. That monster you saw? It's a hideous, slimy creature that eats human flesh. It would have eaten you if you'd stayed there much longer. Here you're safe, though. I got rid of them over here."

Tamara's eyes widened. "Then won't it get Jennifer instead?"

"I don't know, maybe. But there's nothing I can do about it."

Tamara started to cry.

"I'll go run your bathwater now," Valerie said, a little irritably. "Need to get that fever down."

Vonda was in the bathroom mirror. While the water was running, Valerie had gone to the sink to wash her face, and there was Aunt Vonda, not next to Valerie's reflection but in place of it. Her eyes were accusing. "What do you mean kidnapping your cousin's child? Don't you know Elisabeth's out of her mind with worry? Take her back home this instant! She needs her mother."

"Aunt Vonda," Valerie sighed, "don't you understand? I did it to save her. The ones who see or hear them are the intended victims. Tamara would have disappeared anyway if I'd left her over there. And besides, I could use the company. Gavin is dead, and he wasn't much company to begin with."

As Valerie stared at the reflection in the mirror, it became her own, Vonda's features melting away. The old biddy ought to mind her own business, Valerie thought.

She heard Tamara dry-heaving in the spare bedroom, above the sound of the running water. There was enough in the tub now; Valerie turned it off and went to get the girl. After a long soak, the fever would be down and she'd feel like eating those pancakes. Everyone had to eat.

"Nothing yet," Detective Morrison said solemnly. "We're still checking the surrounding area."

Elisabeth collapsed on the couch and put her head in her hands. "Oh God, God, I can't believe this has happened."

Her husband patted her on the shoulder, his face looking much older than his thirty-four years. "They'll find her."

"But what if they don't?" Elisabeth cried miserably, feeling guilty as sin for the way she'd treated Tamara the day before, being angry at her for being sick because of the money it might cost.

Detective Morrison was a tall, sturdy man in his late forties, with a haggard but handsome face, dark hair peppered at the sides with gray. He knew it was not often that children disappeared from their own beds in the middle of the night, but when it happened, chances were they'd find the body later. When it was too late. There were no witnesses who'd seen a strange person or car lurking around the neighborhood, no clues at all, nothing. No ransom note or call, at least not yet, so perhaps that hadn't been the purpose. Frightening to think why else the child had been taken.

"Mrs. Wade, do you know of anyone who could have been responsible for this? Do you have any enemies?"

"No," Elisabeth sobbed.

Morrison put his hands in his pockets and studied the family photograph on the television console. "Well, it would be very unlikely she was taken by a total stranger, not from her own house. I think whoever took her knew her, at least knew who she was, and knew where to find her. Pardon the question, but are there any funny uncles in your family? Someone in the neighborhood who paid too much attention to her, perhaps? Anything, Mrs. Wade. We have to start somewhere."

Elisabeth thought about Valerie, who'd been alone with Tamara yesterday morning for forty-five minutes. Tamara hadn't said anything about talking to her, but maybe she had. Even so, what might she have said that would make Valerie decide to come back and take her? No, that wouldn't make sense. Valerie had her damn writing to do. She couldn't be bothered with a child, especially a sick one, although Tamara should just about be getting over it by now.

"I don't know who the hell could have done it," Elisabeth whimpered.

Valerie read the thermometer and smiled. "There, you see, it worked. Barely over a hundred now. Feel like eating some pancakes?"

Tamara shook her head. She was thinking about her

little sister getting eaten up by the yellow-eyed monster, which naturally was upsetting. "I don't feel hungry."

"That's because your tummy's all shrunken up," Valerie said cheerfully, patting the girl's sunken abdomen. "You should at least eat one pancake. You could eat one for me, couldn't you?"

Just think, Grandmother, the worms eating your body in that dark smelly coffin. Going up your nose. Maggots eating your eyes, crawling all inside your mouth. Think of it, Grandmother. It'll happen soon.

Make her shut up, Herb. Make her leave, get me to the hospital. Isn't Vonda back with the car yet?

What do you think it feels like to be eaten alive, Grandmother? You'll feel it, you know. You'll feel the worms inside you, eating your guts, thousands of them. Eating away that foul tongue of yours. Wonder how long it will take them?

I feel like eating you alive, Doug said, leering, drunk. He always said that when he was drunk. But he never did it, he just expected her to do it for him. And because of the alcohol in his system, it wouldn't get hard. It was like a limp balloon, the smell of it almost making her gag. Good thing he only got drunk on Saturday nights. Sometimes he would go out and stay gone until Sunday afternoon, coming back and saying he'd passed out at Dennis's apartment. As if she cared where the hell he'd been. At least he hadn't been there, forcing her to do this degrading, disgusting act. Sometimes she had an almost irrepressible urge to bite it off and spit it out in his face, like she wanted to do now.

Valerie was mashing her teeth down on her tongue. The taste of blood filled her mouth and she hurried to the bathroom to spit it down the sink.

The horror plot was no good, she decided. Wasn't healthy for her either, to write such things. What she should write was children's stories, stories she could read to Tamara, unless she preferred to read them herself. She was almost finished with first grade now. She could probably read quite well.

Valerie put in a fresh sheet of paper and pulled her

chair up to the desk. The fan was turned on and the wind it made fluttered the sheet, making a crackly sound. Clouds had moved in, so it was cooler. Maybe it would even rain; that would be wonderful. Valerie had her hair up, twisted with a pencil run through to keep it in place, and light clothing on, so she felt comfortable; maybe now she could get some writing done. It was impossible to think when it was so hot.

A child's story. That should be easy to do. She only needed to use three-cent words. Any silly plot would do. She turned on the typewriter and placed her fingers on the keyboard.

its not over yet valerie

Her hands jerked away from the machine. Oh God, Gavin. She knocked over her chair getting out of it and dashed into the hallway. She looked up at the closed attic door.

"Cousin Valerie?" Tamara called from the spare bedroom. "Can I call my mama?"

"No," Valerie said harshly, filling the doorway. "And don't ask me again or I'll tell the monster where you are."

Tamara turned into her pillow and began to sob. "I don't think Mama knows I'm here. I don't think she told you to take care of me like you said. I think you lied."

Valerie took a step into the room. "That's right, Tamara, I lied about that because I didn't want you to be upset, but I still did it for your own good. Your mama doesn't understand what could happen, and she wouldn't believe me if I told her. She doesn't believe there is a monster. She thought you just saw the knobs on your closet door, but we know better than that, don't we? So you're going to stay here and I'm going to take care of you. I wouldn't really tell the monster where you are, but you're going to have to behave or I'm going to get angry with you, and you *don't* want me to be angry with you."

She backed out into the hallway again, eyeing the rectangle in the ceiling, the cord that ran from it to the wall and wrapped around a hook. So it wasn't over yet, was it? We'll see about that, Gavin. We'll see what you have to say when you're all chopped up.

Valerie went to the kitchen and found a box of garbage

bags, a plastic sheet from the back porch, and her sharpest carving knife. She took them all up to the attic, ignoring Tamara's question as to what she was doing.

She was taking care of Gavin, that's what. He wasn't *quite* dead enough.

What a mess. And the smell of the escaped gases was almost enough to make her vomit. But at least most of him was bagged up now. He wouldn't be giving her any more messages on the typewriter. Valerie stood up and looked at herself in the cracked mirror, her face smeared with black blood. It was all over her arms too, and the front of her blouse. Disgusting.

Uncle Herb. Oh, that he should see her like this. But he didn't seem disturbed by the sight. He was frowning, though. "What he said is true, you know, but you just did the right thing."

"What do you mean?"

"Well, I'd keep those bags handy, so you'll have something to feed them. They'll be coming around again, you know. They were here last night too, but I kept them from coming up the stairs, like I been doing except for the time he led them through. But the hungrier they get, the stronger they get. I can't hold them off much longer."

Valerie grimaced. "Feed them? How horrible!"

"Be him or you, I suspect."

He was right, of course, and she believed what he said, even though last night she hadn't heard a thing. And she'd stayed awake again until dawn just to be sure, since Tamara was there. Even so, Valerie still didn't feel the least bit tired, just filthy. She wanted to take a bath.

Herb had walked back into the shadows and disappeared. Valerie tied the bags and took them down to her room, shoving them under the bed. Then she went to the bathroom to get cleaned up, wishing her tongue would stop hurting.

Lynn was trying in vain to comfort Elisabeth, who couldn't stop crying for more than a few minutes. Jonathan couldn't take it anymore, and he'd gone back to the bedroom to lie down.

"There, there," Lynn said, stroking Elisabeth's short blond hair. "Don't worry, I'm sure the police will find her, and she'll be okay."

"You don't know," Elisabeth shot back angrily. "You don't know anything. How can you sit there and tell me not to worry? What if it was Lisa missing? Would you be so confident then?"

Lynn had no answer for that; she looked desperately at Amy. Amy looked at Vicky. Vicky sighed. "Our hearts are with you all the way, Liz. This hurts us too, because you're our friend and we care deeply about Tamara as well. If anything happened to her, it would tear us apart. You're right. Lynn doesn't know, none of us knows if she's all right or if she'll be found, but by God, we're hoping with all our strength. You know we are."

Elisabeth broke into fresh tears. Lynn slumped against the back couch cushion, despondent, thankful that it hadn't been her Lisa. They'd have had to knock her out with sedatives.

Amy snapped her fingers. "What about that guy living with Valerie? Maybe she told him where you lived, or just talked about you, and he looked your address up in the phone book. She might have told him about your two little girls. Maybe he's that kind, and he's the only one I can think of who could fit into the picture that we don't really know anything about. That detective said it almost had to be someone who at least knew about Tamara."

Elisabeth's head jerked up. "Maybe. Call the police station for me, would you? Have them get a message to Detective Morrison to call me."

"If it was him," Lynn said, "then he couldn't have taken Tamara to Valerie's house. She would have caught him."

"He could have hidden her in an abandoned house," Amy offered.

Elisabeth dropped her head in her hands. "They're already checking abandoned houses."

Valerie finally got Tamara to eat some vegetable soup, and for the moment it was staying down. Valerie was pleased. She set the cup and spoon aside and touched the back of her hand to Tamara's forehead. Cool now. Her skin was a little clammy, but she was doing fine.

"Your fingers smell funny," Tamara said, wrinkling her nose.

Valerie frowned. "That's not a nice thing to say."

"What did you do in the attic?"

Children and their endless questions. "Nothing for you to worry about. All you have to think about is getting well. Don't you feel better already? Your fever is gone."

Tamara nodded that she was, but she wasn't particularly happy about it. She couldn't be happy about anything, thinking about that monster eating Jennifer, maybe Todd next, her older brother who was nine, and then little Davie. Maybe it would even eat both her parents as well. She would be an orphan.

"Well then, we'll just let you rest some more, and maybe later this afternoon, if you feel up to it, we'll go downstairs and watch some television in the living room. How does that sound?"

Tamara shrugged, eyes downcast. "Okay, I guess."

"I'm going to close this door so my typing won't disturb you. I'm going to write a story just for you. How about that?"

Tamara turned her face to the wall and drew the covers up to her chin.

Little ingrate, Valerie thought, getting up to leave when the phone rang downstairs. Probably Elisabeth again, calling to tell her that Tamara still hadn't been found, which of course she very well knew. Tamara would *never* be found.

Valerie hurried downstairs and answered the ringing. "Hello?"

"Valerie, this is Lynn Street, a neighbor of your cousin Elisabeth. I believe we met once . . ."

"I remember," Valerie said. "Where is Elisabeth? Have they found Tamara yet?"

"No, but that's what I'm calling about; Liz is too upset to talk right now. But she wanted to know if you ever mentioned anything about her family to that guy who's renting a room from you."

Valerie thought about the implications of that question for several moments, finally deciding on her answer. "You know, seems I did once, as a matter of fact. But he's gone, left yesterday morning for good. Took all his stuff."

"Oh God!"

"What's wrong? You don't think he—"

"There's a detective on his way over to your house right now. Tell him everything you know about that guy."

"Will do," Valerie lied.

Shit! The smell, she had to get it off her hands before he got there. And Tamara. Valerie had to make sure she stayed quiet. Slamming down the phone, she turned and rushed back up the stairs to get a knee sock and a pair of nylons from her dresser.

"I'm going to have to tie this sock over your mouth, Precious. I'm sorry."

What? I can't hear you, Grandmother. You'll have to speak up. Maybe it would help if you took Uncle Herb's tie out of your mouth.

Mmmfff!

What's the matter? Tied too tight? That's a shame, I guess you'll just have to leave it on, then. You don't have anything to say I want to hear, anyway. I think I've been called a bitch enough times, don't you? Your pulse is getting weaker, you know. Probably only a matter of hours now, until you die. I've been cheating you on your heart medicine, you know. You didn't know that? What, didn't think I would dare? Well, just goes to prove, doesn't it, that you just never know about some people, so be careful who you push too far.

"Why? I don't want that on my mouth." Tamara eyed the sock fearfully.

"I know, I know, Tamara, but it'll just be for a little while. There's a man coming. He works for the monster. So I can't take the chance of you making any noise, or getting out of bed. You might knock something over. I'm sorry."

Valerie forced the outstretched sock between Tamara's

teeth and pulled the ends into a tight knot behind her head. Getting the nylons tied around her wrists proved a little more troublesome, as Tamara was actively fighting her by then, but a few minutes later Valerie's mission was accomplished. She closed the door and hurried into the bathroom.

8

It was starting to rain by the time Valerie opened the front door, smelling strongly of Grandmother's rose cologne. Detective Morrison's eyebrows rose when he produced his badge for her inspection. He was probably wondering if she'd taken a bath in it, but there was nothing suspicious about a woman wearing too much cologne, was there? Maybe she liked smelling like a rose. "Yes, I've been expecting you, sir. Please come in."

Morrison took a small notebook from his inner coat pocket and a ballpoint pen from his shirt pocket, all the while looking, taking in her house, judging her personality by it. That was all right, Valerie thought. There was nothing indecent about it. It was very quaint, actually, filled with antiques, handmade afghans on the chairs and sofa, embroidered pillow slips, crocheted doilies on the tables. Let him measure her by the environment—an old maid's lair.

"This man you rent a room to . . . Gavin, is it? Is he here now?"

Valerie shook her head. "No, and he won't be back. He moved out yesterday."

"Oh? Well then, could you tell me his last name, please?"

"Sheffield," Valerie answered.

Morrison wrote the name in his notebook. "Former address?"

Now this was embarrassing. "I'm afraid I don't know that. He never said."

Morrison sniffed; the rose cologne was apparently overwhelming him. "You didn't check him out? Ask for any references?"

"Well . . . no. I'm no good at that sort of thing, you see, and this was the first time I'd ever run such an ad. I didn't really know what I was doing, to tell you the truth. It was a bit awkward for me. I did think of those things later, though. I even thought of hiring a private detective. But Gavin seemed harmless enough. A little standoffish, maybe, a little too quiet, but okay."

"When did you say he left?"

Valerie cleared her throat, brow furrowed in concentration. "Well, I was still in bed, so I can't swear to this, but assuming it was the time he normally left, I'd say it was between eight-thirty and eight forty-five yesterday morning. The library opens at nine o'clock. That's where he worked. That I know for sure." She was fairly certain none of the neighbors, had they even paid attention, would have checked their watches when she'd driven Gavin's Chevy away two hours later than that, and a day had already passed. People's memories got fuzzy pretty quickly about such trivial details.

Morrison looked at her. "Worked?"

"Well, some lady called late yesterday morning from there. I forgot her name, Sara something, but she was looking for him, so I assume he didn't go to work, like I'd thought. I didn't find out his stuff was gone until later, when I went in to dust."

"And you haven't heard from him since?"

Valerie felt herself starting to sweat as she remembered the chilling message from Gavin on her typewriter that morning. "No, but if he does contact me, I'll certainly let you know." She began toying nervously with the watch around her wrist, the one with two tiny diamonds on either side of the crystal. It had belonged to Grandmother.

WHAT'S WRONG WITH VALERIE?

Doesn't your watch look pretty on me, Grandmother? Of course, you won't be needing it anymore anyway, time has run out for you. Now, don't look at me that way. You asked for this. If you'd been nice to me, things would be different. I don't know how you could treat your own granddaughter like a dog, worse than a dog, especially when she made such a sacrifice to come up and take care of you so you wouldn't have to go in a nursing home. I gave up my job, I gave up Doug, just for you, Grandmother, and all you've done is call me a bitch. Well, not anymore. Your last words have already been said, Grandmother.

"Miss Scott?"

Valerie tensed. "I'm sorry, what was that again?"

Morrison was studying her curiously. "I'd like to see his room, if you don't mind. Where he stayed."

"Yes, of course. This way, please . . . " She led him through the doors off the living room. In here, the rose cologne was overpowered by the scent of Lysol. Morrison took a hanky from his back pocket and trumpeted into it; allergies, Valerie guessed. Wordlessly, Morrison slowly cruised the room, looked under the bed, under the mattress, opened all the dresser drawers, then turned up the couch cushions . . . revealing the library books Valerie had checked out. So Gavin had lied about that after all. He'd taken them to keep her from finding out what was going to happen to her. The books might have said something about the hideous flesh eaters.

Morrison picked up the books and studied the covers. "These were his?"

Careful, careful. He could find out she had checked them out. "No, those are library books I checked out the other day. They turned up missing that same night. I asked Gavin if he'd taken them, but he said no."

"You interested in the supernatural?"

"Only for fiction." Valerie smiled. "I'm trying to be a writer. I thought those books might give me some ideas."

"I see. Wonder why he would have taken them and hidden them in here?"

"Who knows? Some people think just reading things like that or talking about them will open the doors to another realm, or attract evil spirits or some such ridiculous thing. Maybe Gavin was one of them."

"He ever exhibit any odd behavior?"

Valerie sighed; this was getting tiresome. "No, I wouldn't say odd. He was just very quiet and kept to himself most of the time."

Morrison nodded and tossed the books back down, then went over to inspect the tapestry Gavin had hung.

"Nice wall hanging," he commented. He moved closer, inspecting the wall around it, though why the wall should interest him so much, Valerie couldn't guess.

"The tapestry yours?"

Valerie nodded. "Everything in the house is mine. I inherited it from my grandmother. She passed away a month ago. In this very room, actually."

"Sheffield know that?"

"No."

Morrison shrugged as if a cold hand had touched his shoulder. "So what was hanging on this wall before you put the tapestry up?"

"What?"

"All these extra holes." Morrison pointed a few of them out.

Valerie forced herself to smile. "Oh, old family pictures, mostly people I didn't even know. Anyway, I didn't think a roomer would care to look at them, so I took them down and put up the tapestry instead."

Morrison nodded, rubbing his chin. "Does something for the room."

"I thought so."

"Why all the disinfectant spray?" Morrison had moved over to the bed, jabbing at a piece of the carpet with the toe of his shoe.

"For germs, of course," Valerie said stiffly. "For all I know, the man had fleas."

Morrison bent down and picked at the carpet with his fingers. Valerie watched, tense. What could he have found? She couldn't see, it was too small. Morrison brought whatever it was up to his nose and sniffed. "Smells like Lysol, but it's a tapioca pearl, I think."

She shrugged, nonchalant. "I suppose he ate in here, I

never found any messes in the kitchen." Her mind was racing furiously but she forced herself not to panic. What if he takes it to the crime lab for analysis? What if there's traces of cyanide on it?

Much to her relief, Morrison flicked the piece of tapioca off his finger and glanced over his brief notes. "He ever mention any friends or relatives?"

"We hardly spoke at all," Valerie answered, wishing he would hurry and leave. She didn't like leaving Tamara tied and gagged upstairs for so long.

Morrison wasn't quite finished. "On any of these rare occasions then that you did speak, did you ever talk to him about your cousin's family?"

"I told Elisabeth's friend who called shortly before you came that I had. It was during our one actual conversation a few nights ago out on the front porch."

"And how was it you got around to discussing the Wade family?"

Valerie crossed her arms defensively. "Well, he wasn't talking much, so I thought I'd draw him out by telling him something first, and Elisabeth's family is the only people I know in town, besides her mother, my aunt."

As she was still talking, Morrison was pushing his way through the double doors back into the living room. Valerie followed him, and was shocked to see the man who had identified himself as her great-great-uncle Armand sitting on the sofa. Morrison didn't seem to notice him.

"So he just left yesterday morning, didn't tell you he was moving out or where he was going. Correct?"

Valerie glared at the pale intruder. "That's correct."

"Was there any sort of argument that preceded this? Any confrontation about anything between the two of you? Could he have been angry, maybe angry enough to get back at you by kidnapping one of your second cousins?" Morrison asked rapid-fire, glancing afterward at the sofa, then back at Valerie's face. "Something wrong, Miss Scott?"

Valerie made a conscious effort to relax her facial features and gave him her full attention. "No, nothing's wrong. And no, there was no fight or anything like that."

She decided to scratch the attempted rape business. Morrison might start wondering if she'd killed Gavin to defend herself, then kidnapped Tamara to provide a reason for his disappearance.

"Did he know where your cousin and her family lived?"

Would this ever end? Valerie sighed, already sickened by the cologne she was wearing. She wanted to stand out on the front porch and breathe the nice rain-soaked air, maybe even stand out in the rain. "How should I know? I mentioned their last name. I suppose he could have looked it up in the phone book."

"One more question, then. I need his description, and a description of his car, and the license number if you know it."

Valerie wearily described Gavin, his car, and told Morrison the license tag number, which was actually a word, FIRST, and in case he was wondering, she didn't know what it meant.

Morrison wrote the information down and put his notebook and pen away. "I guess I'll go have a talk with the people at the library. Thank you for your time, Miss Scott." He reached into his shirt pocket and drew out a business card. Handing it to her, he said, "Call me if you think of anything else. I probably won't be in, but you can leave a message."

Valerie studied the card a few moments, then said, "I hope you find her soon. I'm sure Elisabeth's half out of her mind with worry."

Morrison threw the staircase a perfunctory glance, pushed the screen door open and said, "We'll find her. Eventually," he added with a heavy sigh.

After watching the unmarked car pull into the street from in front of her Datsun, Valerie whirled around and faced Armand, who was still sitting on the sofa. "What do you want?"

"Big mistake," he said, shaking his head. "They're going to catch you, you know. And then they'll put you away, like they did me. Put you away for good."

"Killing Gavin was an accident," Valerie snapped. "I

meant to throw the pudding away. Besides, he wouldn't have eaten it if he hadn't been planning to steal some of my food."

Armand smirked. "I'm sure they'll take that into consideration."

"Why don't you go haunt someone else? I don't need your advice. I've got things under control here."

"Is that so? Well, we'll see about that. Tamara's not a helpless old lady on her last legs, you know. She won't be as easy to control as you think, and when she gets out of control, are you going to kill her like you did Amanda?"

What, you're still alive, Grandmother? It certainly is taking you a long time to die. But it's not surprising, as stubborn as you are. Would you like me to help you along? I could hold a pillow down over your face . . . oh, you don't like that idea. What? I can't understand you. Are you calling me a bitch again? Maybe a goddamn bitch? Stupid bitch? Big or little bitch? I can't hear you, Grandmother, I can't hear you . . .

Tamara was crying. Valerie untied her and took off the gag, then gathered the girl into her arms, attempting to soothe. "I'm sorry, Tamara, I really am, but I had to protect you. Don't you understand? If that man knew you were here, he would have taken you home, and the monster is waiting for you there."

Tamara couldn't stop crying. Valerie shook her gently. "Stop it now. There's no reason for you to cry. Want me to bake you some cookies? It's not so hot today. We could use the oven to bake some chocolate chip cookies."

"I feel something bad in this house," Tamara sobbed.

Valerie pursed her lips. "I know. I misunderstood Uncle Herb when he told me to . . . well, I thought the monsters would go away if I did something, but I was wrong. They're still here. Not here now, I don't think, only at night, but don't worry, Tamara, I'll protect you. I promise. You're such a sweet girl. I wouldn't want anything to happen to you, and that's why I'd like for you to stay with me. I won't even make you go to school; what about that? No more school."

This had an effect, in spite of Valerie's assurance that the monsters would come back after dark. Tamara stopped crying. "I won't have to go to school?"

Valerie smiled. "Never again."

Tamara mulled this over a few seconds. "Then won't I be dumb?"

Valerie laughed; the child was such a delight. "Of course you won't be dumb. I'll teach you lots of things, but it won't be boring, like in school. School is awful, isn't it? The kids make fun of you and call you names, because you're not pretty enough or they think you're weird, and no one will make friends with you because that would make them outcasts too."

"But I have lots of friends at school."

Valerie frowned. "Well, not everyone does. Besides, it's boring, isn't it? Having to sit in a dusty old classroom while the sun is shining outside?"

"Summer vacation starts in four more days," Tamara suddenly remembered. "I don't have to go to school anyway, after four days."

"Well," Valerie said, "summer vacation doesn't last forever, though, does it? Never mind about that, it's just not safe for you to go home. Your parents don't know how to handle these monsters."

Tamara's lower lip began to quiver again. "I don't want the monsters to eat Jennifer or Todd or Davie or Mama and Daddy."

"I know, Precious, but I don't know what I can do about it. If I tell them about the monster, they won't believe me. They might even try to get me put away. And then here you'd be, all alone, with a whole bunch of them. The ghosts too. Are you afraid of ghosts?"

Tamara's blue eyes widened in fear. "Ghosts are here too?"

"Not scary ones. Just our family. You remember Unkie and Aunt Vonda? Them, and one of Grandmother Mandy's uncles, Armand. I can't stand him, but he's not scary. He doesn't even look like a ghost."

"Grandma Mandy isn't here too? How come?"

Look, Grandmother, I caught a mouse by the tail this morning. He's still alive. What do you suppose he'd do if I

put him down your nightgown? Not even a guess, huh?
Don't like him, do you? Wonder what you would do if I put
him in your nightgown. Suppose you'd have a heart
attack?

"I told her to stop calling me a bitch," Valerie answered harshly. "Guess she didn't have anything else to
say."

9

With Tamara tucked under an afghan on the sofa watching *Sesame Street,* Valerie called the newspaper to place another ad for the room. She needed the money; no use letting an opportunity for capital gain go to waste. She raised the price to twenty-five dollars a week.

Five minutes later the phone rang. It was Elisabeth's friend Lynn again, asking if the detective had been there and what he'd said. Valerie recounted Morrison's visit, and told her he had gone to talk to the people at the library where Gavin had worked, then asked how Elisabeth was holding up. Not well, Lynn replied, but that was understandable. Valerie said indeed it was, what a terrible thing, losing a child. She didn't add that Elisabeth was likely to lose more. Very likely.

Armand was still hanging around, going from room to room, inspecting things. Valerie noticed that although he looked solid, he had no problem passing through walls. Tamara couldn't see him, but whenever he walked near her, she seemed to shiver slightly.

Valerie didn't talk to him. She was afraid it might alarm Tamara, her talking to someone the girl couldn't see. Fortunately, Armand didn't say anything either, which would have been hard to ignore.

"Well, I suppose I ought to try to get some writing done," Valerie said. "Don't leave the house, now. Don't even go out on the front or back porches, and don't use the phone. I mean it, Tamara. I will be very upset with you if you do any of those things, and I'll punish you severely, understand? Unkie will come tell me if you do something you shouldn't."

Tamara nodded fearfully.

Valerie smiled. "That's a good girl. Just call for me if you need anything." She turned and went upstairs, convinced the girl was safe during the day. The things only fed at night.

The message from Gavin was still in her typewriter.

its not over yet valerie

Now that he was dismembered, did he have anything to say? She typed the question:

You still around, Gavin?

Her fingers began to move again, like on a Ouija gadget, of their own accord.

what do you think valerie

Damn it, he was still around . . . *inside* her? She closed her eyes, sensing herself. "Are you in there, Gavin?" she whispered angrily. She heard no voice, felt no differently. So this wasn't the way to communicate with him; it had to be done on the typewriter. She replaced her fingers on the keyboard.

Are you inside me, Gavin? Is that where you're hiding? If so, get out.

im afraid i cant

You're afraid? Of what?

im not afraid i just cant

Oh, baloney. You got in somehow, you can get out, so do it.

you cant make me

Valerie growled and slapped the typewriter. The parasite!

So, what exactly did you mean by, "It's not over yet?"

theyre hungry

So what else is new?

nothing except now you have to feed them instead of me

* * *

Lynn went home for a few minutes and brought back a couple of Valiums for Elisabeth. They had already taken effect, and she was no longer crying, just lying curled up on the couch, staring blankly at the fish tank, mesmerized by the flow of bubbles arising from a sunken treasure chest. They were alone now. Vicky and Amy had other pressing obligations, and Jonathan had gone to a local bar to drown his sorrow in whiskey. He'd left the number so Elisabeth could reach him if there were any news.

There was news, but it wasn't good, so Lynn had decided not to call and burden him with it. Were it not for the Valiums, Lynn imagined Elisabeth would have lost all control by now. Instead she had received the information with numb indifference; she was expecting the worst now and had come to chemical grips with it.

Detective Morrison had called saying he'd interviewed Gavin's supervisor at the library. She hadn't been very useful, at least until she remembered a young woman's name; Gavin had gotten her a library card. Terri Blake.

Terri Blake knew Gavin very well, for he had been paying her to have sex with him at least three times a week for the last several months. She refused to go into much detail, but she told Morrison that Gavin had a few "peculiar fetishes" for which he paid extra. On several occasions she admitted he wanted her to pretend to be a little girl, to dress like one and talk like one, and he would pretend to seduce her.

And so, Morrison had concluded, it looked like the guy did have pedophile tendencies. Could be their man. If they were lucky, he still had Tamara with him, but if she was in fact with Gavin Sheffield, chances were she had already been molested. There was an APB on their descriptions and the car. Something should turn up soon.

And by the way, did Valerie Scott always wear so much perfume?

"I don't remember that she ever wore any," Elisabeth said to Lynn, her voice low and very calm.

Lynn sipped her coffee, thinking it was high time for Lisa's nap. "Guess that's neither here nor there," she said, wanting to take a nap herself. "Kind of a strange thing for him to ask, though, isn't it? But he sounded hopeful, about finding Tamara alive at least. He thinks she'll be home soon. Well, I hate to leave you, but I'd better get Lisa home for her nap. She won't go to sleep unless she's in her own crib or riding around in the car."

Elisabeth nodded. "Yes, soon. Is it still raining?"

Lynn looked toward the window. "Yes, but it's slowed up. Don't worry, I'm sure she's not out in the rain. So, are you going to be all right? I'll come back later this evening, after Gary gets home to watch Lisa. Call me if you need me."

"I'm okay. Go on home. I think I'll take a nap too."

"Promise to call if you need anything, anything at all."

"I promise."

"No you won't," Valerie said sternly, her hands placed challengingly on her hips. "Writing them a letter would be the same as calling. Now eat your dinner, you've barely touched it."

"I still feel a little sick," Tamara mumbled, pushing at her peas with her fork. Why did there have to be such things as monsters? Daddy said they were just movie actors with makeup on, but he just didn't know. There were real ones too. Cousin Valerie said so.

"Then I guess I'd better put you back to bed," Valerie said, washing down the last of her meal with a gulp of iced tea. She'd made a new pitcher, of course. She wasn't about to drink what that thing had been in, that mouse or innard or whatever it had been. Disgusting.

"By the way, I'm going to put you in my room tonight. You can sleep with me. I can't take the chance of leaving you alone."

Tamara shuddered. "I don't want to sleep here."

"Don't worry, it'll be all right," Valerie assured her with a smile. "I'm ready for them, when they come."

Tears formed in the corners of Tamara's eyes. "I'm scared."

Valerie shrugged. "They're just hungry. Once you really think about it, it's not that scary, as long as it's not you they're going to eat."

"So what are they going to eat?" Tamara asked desperately.

Valerie sighed. "Well, I probably shouldn't tell you this, but you're a big girl now, and you know about the monsters anyway, so I guess I should, so you'll know what you have to do if something should happen to me. They're going to eat Gavin. You never met him, so it's no one you know. He's already dead anyway, so it won't be like he suffers or anything."

Tamara had gone as white as a sheet. "Where is he?"

"Under my bed. In bags. But don't even think about it; he certainly can't hurt you."

"A dead man's under your bed! We have to sleep with a dead man under the bed!" The seven-year-old was horrified.

Valerie slapped the table. "No need to get hysterical, Tamara. These things happen. You just have to deal with them as best you can. Gavin's body just would have gone to waste otherwise."

I think I'll have your body cremated, Grandmother, and I think I'll have them put your ashes in a paperweight for me. You wouldn't want to be totally useless, would you? Nothing to do but rot? Where's the mouse, Grandmother? Did he go to sleep? How sweet, now you have a pet.

"Come on, let's go upstairs and get you ready for bed. Need to brush your teeth and wash your face."

Tamara shook her head adamantly. "I don't want to go upstairs with the dead man!"

Boy, that had been a mistake, telling her about Gavin. She should have known it would upset the child; she wasn't mature enough to handle these things very well. Damn, what now? She had to get some writing done, those books weren't going to write themselves. Suddenly Valerie had an idea. If Gavin insisted on possessing her, why not make him write the books? He had worked in the library, he ought to know how to write. It was the least he could do.

"Tamara dear, you were upstairs a while ago with him, and nothing happened, did it? What's under my bed is going to save us. Just think of it that way because if we don't feed them Gavin, they'll eat us instead. Unfortunately these monsters have a very particular appetite, or I would just go buy them some hamburgers. Just think of Gavin up there as food."

Tamara looked ready to start retching, trembling from head to toe. Valerie felt a rush of pity for her and got up to put her arms around her. "Everything's okay, Precious. Try to think of something else, something pleasant. How about horses? Have you ever ridden a horse?"

Tamara only shuddered. Valerie picked her up and carried her upstairs to her room.

"You just rest for a while. I'm going to try to get some work done, okay?" Without waiting for Tamara's reply, Valerie stepped back into the hallway, closing the door behind her.

Seconds later Tamara heard a key being twisted in the lock. She immediately sat up on the bed, clutching the pillow for comfort.

There was a dead man under cousin Valerie's bed.

A real dead man, right in the next room.

She wondered how he had died. Had Valerie killed him? Tamara buried her face in the pillow and shuddered violently, wishing she were at home with her parents, home where she knew she was safe, at least in the daytime.

She didn't feel safe at all in Valerie's house. Only scared. More scared than she'd ever been in her whole life.

Seated at her desk, Valerie typed on a fresh sheet of paper:

All right, Gavin, get to work and write me a book. All the time that's gone to waste is your fault, anyway.

they used to be human

I don't want conversation, Gavin, I want you to write a book for me, a children's book, you know, like *Cinderella* or *Beauty and the Beast*. You can handle that, can't you?

they cant get loose

Gavin, quit stalling. Write something amusing for Tamara.

they want her she is young

Well, they're not going to get her because I'm going to feed them your stinking corpse. Now would you please get on with it? You're wasting paper.

You're wasting air, Grandmother, so why don't you stop breathing? I'd like to get on with things, if you don't mind. My new career as a writer. Didn't know I was creative, did you? How else do you think I stood living here? You wouldn't believe some of the people who've dropped by to visit me, all kinds of royalty, and movie stars. And you, you'd never guess all the things I did to you in my mind. I'll tell you all about it if you'd like. It looks like you're going to be around for a while . . .

"I did some writing myself once, but Vonda told me it was no good."

Startled, Valerie turned and saw Uncle Herb sitting behind her in his favorite chair. It was good to see him. He was the only one she could stand. "Really? What did you write about?"

"The war," he said. "I was a pilot, you know, shot down twenty-three German planes. I was decorated."

"But Aunt Vonda said you were a mail clerk."

Herb scowled. "What did she know? Was she there?"

"Well, it doesn't matter, if you say you were a pilot, I believe you. Anyway, Gavin was just telling me a few things about our hungry friends. Said they used to be human, and something about them not being able to get loose. You know what he's talking about?"

"I wasn't no mail clerk," Herb grumbled, then said, changing expressions, "About those hungry characters, I don't know. Don't see them around in the day, that's all. Ugly things, like us only sort of melted down. Some of them, though, wouldn't think they'd ever been human, hideous as they are. No shape like I ever saw before, all lumpy and deformed, big yellow eyes—"

"I saw one of those in the living room," Valerie interjected. "My hand went in its mouth. It was horrible."

Herb lit his pipe and puffed thoughtfully. "I'll bet. They came with that fellow Gavin, guess you know."

"Yes, I'd figured that much out."

"Valerie!" The high-pitched voice came from the attic, resounding, hollow, near and yet far, but Valerie knew it came from the attic, and whose it was.

"Aunt Vonda," she sighed.

Herb grunted. "Just ignore her. I always did."

"Valerie!"

"She wants you to take the little girl home," Herb said, still puffing on his pipe, teeth clenched on the stem. The room was filled with the aroma of cherry tobacco. Valerie loved that smell. "But like you say, that wouldn't be any good for her. At least you saved one of them."

"Damn right. But do you think anyone will ever thank me for it? Idiots. Why doesn't Vonda come down?"

"Likes to stay in the attic most the time," Herb replied. "With all her stuff. Keeps thinking she can get it over to the other side, I 'magine. Be like her to think something stupid like that."

"What's the other side like, Uncle Herb?"

Just think, Grandmother, when you get to the other side you'll probably burn in a lake of fire, or have little red devils running after you with pitchforks. Or what if it's nothing but blackness, pitch-blackness forever and ever and ever.

She was still looking at the chair, but Uncle Herb was gone, her question left unanswered. There was only a trace of his cherry tobacco lingering on the air. Probably Vonda had grabbed him by the ear and made him go up in the attic with her so she could bitch at him in private for being on Valerie's side. Valerie turned back around to the typewriter.

All right, Gavin, get busy on a book.

A few minutes later Valerie went down the hall to check on Tamara. Gavin had refused to write anything at all. Tamara was asleep with her thumb in her mouth, her arms clutched tightly around a pillow, her legs drawn up in a fetal position. It was sweet, Valerie thought. She looked just like a baby. Valerie had thought many times in the past about having her own baby, and had even tried to get pregnant by Doug, but it never happened. He was probably sterile with all that pot he smoked. She should have slept around. It wasn't as if she hadn't wanted to. She just hadn't had the nerve. All the experience she'd had other than with Doug was the first time, during her junior year when she'd been raped by two seniors under the bleachers during a football game, and then that time with Steve at the class reunion when she was drunk. Normally she didn't care for alcohol; it made her confused.

Elisabeth told her husband the news. Morrison had called and said Gavin's car had been found abandoned in Charleston near the bus station. So it was possible he had taken Tamara on a bus somewhere, if he still had her. Elisabeth had to believe he did, because if he didn't, Tamara was surely dead. But no one remembered someone fitting Gavin's description traveling with or without a little blondheaded girl. The ticket clerk thought he'd sold a one-way ticket to Cleveland to a man with a scar on his left cheek, but was fairly certain he hadn't been tall. Nevertheless the driver had been notified, and when the next stop was made, police would be waiting to check IDs. No need to panic. It probably wasn't Gavin.

And incidentally, would Elisabeth describe her cousin as basically unemotional?

Todd, Jennifer, and Davie had been disbursed to Elisabeth's friends, as she was in no condition to care for them, and Jonathan didn't feel competent in that area. Elisabeth didn't miss the usual amount of noise, but she would have welcomed it if Tamara could be there, making her share.

Jonathan lost himself in the television, as usual. There was nothing more to say, nothing more to do but wait.

The phone rang just before ten. Jonathan answered it since Elisabeth had passed out on the couch.

"Mr. Wade, this is Detective Morrison. I just found out it wasn't our man on that bus. I thought you'd want to know. Not even close. At any rate, we're checking all the motels in Charleston, the car rental agencies, et cetera. He could have stolen a car, but we're looking for those anyway. Sorry I can't give you any better news."

"You're doing all you can do," Jonathan said. "We appreciate it."

They hung up. Jonathan went back into the living room. "Let's go to bed, hon."

Elisabeth moaned groggily in her sleep. Jonathan sighed and went to the linen closet in the hallway to get her a blanket. No sense in waking her up. Let her have all the escape from reality she could get.

As much as she wanted to leave the light on, Valerie finally decided it would be best to turn it off, thinking it would be much worse to see the creatures when they appeared. She wished they would hurry up and come so she could go to sleep; the lack of it had finally caught up with her. She could hardly keep her eyes open. Also, she wanted to get up early and start to work before it got too hot. The rain had stopped, so it probably would be. Rather, she wanted to get up early and put Gavin to work; no more of this horsing around, changing the subject. Grandmother's money wouldn't last forever, and she could hardly be expected to write if she had to hold down a full-time waitress job, which was probably all she could get. There would be no energy left over. Her mind would be sapped by the end of the day.

Tamara whimpered next to her in the dark. Valerie reached over and patted the small form beneath the sheet. This couldn't go on forever. And she had no intention of ending up as a meal for these things herself, so something was going to have to change. What she had to do, she supposed, was find someone else to take over the job. Make Gavin go into them. He could probably completely take over a person's mind if he wanted to. Then she'd send the whole horrid pack off to somewhere far away. Tamara could then sleep in her own room and wouldn't have to dream about chopped-up bodies under the bed.

Unreal, Valerie thought. A chopped-up body was under her bed, the very bed she was lying on right now, and she was the one who'd done the chopping. Yet she didn't think it was all that odd. Was she going crazy after all?

No, she answered herself after a moment's consideration. She'd always heard that crazy people never questioned their sanity. So then, all this meant was that she was extremely adaptable. And that was good, with all the goings-on in this house.

She heard the first sound at ten thirty-five. Wet liver dropping on a hard floor. They had already come upstairs; must be pretty hungry now, they had gotten past Uncle Herb. She hadn't heard them come up because she'd drifted off to sleep, but she was awake now, listening to the slurping, smacking of lips, their bodies bumping against the door, which sounded like dough being repeatedly pulled off sheets of waxed paper. Tonight she hadn't blocked the door. All they had to do was turn the knob. It wasn't locked. Surely they could turn knobs. Valerie reached under the bed for one of the bags. Though it was closed tight with a green twistie, she could still smell the sickening odor of what was inside. How to describe a smell like that? Like creek mud, sort of, with algae. Only knowing what it really was made it seem worse.

They could smell it too. They were coming in. Valerie couldn't see them clearly, but she could tell what they were doing—oozing through the cracks around the door. So maybe they couldn't turn knobs, but what did it matter if they could squeeze through such a small space? Moonlight played upon a shimmering line that expanded quickly, became oblong, and once it was all inside, plopped to the floor in a vaguely human shape, only squashed like Herb had said, sort of like a dwarf with a big head. Others were oozing in above it. Valerie felt a little sick. The sounds they made were revolting enough, and on top of the creek-mud-algae smell of the bag, it was almost too much. Definitely, this job had to be passed on to someone else, and the sooner the better.

There were six of them, only one with big yellow eyes, the kind Uncle Herb couldn't describe they were so horrible. The one that had followed her over to Elisabeth's. Now it had come back. Maybe it had a special craving for Tamara for some reason, but Valerie couldn't imagine what that would be.

They began to approach, making their sloppy sounds. Fearing they would get on the bed, Valerie tossed the sack on the floor near the foot. They slowly converged on it, and she could hear the crackle of plastic.

She listened while they fed. Sickening, the sounds they made, worse than pigs, slimy lips smacking together, licking, slurping, sucking. When they finished, they started moving toward her again, wanting more. Valerie got another bag and tossed it over to them. At least they didn't have to be fed by hand; that she strongly doubted she could do. How much were they going to eat? There were only five bags left; she was going to have to conserve.

After devouring the second bag, she ordered them to leave, not knowing what she would do next if they refused; give them more, give them all they wanted, she supposed, and hope like hell Gavin was enough.

But they did leave, vanishing into thin air, leaving only their horrible smell behind. Valerie sighed with relief and nestled against Tamara, asleep in less than a minute.

Tamara was wide awake.

Through half-open lids she had fearfully watched Valerie reach under the bed, then throw something out on the floor.

Pieces of the dead man, in a bag, for the monsters to eat.

Immediately Tamara had squeezed her eyes shut, knowing she couldn't bear to see the monsters, let alone watch them eat pieces of a dead body. Having to smell the stink was bad enough.

But as far as she could tell, nothing else had happened, other than Valerie tossing over another bag and soon afterward telling someone to leave.

Now thoroughly confused, Tamara tried to sit up so

she could see if the bags were gone, but Valerie's arm around her tensed, keeping her pinned.

"S'all right, they're gone," Valerie murmured sleepily.

"The dead man too?" Tamara asked, her voice quivering.

Valerie responded with a snore.

10

The sound of the telephone ringing so near startled Valerie out of sleep. What was she doing on the sofa in the living room? Sleepwalking again? Tamara jumped out of the rocker and ran to answer it before Valerie could stop her. Fortunately, it was only someone calling about the ad. Clearly disappointed, Tamara held the phone out toward Valerie. "It's about the room."

Valerie bounded over to her, took it and covered the mouthpiece. "Don't you ever, ever answer the phone again, do you hear me? Ever!" she ordered in a harsh whisper.

Tamara's face screwed up in dismay, and she dashed back into the living room, tossing herself on the sofa. Valerie raised the phone to her ear. "Yes, this is Valerie Scott. You were interested in the room?"

"I was wondering if I could come look at it," a woman said. She sounded kind of old, at least in her sixties.

"Of course. This morning? I just got up, if you'd give me about an hour before you come."

That was fine with the woman. Valerie gave her the address, exchanged parting amenities and hung up.

"Well, at least it was a woman," Valerie said as she

walked back into the living room. "Sounded old, though. She might be the nosy type so we'll have to be careful what we say around her. Wouldn't be a good idea to tell her about Gavin or the monsters or our ghosts. She probably wouldn't want to stay then, and I need the money. We'll just say that you're my daughter. That would make it nice and simple and there wouldn't be a lot of questions to answer."

Then Valerie had a startling thought. What if pictures of Tamara had been posted all over town, or even put in the newspaper? Valerie didn't take the paper so she wouldn't know. She would have to change Tamara's appearance. Cut her hair, dye it. Vonda had left some brown hair dye; it was still in the bathroom.

"Come upstairs with me, Tamara. I'm going to change your hair. Make it prettier."

Tamara looked at her sullenly. "I don't want to. Just leave me alone."

Valerie took a threatening step closer to the sofa. "I'm your mother now, and you'll do what I say. Now come upstairs with me. I'm going to make you look really pretty."

"Am I ever going to get to see my real mother again?"

"Why would you want to?" Valerie asked, closing the gap between them and pulling Tamara off the sofa. "I'll bet she wasn't a very good mother anyway, bitchy as she was. Now you come along with me and let me do what I want with your hair. And no more arguing or I'll make you sit up in the attic with Gavin's skeleton."

A look of terror seized the girl's face.

"I'm afraid so," Valerie said, pulling her toward the staircase. "I wouldn't want to, but I can't have you misbehaving, can I? I want you to be a nice little girl and do what I say. We'll pretend I'm your real mother, and as long as you do what you're told, I'll be very nice to you, and we'll be very happy, as soon as I get rid of the monsters for good. Now stop dragging your feet. We have to hurry. That lady is coming over to look at the room, and I want you to look pretty for her."

* * *

Jonathan wasn't alarmed when he woke up and discovered that his wife wasn't in the house; she was probably over at one of her friends' houses, maybe Lynn's, to see Davie. He saw no point in staying home from work today; there was nothing he could do. He needed something to get his mind off Tamara, what might be happening to his little girl. It made him angry, being so helpless, especially when the well-being, if not the life, of one of his children was at stake. He felt he needed to explain to Elisabeth why he was going on to work before he left, so he called Lynn's number. Lynn was still in bed. She hadn't seen Elisabeth this morning yet.

Jonathan began to feel apprehensive. Next he dialed Amy's number; Todd was with her. No, Amy was just getting ready to come over there. Liz wasn't home?

Jonathan was extremely nervous as he waited for Vicky to answer. She didn't, but her husband answered on the sixth ring. Vicky was in the shower, he was running late, but he was sure Elisabeth wasn't over there; Jennifer was still asleep.

Jonathan hung up and parted the curtains over the kitchen window. The station wagon was still parked in the driveway, and so was his pickup. Maybe Elisabeth had just decided to take an early morning walk around the neighborhood, perhaps over to the park several blocks away. He had to believe this. If she'd gone looking for Tamara, she would have taken the car. She hadn't been kidnapped too. Out walking, that was all.

He wrote her a note and pinned it to the refrigerator with a magnet. By the time Detective Morrison called at eight, there was no one home to answer.

Morrison wanted a picture of Valerie.

In a second interview with Sara Hensley of the Huntington Public Library, he'd found out a Mrs. Peachtree had called looking for Gavin, wanting to know if he was still interested in the room she had for rent. She'd left a number.

In his conversation with her, Morrison learned that Gavin had left a fifty-dollar deposit, and had also hinted that his present landlady was out of her tree, his reason for wanting to move.

This didn't jibe at all. Why would Sheffield put down a fifty-dollar deposit on a new room if he was planning to kidnap the girl and head for Charleston? Had it merely been a contrived effort to throw suspicion on Valerie, or had something happened to Sheffield? He had disappeared a good many hours before the kidnapping.

Morrison was beginning to wonder. No one at the bus terminal in Charleston remembered seeing Gavin Sheffield. It would be interesting to see if they remembered Valerie Scott.

The phone was still ringing. Frowning, Morrison hung up. Maybe it was time he paid another visit to the house on Thirteenth Street.

The woman was, as Valerie had suspected, in her sixties, sixty-seven to be exact, but still "strong as a horse" she assured Valerie. She definitely was no invalid, just a poor woman who wasn't making ends meet with her Social Security checks, and couldn't afford her own apartment any longer. Valerie was very sympathetic. Rough world, all right.

The woman's name was Mary Shaw, and she was very impressed with the dining room, how large it was, and so well-furnished. Clean too, smelled like. A steal for twenty-five dollars a week. She wanted to move in that very afternoon, which was fine with Valerie. Mary didn't ask to see the rest of the house, so she didn't see Tamara, who was in the living room sulking about her hair, but Valerie told Mary that she had a little girl, eight years old, instead of Tamara's real age, seven. There was sure to be a story in the paper, if not a picture. Mary remarked that Valerie didn't look old enough to have an eight-year-old child. It was false flattery, but Valerie thanked her anyway. Mary left to go pack her belongings at the apartment house she was living in, with "too many blacks" she'd whispered, as if they might hear from across town.

Valerie fixed a nice breakfast for herself and Tamara, cheese omelets, bacon, and toast with strawberry jam.

Tamara sat with her at the little metal table, but wouldn't eat.

"What's wrong with you?" Valerie asked irritably. "I wouldn't have gone to all this trouble for just myself, I would have been just as happy with a bowl of cereal. What's the matter?"

"I hate my hair," Tamara pouted. "It's ugly now and I hate it."

Valerie had to admit she was no beautician; Tamara now had what they called a bowl cut, probably a little too short, but the color had turned out nicely, she thought. Mary would never recognize Tamara even if she had seen her picture in the paper, or on a poster somewhere. Elisabeth was probably plastering them all over town.

"Well, you'll get used to it. I think it's pretty. Now eat your breakfast. You need your vitamins."

Tamara slowly picked up her fork and half-heartedly jabbed at her omelet. "I won't ever get used to it."

"Just don't look in any mirrors, then, and forget about it. Now eat."

Tamara glared at her. "I hate it, and I hate you! You're mean."

Valerie threw down her napkin. "All right, if you have to learn the hard way."

Tamara pressed against the back of her chair and screamed, "No!"

"It's too late for that now. Come on, you're going."

Tamara kicked, screamed, and flailed her arms, but she was no match for Valerie. By the time Valerie got her up to the second floor, all Tamara's energy had been spent. She was only crying now, and repeating the word no, but weakly. Her body had gone limp, making her seem twice as heavy, but Valerie managed to get them both up the ladder without mishap.

God, but the attic stunk. Ripe decay; horrible odors. Valerie sat Tamara down in front of the cracked vanity mirror. The terrified girl brought up her legs and hid her face behind her knees, sobbing, occasionally gagging from the smell. Valerie felt sorry for her, but this had to be done. At least it would only have to be done this once and never again, probably.

"How could you do this? How could you?" Aunt Vonda shrilled from the mirror as her face came into it.

Valerie bristled. "Mind your own business. I told her this would happen if she misbehaved."

Tamara's head jerked up, her eyes red and puffy from crying. "Who are you talking to?"

She was afraid it was the skeleton; that maybe it could still move around and talk, and would, right in front of her. If it did, she would surely die of fright when she saw it.

"Aunt Vonda," Valerie answered. "She's in the mirror. Can't you see her?"

This was something of a relief, but not much. Tamara looked into the mirror, hoping to see Auntie Vonda. Tamara remembered her. She was nice; she always gave them lots of candy at Easter, and little windup bunnies. But all she saw was her own reflection. "I just see me."

"Well, she's right there, right next to you. Say something to her, Aunt Vonda, so she'll know."

"You're a wicked, wicked girl," Vonda hissed at Valerie.

"There, did you hear that?" Valerie asked Tamara. "She said that I'm a wicked, wicked girl. Did you hear?"

Tamara was too afraid to say no, certain that Valerie would get very angry with her if she didn't agree. Also, if she went along, maybe Valerie wouldn't leave her up here all alone with the skeleton. "Yes, I heard her."

"So can you see her now too?"

"Yes, I see her."

"Well, don't pay any attention to her. She's just a self-righteous old biddy. Talk to Uncle Herb. He'll set you straight on what's what. Anyway, I'm going to go down and write for a while. I'll let you come out in fifteen minutes."

"Don't leave me up here alone!" Tamara shrieked.

Valerie ignored her and climbed down the ladder, closing the lid on Tamara's terrified face, muffling her continued screams.

Are you afraid, Grandmother? Terrified that mouse is going to bite you? It might, you know. They have nasty

*little teeth too, probably cause an infection, or even rabies.
But I doubt you'll live long enough to worry about rabies.
You want me to take the gag off, so you can tell me what a
bitch I am? I'll bet. Well, that's too bad, I'm not going to
do it. Not until you're dead, which should be pretty soon. I
wish you would hurry up.*

Tamara stopped screaming after a while; apparently
her throat had become too raw to utter any sound. Gavin
was still giving Valerie the silent treatment, refusing to
type a single word. Maybe he was gone, but she didn't
think so. Just laying low, making her think he was gone
so he wouldn't have to work. Valerie wondered what
Tamara was doing now. It was pretty mean, she admitted
to herself, sticking Tamara up there with that smell and
all, and she was feeling a little guilty, but the lesson had
to be taught. After the fifteen minutes were up, she would
take Tamara downstairs and give her a treat, be extra
nice to her, and she would quickly come to understand
how things were—what happened when she was bad and
what happened when she was good. What was that called
in psychology? Positive and negative reinforcement?
Whatever. It would work.

The fifteen minutes were almost up when the doorbell
rang. Mary back so soon? Valerie went downstairs to see.

She was most dismayed to peek through the curtain
and see that detective standing out there again; she'd told
him all she knew, at least he should think she had, so
what was he doing back here? She pasted on a smile and
opened the door. "Well, hello again. Something else I can
do for you?"

Apparently there was. He stepped past her without
being invited in and sauntered into the living room with
his hands in his pockets. Valerie left the door standing
open and followed him, fervently hoping Tamara didn't
start up with the screaming again. That would certainly
be difficult to explain. He would want to check it out no
matter what she said.

"Can I get you some iced tea? Coffee?" Tapioca
pudding? she smirked to herself.

"Nothing, thanks," he said, turning to her. "There's no one home at your cousin's. Do you know where they might have gone?"

Valerie shook her head. "No idea. Why? Have you found Tamara?"

"Not yet, I'm afraid, but we haven't lost hope yet. Mind if I ask you a few more questions?"

"What if I did?" Valerie laughed, making it a joke. She did mind, all right. Very much. But he couldn't know that, unless he thought it was only because he was wasting her time, which he was.

Morrison looked at her thoughtfully a second or two, then smiled. "Well, no one's forcing you to cooperate, but I would assume you'd want to be as much help as possible in this case."

Valerie received the underlying message very clearly: no one's forcing you to cooperate *yet*. No more jokes with this one.

"Of course I do. Forgive me for making light of the situation. I'm just trying to get some work done, but of course I'm very concerned. I'll do anything I can to help. What was it you wanted to ask me?"

"Well, I found a friend of Gavin's, a Miss Terri Blake. Know anything about her?"

"No, as I said, Gavin didn't give much information out about himself, and none about anyone he knew. Told me he used to enjoy riding horses, that was about it."

Morrison nodded, mulling over his next question. "He ever make any sexual advances toward you? Offer you money for sexual acts, anything like that?"

Valerie's eyes narrowed. "No, he did not. Never came near me and certainly never offered me any money except for his rent. Do I look like a prostitute or something?"

"That wasn't what I was suggesting," Morrison said, "but it seems Gavin was in the habit of visiting one, so it wouldn't be out of the bounds of his character to approach you with such a proposition, or any other woman he felt attracted to, for that matter. I was only asking if he had. Why so defensive, Miss Scott? Do you have something to hide?"

Valerie knew, then, that he suspected her of being involved in the kidnapping, of being involved with Gavin much more than she'd admitted. But he couldn't prove a damn thing! He was only fishing. He didn't even have enough to obtain a search warrant or he would have shown up with one. "Such as?"

"Anything, Miss Scott, anything at all. I notice you're not wearing your perfume today."

Nothing escaped him, apparently. She had to admire his analytical cunning, but it was a danger to her, and she hated him all the more for it.

"Actually, I don't wear perfume," she replied stiffly. "Yesterday I accidentally broke a bottle and it got all over me. What does that have to do with anything, anyway? Is it a crime to wear too much perfume? People wearing perfume are hiding something? Why don't you come right out and say it? You think I had something to do with Tamara's disappearance, don't you? That maybe I planned it out with Gavin and sent him to do it? Maybe you think I'm even hiding them both here?"

"Oh no, no," Morrison said with an exaggerated frown, shaking his head. "Just like to know all there is to know. You'd be amazed at some of the little things that break cases sometimes. Seemingly insignificant things."

"I still don't know why my wearing perfume—it was cologne, by the way—would interest you."

"You friendly with any of your neighbors?" he asked, sidestepping the issue.

What was this game he was playing? He should be out searching for Gavin, for all the good it would do him.

"I know Mrs. Rothford next door, on the right. She hardly knows me, though. She never gives me a chance to talk. You'll be sorry if you go over there. She'll wear your ears out telling you about all her operations before you can even get your questions asked."

Morrison grinned slightly. "Well, maybe I should chance it anyway. Did Sheffield ever talk to her?"

"Like I said, you don't talk to Mrs. Rothford. She talks to you. But no, Gavin never went over there, that I know of. He was hardly ever here, for that matter, except to sleep."

"Well, I won't waste any more of your time, Miss Scott. Oh, one more thing . . . you ever been married?"

Where were those hideous creatures when she needed them!

"No, I was never married. I lived with someone for two years, though, if that means anything to you."

"Here in Huntington?"

"Savannah. Is that all?"

"Just one more thing. Mind if I ask his name?"

The man was relentless! But so what if he wanted to talk to Doug, to find out if she was as strange as he imagined? Doug had nothing bad to say about her. "Doug Chambers. Would you like his phone number too? His address?"

Morrison smiled, taking out his trusty notebook. "If you don't mind."

Barely able to conceal her contempt, Valerie recited her old phone number and address, warning Morrison that it might be invalid because it had been three years since she had seen or talked to Doug, and he wasn't the greatest at holding down a job. Morrison thanked her kindly and left. Valerie closed the door behind him and leaned against it, breathing a little hard. Damn that man, she hoped she'd seen the last of him.

Morrison paused on the last porch step, head bent, rubbing his chin thoughtfully. For such a concerned relative, Valerie was certainly displaying the wrong reactions. She clearly resented his presence, and he couldn't quite believe it was just because he was interrupting her work.

He glanced back at the closed front door. After twenty-two years on the force, he'd learned a thing or two about human nature. She was hiding something, all right. People didn't get that defensive if there was nothing to defend.

As he ambled toward his car, he hoped her old boyfriend wouldn't be hard to track down. Maybe he knew something about Valerie juicy enough to justify a search warrant.

11

Tamara was curled up in a little ball, repeating a strange noise, like a short hum with one low tune, over and over. Valerie truly felt bad, seeing her that way, but now it was all over. Tamara wouldn't be making any more trouble, saying things like "I hate you, you're mean."

Armand was up there, sitting on the cedar chest, shaking his head. "I think you overdid it a bit," he said. "You're going to get caught anyway. This will just make it worse. They'll throw away the key."

Valerie wished he would stop bothering her, but at least Aunt Vonda wasn't making an appearance, chipping in her two cents' worth. "You don't know anything. You're dead," Valerie retorted. "All you can do is guess, like anybody else, and you're wrong, because I'm too smart for them."

"You're not smart, you're diabolical. Just because Mandy put you in the attic when you were a kid doesn't mean it's all right to do it to her."

"You liar! Grandmother never did such a thing," Valerie growled. "I was a good girl."

"Oh yes she did," Armand insisted. "Told me all about it once when she was visiting me in the sanitarium. She was the only one who ever did, you know. Everyone else just forgot me. She told me how much she hated you, because she didn't think you were really her granddaughter. Of course she had to be nice to you when others were around, but sometimes your parents left you alone with her, and she'd do things to scare you and make you cry. Stopped doing it after you could talk good, because she was afraid you'd tell on her, so you were too young to remember. Ask Herb, he'll tell you. Came over once while Vonda was at her sister's making a quilt and caught her in the act. She had you in the kitchen, pretending she was going to make you eat a dead mouse. I don't know, maybe she'd already made you eat one, she didn't say. Herb was really mad at her, though. Mandy said he slapped her across the face and made some threats."

Valerie still refused to believe it. Armand was just trying to convince her she was crazy, like him. "Come on, Tamara sweetie," she crooned, reaching for the trembling child, who was still humming her one note. "Let's go downstairs and get you some ice cream. You like chocolate?"

Mary Shaw had returned with her old Rambler loaded with her personal belongings, which she insisted on carrying in by herself, as if to prove to Valerie she wouldn't be expecting nursemaid service along with the room. That was fine with Valerie. She had other things on her mind, mainly getting Gavin to communicate with her. Tamara was lying down in the extra bedroom, sucking her thumb, appearing to be in some sort of shock, which was better than her misbehaving, but Valerie didn't much like the looks of it. Maybe she had gone too far, putting Tamara up there with what was left of Gavin, besides what was still under the bed. But what was done was done, no changing it now. Surely in a little while Tamara would snap out of it. Sensitive child, apparently. A little too sensitive perhaps.

Valerie typed the question again, this time in caps:
DO YOU READ ME, GAVIN?
This time he answered.
what do you want

You know what I want, Gavin. I want you to go in to Mary and get these things out of my house. Tamara can't take it. I can always get another roomer.

youre afraid arent you

I'm not afraid, Gavin. I just don't want the responsibility, and Tamara's all freaked out. It's no good for her. And how am I ever going to get any writing done if I'm always having to come up with human flesh? I'd have to get a new roomer every few days. Do you know how much those ads cost? They're not exactly cheap.

Valerie hadn't thought about that until just now, what to do in case Gavin refused to cooperate. There was no choice, really; the hunger had to be fed, and if there was nothing else, that left her and Tamara, and Yellow Eyes *really* had a craving for Tamara. Roomers would be good. They were usually transients, or loners, people who wouldn't be missed. But Gavin was going to cooperate, by God, if Valerie had anything to say about it. It was all his fault anyway. She hadn't asked for this, and it wasn't as if she had all the time in the world to fool around. She wanted to be a writer more than anything. That was her hunger, and it wouldn't be denied on account of some scar-faced jerk.

Gavin, you haven't answered me. Will you go into Mary or not?

no

And why the hell not? You started this. It's the least you can do. All I wanted was some peace and quiet, and a little extra income, so I could write without having to worry about money. And now look what I'm having to deal with! You and that stinking skeleton of yours up there in the attic, having to feed the rest of you to those disgusting things. Give me a break.

i cant

What do you mean, you can't? You got into me somehow. Why can't you just get into her?

i just cant

Well, that's just great. You expect me to keep doing this forever? What if I sell the house and move? Would they stay here, or follow me?

follow

I probably could have guessed. Are you sure you can't? Couldn't you at least try? Maybe if I touched her, on the arm or something. Think you could then?

maybe

Well, I'd damn sure appreciate it. This situation is really getting on my nerves, plus I've got that stupid detective to worry about. I know he's checking me out; he suspects. But I can't give her up. Yellow Eyes would get her for sure. Morrison probably suspects everyone, though, maybe even Elisabeth and Jonathan. Like maybe four mouths to feed was too big a burden, you know what I mean? I might just mention that if he comes around again. That'll give him something to think about, won't it? But I'm not really that worried. Doug might tell him I was frigid, maybe too much of a homebody, but that's about all he can say without making something up. He'd better not say anything about Dennis. I never did anything with Dennis. I was wondering, though. How did these things latch on to you in the first place? I've been kind of curious about that.

one was already here

Valerie stared at the words, her brows bowed in dispute.

Are you sure?

the one with yellow eyes

Suddenly Valerie gasped.

Grandmother. I'll bet it's Grandmother! No wonder I haven't seen her around here. Do you know if it is?

yes

Yes what? Yes you know or yes it's Grandmother?

grandmother

"Holy shit." Valerie cringed. That her grandmother had turned into such a thing after death wasn't very surprising, but if that were the case (and undoubtedly it was), then why hadn't she gone ahead and eaten her before Gavin came?

You really hate me, don't you, Grandmother? I bet you'd like to tear me limb from limb. Slowly. Or maybe you'd prefer burning me alive, or hey, what about eating me alive? Yes, I can see you like that idea. Only you don't have

*teeth anymore. Guess you could gum me to death. Would
you like to do that, Grandmother? Would you?*

It was Uncle Herb, of course, who had kept her from
doing it.

Gavin, why do you suppose Grandmother followed me
over to Elisabeth's? She liked Elisabeth and her kids. I
don't think she really intended to eat Tamara, unless they
just don't give a damn anymore, in that state. To set me up,
maybe? Say she made Tamara sick so Elisabeth would ask
me to come over and watch her, then made Tamara tell me
about the yellow-eyed monster in her closet. What would I
do? She knew what I'd do. She knew I'd take Tamara to
protect her. Now I've got that detective on my back. What
do you think—too elaborate? But if Uncle Herb wasn't
letting her eat me, what else could she have done to get
revenge? I know she wants to do me in somehow. What do
you think?

vampire

What are you talking about? Are you even listening to
me? What are you talking about vampires for? There's no
such things.

the creatures are like vampires

Oh, because they don't just go for the blood. They want
it all.

flesh

That's what I meant, Gavin, and I already knew that
anyway. Like vampires, huh? Well, I guess that explains
why they only come out at night, smacking their lips
instead of baring fangs. So, what about it? Is there any use
for that little tidbit of information?

drive a stake in they go back to their bodies during the
day

Very funny, Gavin. Glad to see you've got a sense of
humor. Now cut the crap.

drive a silver stake through her brain

Brain? You need to brush up on your monster trivia.

Valerie wondered if he thought she was actually going
to fall for this. How ridiculous could you get? She added:

That's heart, you dumb-ass, and silver's for werewolves.

silver stake through the brain

Listen, Gavin, the bitch is dead. What good would it do to drive a damn stake through her rotting brain? You just made that up, didn't you?

cord wont break

Cord? Now that makes a lot of sense. What cord?

from body to soul thats why they still have to eat

Valerie thought about this. It was starting to make sense, sort of. Maybe Gavin was really trying to be helpful after all.

So, if I drive a silver stake through Grandmother's brain, I guess a butter knife would have to do, the cord will break and she'll go away? Some other realm or something?

yes

Sounds easy enough, I guess. She's buried in a crypt, at least I wouldn't have to dig. Too bad I don't know who the others are. Do you?

one is my twin brother

Really? What happened to him?

overdosed on heroin

Oh. Well, he should have known better. Drugs are bad news.

Lynn was relieved to hear Elisabeth's voice. "Liz, where have you been? We've been worried sick about you. Jonathan was looking for you this morning, but now he's gone. I guess he went to work."

Elisabeth sighed into the receiver. "He did, left me a note on the refrigerator, said he had to keep busy to keep his mind off things, which I can understand. No sense in using up all his sick pay to sit around and worry. I woke up last night around one or so. He'd left me on the couch. Anyway, I had to get out of the house, so I decided to take a walk. I guess I was hoping if Tamara was still near enough, she could guide me to where she was; I walked all over town, but I never sensed her and finally ended up at Mom's. I woke her up early this morning. We drank a lot of coffee and cried, then she gave me some sleeping pills and made me go to bed. I just woke up an hour ago and she brought me home. How's Davie?"

"Oh, he's just fine. I left him and Lisa with my mother today so I could put up those posters for you. She said she didn't have a bit of trouble with him. Have you talked to Detective Morrison? Any luck with him yet?"

"He called right after I walked in the door a few minutes ago," Elisabeth said numbly. "He's on his way over now. Wants a picture of Valerie. By the way, thanks for getting Tamara's pictures distributed. I really appreciate it. I don't think she's in Huntington anymore, though."

"Well, I guess there's no telling. Anyway, did he say why he wanted Valerie's picture?"

"No, but he said I shouldn't mention it to her. I wonder if he thinks she had something to do with Tamara's disappearance. Maybe she knew that guy Gavin a lot more than she's admitted. That morning she came over to talk to me about something, she seemed upset . . . but she never said what was on her mind. Guilt? Like maybe they'd already planned this but she wasn't sure if she wanted to go through with it?"

"Then Tamara could be at her house?" Lynn asked, excited.

"Well, Morrison's been over there twice, so I wouldn't think so . . . I don't know. It's hard to imagine Valerie getting involved in something like this. There's a lot of things I wouldn't put past her, but taking Tamara, or conspiring with someone else to take her . . . Anyway, I just have this gut feeling that Tamara is very far away, somewhere with that Gavin creep. If Valerie knew anything about this beforehand, I doubt very strongly she knows where he took her. And if she does, she has no intention of telling, so it certainly wouldn't do any good for me to go over there and demand some answers. I'd probably end up beating the life out of her and then I would be the one in jail. Morrison's no Keystone Kop, so I'll leave it in his hands. If Valerie's guilty, he'll nail her. I just want my little girl back."

"I know," Lynn said sympathetically.

"Anyway, I just called to check on Davie, and ask if I could have a couple more of those Valiums, if you don't mind. I don't think I can handle this without them."

"Sure, Liz, all you want. I'll be right over."

* * *

Valerie had the silver butter knife and a hammer in her purse, ready to leave; if Gavin knew what he was talking about, this had to be done today, before sunset. It was a stretch of the imagination, thinking that Grandmother had turned into a hideous vampire-like thing, but Valerie was prone to believe it. Why should horrible people be any different when they were dead? So awful their cords wouldn't even break, confining their nefarious souls to their bodies, so they had to eat human flesh to ease the torment of decomposition. If it happened to anyone, it would certainly happen to Grandmother.

Maybe she *had* done horrible things to her as a child.

Valerie suddenly remembered the Thanksgiving weekend her parents went to look for the new house in Savannah, where her father was being transferred. She was eleven at the time, and they'd left her in Huntington with Grandmother, saying they couldn't afford the extra plane ticket.

That first night at the dinner table, Valerie had found a sewing needle in her mashed potatoes. Grandmother had sworn up and down she didn't know how it had gotten there.

Sure.

Valerie went back upstairs to check on Tamara before leaving. Tamara was asleep now, still sucking her thumb. When she woke up, she probably wouldn't remember about the attic, or else would think it had just been a nightmare. She'd be all right as she was for an hour or so; Valerie knew that what she had to do shouldn't take much longer than that.

She had just stepped back into the hallway, quietly closing the door behind her, when she heard Uncle Herb call her name from his old room.

He was sitting in his chair, smoking, a look of concern on his face. "You'd better be careful."

Valerie moved to stand in front of him, a little angry. "Why didn't you tell me? You knew, didn't you?"

He took his pipe out of his mouth and met her open stare. "Didn't think you'd want to know. I heard Vonda telling Sadie at my funeral that she was going to ask you to come up and take care of Mandy so she could travel a bit, so I thought I'd better stick around for your sake. I knew the way Mandy felt about you. Watched her when she died. It was terrible; she came across all grotesque, screaming like she was in this terrible pain, and I could tell something had hold of her on this side and wouldn't let go. Guess the ones like her, they can feel their bodies coming undone. When they eat flesh, I guess that helps it, maybe stops it, couldn't say for sure. Well, I could tell she was going to eat you right away, after all, you *had* killed her, but I wouldn't let her get close; she's not any stronger than me, even with that hunger of hers. Then I'll be damned if that fella didn't show up with five more of the sons of bitches. Like I told you, I was having a hell of a time keeping 'em all at bay, and they were getting pretty desperate."

Valerie bent over and tenderly kissed his cheek, her lips tingling coldly in touch with his ethereal body. "Thank you, Uncle Herb. Well, I'd better be on my way." She turned back at the door. "So Grandmother really did do awful things to me when I was little?"

But Herb was already gone, and Mary was calling from the bottom of the stairs. "Yoo-hoo!"

Valerie held a finger to her lips as she quickly descended the stairs, whispering harshly, "Quiet, my daughter is asleep."

The tall, gray-headed woman with sagging skin grimaced in apology. "Oh dear, I'm sorry. I just wanted to ask you if you cared for some iced tea. I just made some fresh."

It was hot, and Valerie felt thirsty, but she didn't want to take the time. It was sure to include a lot of chatter she was in no mood for. All she could think about was getting that crypt open and hammering the silver butter knife through Grandmother's skull.

"Well, that's very thoughtful of you, Mary, but I'm sort of in a rush. Would you mind keeping an eye on my daughter while I'm gone? She probably won't even wake up until I get back, but you weren't planning on going anywhere, were you?"

Mary put a flabby arm around Valerie's shoulder, which Valerie didn't like a bit. It was too familiar a gesture for a perfect stranger, and besides, the woman smelled.

"Be my pleasure to watch after your little girl," she said with breath the odor of tainted eggs. "If she wakes up, I'll just give her some tea and cookies I brought and we'll have ourselves a good time. Don't you worry about rushing. She'll be just fine. Is she sick?"

"Touch of flu," Valerie said, nodding, trying to pull away without seeming impolite or showing the revulsion she felt. "That's why she's not in school, of course; guess she'll be missing her last few days. But there is one thing, Mary. Don't open the front door unless it's someone you know. There's a strange man that's been lurking around the neighborhood, dressed in a business suit, and there's some rumor about him possibly being this rapist they've been looking for."

Mary's eyes bulged from their turtle pockets. "You don't say. Well, I'll keep it locked up, certainly. Doorbell ringing wouldn't be done by anyone I know, anyway. They're all dead or moved away."

"That's too bad," Valerie said. So Mary wouldn't be missed if something should happen to her. That was nice to know.

12

Fortunately there were no visitors in the cemetery. Valerie parked behind the crypt and took her crowbar out of the trunk. Then, with a final glance over her shoulder, she pushed open the creaking metal door of the crypt and went inside.

The heat was sweltering in there, and the dry, stale air was faintly tinged with the unpleasant odor of decomposed flesh. There were twelve drawers, six on each side, sealed with dusty brass plates bearing the vital information of their deceased, the immediate Kellerman family, all accounted for. Since Grandmother had been the last of them to die, she was in the left corner on the bottom row. Valerie was already sweating profusely, laboring to breathe the oppressive air, hoping like hell it didn't take too much effort to get that plate off.

"What do you think you're doing now, Valerie?"

Armand stepped out of the shadows next to Grandmother's drawer, his expression menacing. "Come to pay your respects to the dead?"

"Just stay out of my way," Valerie said angrily, taking the silver knife and hammer from her purse, which she put down on the dull marble floor. "I guess you probably know what I'm here for, and there's nothing you can do about it. You probably know what she is too. Trying all this time to make me think I was just crazy."

Armand glowered at her. "You are insane, crazier than a bat. Those creatures that you think exist aren't real. You're nuts! I loved Amanda. I won't have you desecrating her body."

Valerie ignored him, knowing there was nothing he could physically do to stop her, and with her tools moved toward the corner, passing right through him. A strange sensation, like stepping through a freezer. But the next step she took, he was right in front of her face again. She was certain that if he could strangle her, he would now do so on the spot.

"Get out," he growled. "Leave her alone."

I'm leaving you, Grandmother, all alone. I'm tired of waiting for you to die. I think I'll go out and see a movie. It's been a long time since I've been to a movie. What's that smell? You filthy old woman, look what you've done. Well, you can just lay in it, I don't care. I'm leaving you, Grandmother. You'll be all alone, just your mouse to keep you company. Unless he died in there. Think he died in there?

"Get lost, Armand. I'm actually doing her a favor. You think she likes being what she is?"

His lips curled in rage. "You're doing yourself a favor is what you think you're doing, but you might be in for a nasty surprise."

"What's that supposed to mean?"

"Go ahead, do it, you'll find out."

Uncle Herb's warning: be careful. Valerie wiped the sweat from her forehead with the back of her hand, the one in which she clutched the silver knife. "You're just trying to scare me out of it."

"You'll see," Armand taunted with a malicious gleam in his eyes, and melted back into the shadows.

Valerie coughed, tickled by sweat running between her breasts. She scratched, undid a few buttons of her blouse, wondering. Could Grandmother turn into anything worse?

"Gavin? Gavin, can you hear me? Are you sure about this?"

Gavin couldn't answer, of course. She hadn't brought her typewriter along, and even if she had, there was no place in here to plug it in. Armand had just been trying to scare her out of doing it, anyway. Playing the concerned relative all this time, all the while rooting for Grandmother, hoping she'd get what she wanted: revenge. After a month that hunger of hers had to be getting pretty bad, which was probably why she'd gone over to Elisabeth's; Herb couldn't be in more than one place at a time. Sure, she just couldn't stand it anymore. Grandmother wasn't smart enough to think up any elaborate plans for getting her into trouble with the law. The hungry witch decided to feed on one of her great-granddaughters. So why hadn't she eaten Jennifer instead, Valerie wondered, after she took Tamara away? Or the baby or Todd? What was so special about Tamara that Grandmother had to have her?

Well, she wasn't going to have anyone now. Valerie positioned the crowbar into the small crack behind the plate and pulled with all her strength. Not being prepared for the thing to come off so easily, when it did, clattering heavily on the marble floor, she fell backward and hit her head. The pain was excruciating. "Shit!"

When she sat up, she saw stars, which passed in a matter of seconds, but the pain got worse. The lid was off, though. Now all she had to do was pull out the drawer, open the coffin, place the knife and hammer it in. Was she really doing this? If this was just Gavin's idea of a practical joke . . .

But no, Armand had virtually admitted the truth about Grandmother.

Wincing from the pain—what a headache (did she have a concussion? There was a nasty bump, and her mind was becoming less clear; better not sleep for a while)—she positioned herself in front of the oak coffin, gripped both sides, and heaved. The box came rolling out and came to a sudden jolt on the end of its rail. Time for Truth or Consequences. Dead for a month. Shouldn't look *too* bad—that embalming fluid kept them fresh much longer than that, surely. Valerie straightened up and took a deep breath, which she instantly regretted.

The smell of decay was suddenly overwhelming. They *had* embalmed her, hadn't they? By God they better have, she'd paid for it.

Well, she could stand there looking down at the coffin all day; it wasn't going to open itself. And if Grandmother did start to open it from within, well, that would be Valerie's cue to get the hell out of there fast. Head splitting, nerves on end, muscles rigid, she lifted the lid. And nearly lost her lunch.

Maggots were swarming all over the corpse; they were practically all she could see besides clothing. Damn, that mortuary had ripped her off. Or maybe they hadn't. Maybe this was happening because Grandmother hadn't been eating flesh. Either way, it was too horrible a sight to bear. Looking up as much as possible, Valerie quickly placed the silver butter knife in one of the empty eye sockets and brought the hammer down, squeezing her eyes shut at the same instant. There was a sound, not what she'd expected, kind of a popping sound. She didn't want to see the effect the knife had made. Eyes still shut, she reached over and slammed the lid down. It was done.

The tomb was very quiet.

And very hot. Valerie struggled with the brass plate, finally got it back in place, secured it with the hammer, then picked up the crowbar and her purse, her blouse literally drenched now, as well as her hair, with rancid sweat. First thing she had to do when she got back home was take a cold bath.

The back of her head throbbing, she walked out into the blinding sunlight, thinking some of Mary's iced tea would sure be good right about now.

Mary was rocking Tamara in the living room when Valerie got home. Tamara's eyes were closed, but she was sniffling and breathing raggedly as if she had been crying, her thumb planted firmly in her mouth. Seven was far too old for thumb sucking, Valerie decided.

"She woke up yelling her head off about fifteen minutes ago, and crying, must have had some kind of nightmare," Mary explained when she saw the look of displeasure on Valerie's face. "But I got her calmed down. She's all right now. Seems to be running a bit of a fever, though. Didn't give her any aspirin; didn't know if it would be all right. By the way, I wanted to mention that I noticed there's some sort of smell upstairs. I couldn't tell where it was coming from, though."

"Probably a dead mouse," Valerie said, knowing she was going to have to do something else with that skeleton now, or Mary might catch on. There had been mice all over it when she'd put Tamara up there, but they weren't cleaning it fast enough. "I'll look for it after I take a bath. It's probably behind a dresser or something." She reached for Tamara. "I'll take her now."

But Tamara kicked her and yelled, "Don't touch me!" Her eyes flew open and glared at Valerie with raw hatred.

So she hadn't forgotten about the attic, and now matters were worse. She'd definitely gone too far.

Valerie smiled patiently for Mary's benefit. "Now Tamara, you know that wasn't nice. You hurt me. Come upstairs with me now and I'll give you some aspirin for that fever."

"No," Tamara hissed, snuggling closer to Mary.

"I mean it, Tamara," Valerie warned with more firmness in her voice. "Come upstairs with me right now or I'm going to get angry with you."

"I don't mind holding her," Mary said, patting Tamara's arm. "You can bring the aspirin down, but I've got some on the dresser in my room. That would be handier."

"She's coming upstairs," Valerie said stonily. "Upstairs, Tamara."

Tamara suddenly bolted from Mary's lap and dashed through the dining room doors. Her face set, Valerie said to Mary, "Excuse me," and followed her. But when she stepped into Mary's room, there was no sign of Tamara. Was she hiding in here, or had she gone straight through to the kitchen? The brat. "Tamara, are you in here?"

Of course there was no reply. Only one place to hide, under the bed. Valerie got down on her knees and looked. There she was.

"Tamara, come out from under there this instant!"

Tamara spat at her. "You're mean. Go away. Leave me alone."

Valerie glanced over her shoulder, making sure Mary wasn't standing in the doorway. She wasn't, so Valerie turned back to Tamara and said softly, as nicely as she could, "I'm sorry about putting you up in the attic, okay? I know that was mean, and I promise to never do it again. So will you come out now? I'll buy you a new toy."

"I don't want a new toy!"

"Well, whatever you want, then. Come on, I've got a splitting headache myself. I need some aspirin if you don't, but I can't leave you here under Mary's bed. By the way, you didn't tell her anything, did you?"

Tamara grinned spitefully. "Maybe I did. Maybe I told her you kidnapped me and won't let me go home."

Valerie knew she hadn't. "If you'd told her that, Tamara, she would already have called the police, and she wouldn't have been so nice to me when I got home. Probably would have taken you to the police station herself. Don't try to bluff me, you're not smart enough. Now get out here or I'm coming under there after you. Besides, I did not kidnap you. I saved you from the monster."

"You're the monster," Tamara hissed.

Fresh out of patience, Valerie groped under the bed, hoping to reach one of Tamara's limbs, when she suddenly felt an acute stab of pain. Tamara had bit her. That was the last straw. Fingers throbbing, Valerie said in a low mutter, "Let's see what I can do with the broom handle."

Valerie went to the kitchen to get the broom out of the pantry, cursing under her breath. So this was the thanks she got for risking jail to save the kid's hide, literally. Tamara was just like her mother: two-faced. If this kept up, Mary was going to get suspicious; she probably should have waited until Tamara was settled to run the ad. But she needed the money, and besides, Gavin wouldn't last forever.

Mary had turned on the television to watch a soap opera, which irritated Valerie because that part of the house was private, and the television wasn't for Mary's use. Yet for the time being Valerie was glad that Mary was occupied. This was going to be some scene. Damn that little brat.

When she got back to the dining room with the broom, Tamara was no longer under the bed. Valerie gritted her teeth. She should have known better than to say what she was planning to do. She pushed one of the dining room doors open slightly and asked pleasantly, "Mary, did you see Tamara come through here?"

Mary jumped slightly in the rocking chair and turned around. "What was that?"

"Did Tamara come through here?"

"Didn't see her," Mary said, pushing herself up out of the chair. "You can't find her? Want me to help you look?"

"No." Valerie smiled. "Don't bother yourself. Just watch your program. She plays this little game with me sometimes."

Mary nodded, still looking concerned. "All right, then."

Valerie closed the crack between them and gripped the broom handle tightly, eyes narrowed. Damn brat, where the hell was she? Must have slipped upstairs without Mary noticing. Well, if she wanted to play hide and seek, she would certainly seek Tamara, and when she found her, Tamara was going to be very sorry. But it would have to wait until she had her bath, Valerie decided; she could probably outdo Gavin in a smelling contest right now, from sweating in that crypt.

But she couldn't take a bath because Tamara had indeed snuck upstairs and had locked herself in the bathroom. After trying the knob and finding it locked, Valerie knocked softly on the door. "Tamara, I know you're in there, so unlock this door. The game's over. If you come out right now, before I count to ten, I promise I won't punish you."

I'm going to count to ten, Grandmother, and on ten I want you to die. By the way, that was a pretty good movie. I even cried. So now, are you ready? One . . .

". . . Two. Tamara, are you listening?"

Three. Get ready, Grandmother, only seven more to go . . .

". . . Four. Are you going to unlock this door or not? I promise I won't be mad. Five."

Six. Grandmother, death's so close now. Six. You're dying, dying . . .

". . . Seven. Can you hear me, Tamara? You haven't climbed out the window onto the lower roof, have you? You could still fall and break your neck from there."

Eight. Get ready. Only two more to go . . .

". . . Nine. This is your last chance, Tamara. If I have to break this door down, I will, damn you, and you'll be sorry. You hear me? You'd better be getting ready to unlock this door."

TEN!

The door opened, and Tamara stood there, smiling.

"That's better," Valerie said, expelling a heavy breath. She didn't want to have to punish Tamara anymore. "Don't do that to me again," she warned, her voice no longer angry, but firm. "Absolutely no more biting or kicking, and you do what I tell you, and we'll get along just fine."

"I want to go sit with Mary some more," Tamara said.

Valerie sighed. "All right, I need to take a bath anyway, but behave yourself. You know the things you shouldn't say, don't you? Because if you tell Mary anything you shouldn't, then I would have to kill her, and you like Mary. You wouldn't want me to kill her, would you?"

Tamara quickly shook her head, eyes wide.

"All right, go on down, then, and if I can get rid of this headache, I'm going to try to write for a while after my bath. A story just for you, won't that be nice?"

Tamara turned and scampered down the steps.

13

Looking weary, Morrison handed the photograph back to Elisabeth. "Faxed it to Charleston and had them take it around the bus depot, but no one remembered her. So I guess that's another dead end. We can't prove your cousin was involved without a confession . . . guess I could take her to the station and try to scare her up a bit, but I get the impression that even if she's guilty, she wouldn't crack an inch. I'm sorry, Mrs. Wade. We don't seem to be getting anywhere."

Elisabeth looked at the photograph of Valerie standing behind Grandma Mandy in her wheelchair, taken the previous Christmas. Valerie was smiling, her shoulder-length black hair hanging limp, her eyes, normally very pale ice blue, so pale they almost looked like an albino's, glowing red because of the cheap camera. Grandma Mandy's eyes were squeezed shut and she was scowling. "So you do think Valerie had something to do with it?" Her voice was breathy, almost without tone. The Valiums were doing their job.

"Never know," Morrison sighed. "There were some suspicious things about her. Her attitude, for one thing. Didn't seem all that concerned about your daughter's disappearance."

Elisabeth stuck the photograph in between the pages of a *Reader's Digest* on the coffee table and frowned. "That's just her. She never did care about anyone but herself. I asked her to come over and sit by the telephone for me that morning, but she was too damn busy. It's a wonder Grandmother lived as long as she did, with Valerie taking care of her. Let her get terrible bedsores, not turning her often enough."

Morrison took mental note of that and shook his head. "Poor old people. I can't imagine what it would be like to depend on someone else for everything, like a baby. It has to be terribly humiliating. I ever get to that point, I think I'd prefer to take a bullet." He suddenly realized what he'd said in front of such a distraught woman. "Sorry, I forget sometimes."

Elisabeth required no apology; with the Valium, nothing seemed to bother her much. Her house was a disaster, but she couldn't have cared less.

Continuing with the previous subject of Valerie, Morrison said, "I also thought something was funny about all that perfume she had on the first time I went over there. Well, not until I smelled that room Sheffield had been living in, all sprayed down with Lysol. Got the feeling she was trying to cover something up. But I couldn't dig up any dirt on her, so there's no grounds for obtaining a search warrant. Just a wild hair, anyway, but I didn't want to leave any stone unturned. If she's a liar, she's the best damned one I've ever seen. We'll keep looking for Sheffield, though. We catch him, he might implicate her. But like you say, maybe she's just odd."

"Odd isn't the word for Valerie," Elisabeth muttered.

youre really in trouble now get rid of her
Valerie read the message from Gavin and frowned.
What the hell are you talking about now, Gavin? You're supposed to be helping me come up with a story for Tamara. Who should I get rid of? Mary? Does she suspect?
not mary get rid of tamara
Get rid of Tamara? Why?
grandmother

What? I'm getting pretty sick of this, Gavin. What's this about Grandmother? I put the silver knife through her brain, just like you said. You telling me now that was all a joke, or what?

grandmother is in tamara now

Valerie felt the blood drain from her face.

No. Tell me you're kidding about that, Gavin. Please. Not Tamara.

yes

"Damn." Valerie dropped her face in her hands. "This is terrible, just terrible." She placed her fingers back on the keys, feeling a sickness in the pit of her stomach.

How can I get her out?

kill tamara

Valerie gasped, looking furtively around the room. If Aunt Vonda saw this, she'd throw an absolute fit.

I can't kill Tamara, Gavin. I did what you told me to do, damn it, so that should be that. Why didn't you warn me this might happen?

didnt know it would

God, you are incompetent. No wonder you couldn't get a better job than working at the library. But get serious here. I can't kill Tamara. What would Mary think?

kill her too

Valerie tried to think. She supposed she was going to have to do that anyway—kill Mary, that is—if Gavin really couldn't get out. After all, there were still those things to feed. She could lessen their number by one, but she decided not to bother with digging up Gavin's twin brother to give him the silver treatment—too much work, and it would be easy to get caught, digging up a grave in broad daylight. And that would still leave four she couldn't do anything about because she didn't know who they'd been or where their bodies were buried. What was one more, so long as it wasn't Grandmother?

Who was inside Tamara now, according to Gavin. Damn it all, things just kept getting worse. She typed:

Well, Tamara's just a little girl. She can't hurt me.

Valerie didn't want to do what Gavin suggested. Not at all. She didn't save Tamara so she could kill her herself. There had to be a way to get Grandmother out of her; it wasn't as if Tamara had been totally displaced. She was still in there too, like Valerie was still in her body with Gavin. There had to be some way to get rid of them both, Grandmother and Gavin, short of Tamara and herself dying.

wanna bet she cant hurt you

Valerie moaned, popped two more aspirin in her mouth and chewed them, wincing at the taste, and answered:

Grandmother will probably make her try to hurt me, but at night I could tie Tamara up so she couldn't do anything to me while I'm sleeping, and the rest of the time I'll just have to be on my toes, until we get this figured out. There's got to be some other way.

no other way

They were out of room on the paper. Valerie removed the sheet and placed it in a folder next to the typewriter, then rolled in a fresh one.

What do you know? You don't know a damn thing. That means I'd have to kill myself to get rid of you.

maybe not

Well, I'm getting pretty tired of all this, and I don't plan to put up with it much longer. Now what about a story for Tamara?

No response.

Gavin?

Still no reply.

Damn you!

"I'm afraid he's right, unfortunately," Uncle Herb said behind her. Valerie turned in her chair to face him.

"Uncle Herb, this is getting to be a bit much. Now I have to kill Tamara? Wouldn't Grandmother just go into someone else then? I can't kill everyone on the planet."

Herb tamped his pipe thoughtfully. "I suppose maybe I could latch on to her when she leaves the body, keep her from doing that. Only problem is, can't make 'em leave if they don't really want to. Won't stick around inside a dead one, though. No way."

This was very upsetting. "Well hell, then, looks like I'm stuck with those things forever, since it's obvious

Gavin doesn't want to move into Mary. I think he knew this would happen. He's trying to get me back for making him that tapiocá pudding."

"Could be," Herb agreed, nodding solemnly. "Could be, but I never would've guessed Amanda would do that myself; thought she'd want to move on to wherever it is we go from here."

"She must really hate me."

"I expect so, after all you did to her, even though you were just paying her back for what she did to you without really knowing it. But I guess that makes no difference to her. She wants to get you, all right."

Valerie slumped in her chair. "I could see the murder in her eyes the moment she died. I'd never seen such a hateful stare in all my life. It chilled me to the bone. You know, come to think of it, Tamara had that very same look when I got home. Oh well, we know why. Grandmother. I should have known all this was going to happen, that she couldn't die with that much hate in her to leave me here in peace. She couldn't have stood it. Damn, I sure hate the thought of killing Tamara. Maybe I won't. I'll just know when she's acting up that it's because of Grandmother, and put her away someplace until she quiets down."

"That's a young mind in that girl, though," Herb cautioned. "Easy to control. Even when you think she's being good, Amanda could be in control, up to something sneaky. Never could trust her."

Valerie supposed he was right, remembering the smile on Tamara's face when she'd opened the bathroom door. Smug. *I know something you don't.* Evil. *I'm going to get you.*

But that wasn't, unfortunately, the extent of her problems. It could wait on the back burner for the time being. "So what about those other things? Honestly, I can't keep this up. I don't want the responsibility. You said you kept them at bay. Can't you drag them out of here? Maybe lead them to another house?"

"Hmmm." Herb thought the idea over for several moments while he lit his pipe. When it was going, he settled down in his chair with a low grunt. "Well, I don't see how I could force them out, not that many, but if they were enticed . . . you'd have to do it, though."

Valerie craned forward. "Enticed? How?"

Herb nodded toward her bedroom. "That stuff you've got under the bed. Maybe make a trail with it or something."

Valerie frowned. "But there isn't that much, really. The farthest I could get would be to Mrs. Rothford's house."

"Well, there you go."

"But that's right next door!" Valerie complained. "They'd eat her up and come right back."

"But maybe not."

"Just like cats," Valerie insisted. "They know who feeds them."

Herb shrugged. "What about Mary, then? Get her chopped up. You could make a longer trail."

"But I need the money she's paying for that room. If I don't have to kill her, I'd rather not."

"Don't know what else to tell you, then. Try it over to Mrs. Rothford's and see. Maybe they won't come back. That stuff you're feeding them here is pretty rancid anyway. It doesn't help near as much. They prefer fresh."

"I guess it's worth a try." Valerie sighed. "It's stinking up the house anyway. Ought to move the skeleton while I'm at it. What do I care if the damn mice starve."

Herb nodded. "Yeah, Vonda's not fond of it one bit. She's been complaining."

Mary insisted on cooking dinner, to show her gratitude. Valerie raised the dropleafs on the metal kitchen table so they could all sit together. It was fried chicken, crisp like Valerie could never seem to make it, and mashed potatoes with no lumps, the way hers always turned out, green beans, and a Jell-O salad Mary had made that afternoon with Tamara's help. Valerie decided she wouldn't eat any of the Jell-O salad. Herb was right. Tamara could never be trusted. Valerie only hoped Mary didn't die from eating it—she was a great cook, and maybe Valerie could knock that extra five dollars off her rent if she cooked all the meals.

She tried not to think of what she would probably end up having to do to Tamara. Valerie had been watching her very closely, trying to see if she could detect any more spark of Grandmother's hatred in her eyes. But Tamara just looked like Tamara—the new Tamara anyway—with the short brown hair, her eyes only the eyes of a child. Valerie waited to see if she would eat any of the fruit salad herself. Would be a shame to kill such a pretty little girl. And how would she explain Tamara's disappearance to Mary? She supposed she could say that Tamara had gone to spend the summer with her father, off in some other state, and then pretend he won custody.

"Would you like some Jell-O for dessert, honey?" Mary asked Tamara, holding up the dish. "I see you've finished your supper."

Valerie watched the girl's face. "I'm full," Tamara said, looking back at Valerie with a blank stare. "Can I be excused?"

"I think you should try some of the fruit salad." Valerie smiled, testing her. "You helped make it. You should eat some."

"But I'm full!"

Valerie clenched her napkin under the table. "I said, eat some of that fruit salad."

"If she's full—" Mary began, but Tamara, now glaring at Valerie, grabbed the spoon in the dish and plopped some on her plate. Valerie relaxed a little. Maybe Tamara hadn't poisoned it after all. Best to flush the rest of the cyanide anyway, in case the idea just hadn't occurred to her yet. Valerie's smile returned.

"That's better. Now eat it."

"Yes, Mother," Tamara spat sarcastically, taking her own spoon and shoveling it into the pile of Jell-O on her plate, capturing a mandarin orange. She stuck the spoonful in her mouth, but Valerie could tell she didn't swallow. Wouldn't matter anyway, if cyanide was in it. But apparently there wasn't.

"Now swallow it."

Instead, Tamara spat the mouthful back onto her plate. Mary stared in shock. Valerie brought her fist down on the table, making everything on it jump. "That's it, young lady, upstairs."

"Make me," Tamara challenged, and dashed through the side kitchen door into Mary's room.

This crap again. Maybe Grandmother was just bent on making her life a living hell through Tamara, putting her up to stunts like this all the time. She would see about that.

"The divorce has been hard on her," she explained apologetically to Mary. "If you'll excuse me." She left Mary sitting there looking very distressed.

Tamara had gone through to the living room and was rocking in front of the blank television screen. Valerie stopped the rocker with her foot, arms crossed angrily on her chest. Keeping her voice very low, as Mary could be in the dining room now, trying to listen, she said, "Now I know it's not your fault, acting like that, but you're just going to have to get stronger, Tamara, so she can't make you do those things. Gavin can't make me do anything."

"You told me Gavin is dead," Tamara said loudly. Valerie clamped a hand over her mouth and whispered in Tamara's ear, "Keep your voice down! You want Mary to hear?" She could bet her ass that was exactly what Grandmother wanted, she thought suddenly. Tamara fought wildly as Valerie pulled her out of the chair to take her upstairs, screaming behind Valerie's hand, trying to bite it, but she couldn't. With much difficulty, Valerie finally got her up into the spare bedroom and flung her down on the bed.

"Scream all you want now," Valerie growled. "I'll just put that sock back in your mouth and leave it there all night."

This shut Tamara up. She looked up at Valerie sullenly, and Valerie could see it again, the explicit hatred. Grandmother's hatred. "You've been hearing Grandma Mandy's voice, haven't you, Tamara?"

"No," the girl shot back defiantly.

"She's inside you, you know," Valerie said gravely. "Inside your body with you."

Tamara's eyes opened wider, her expression losing some of its viciousness. "She is not."

"She is too, and that's why you're behaving like such a brat. Now why did you spit that fruit salad back on your plate? You shouldn't do things like that in front of Mary. For that matter, you never should. Now why did you?"

"Because I was full! I told you! Mama didn't use to make me eat when I was full!" Tears formed in the corners of her eyes and she began to sob quietly.

Valerie noted Grandmother's release of the girl's mind with wonder. She was really talking to Tamara now. Best to convince her of what was going on, now while she had the chance. Valerie sat down on the bed.

"Tamara, listen to me very carefully. Now I know this is going to be hard for you to understand, but what I'm telling you is the truth. Remember that monster you saw in your house? Well, that was really Grandma Mandy. She turned into a monster after she died. When I found out it was her, I also found out there was a way to make her stop being a monster, so I did it today. That's why I went out. Only you see, when I did what I did, Grandma Mandy jumped into your body. That's why you woke up screaming from your nap. She's not a monster anymore, just a spirit, but she's very, very mad at me, and she's using you to get back at me. Understand?"

Tamara looked ashen. She understood, all right, and it left her speechless.

Valerie patted her arm. "Don't worry, though, she won't hurt you. She just wants to hurt me. So if you ever have the urge to give me a bad time, or put poison in my food or come after me with a knife or something, that's Grandma Mandy trying to get you to do it. So what you do is, just ignore her. Don't do what she wants you to do. That shouldn't be too hard, should it?"

Tamara shook her head slowly.

"Well then, now that we've got that settled," Valerie smiled, "I think it's about your bedtime, isn't it? I'm going to have to lock your door, of course, in case Grandmother tries to make you do something in your sleep. And don't worry about the other monsters, I'm getting rid of them all tonight, after Mary goes to bed.

Then everything will be fine, long as you can keep Grandmother from pushing you around."

Soon after Valerie had closed and locked the door, Tamara jumped out of bed and hurried over to turn the light back on. She was far too frightened to stay alone in the dark.

The threatening shadows fled, but Tamara didn't feel much better. She haltingly approached the dresser, a deeper dread keeping her eyes lowered so she couldn't see her reflection in the mirror. She might find a wrinkled old woman staring back at her, which would surely bring on an endless scream.

Nevertheless, she slowly lifted her gaze, teeth mashing on her lower lip.

Her hair looked awful, but her face, she was relieved to note, still looked the same. For several moments she stared into her own haunted blue eyes, then suddenly felt the urge to scream anyway.

She didn't want Grandma Mandy inside her. She didn't want to be there at all, and she never wanted to see her cousin Valerie again. This was all wrong, like a bad dream she couldn't wake up from.

Turning from the dresser, she threw herself on the bed and smothered her scream in the pillow.

Valerie was getting madder and madder at Mary, sitting in her living room like she owned the place, watching program after program on her television. She wanted to tell Mary that it would be greatly appreciated if she stayed in her own room, but she couldn't call up the nerve, not knowing if she could pull it off without hurting Mary's feelings. So she waited and waited, tramping downstairs occasionally, making an obvious show of looking at her watch whenever she passed on her way to the kitchen. Mary finally got the hint around ten o'clock, turned off the television and went to bed.

Nearly gagging from the smell, Valerie hauled out the remaining plastic bags from under her bed and slipped quietly back downstairs at ten-thirty. The house was dark and silent, but she knew it wasn't empty. The things were already gathered, waiting for their meal.

Valerie held up one of the bags and shook it. "Hungry?" she whispered to the darkness.

Then she heard the sounds. They started to move, coming from the direction of the fireplace. They were all stuck together. Like pets—like cats one called to dinner by shaking the cat-food box. Here, kitty kitty. They came and Valerie led them through the kitchen, hoping Mary was a sound sleeper.

Through the back porch. Out in the yard. They didn't seem to like it outside, and for a moment she feared they would go back in the house after Mary, so she quickly opened one of the bags and let a piece of Gavin's thigh fall to the ground. After what seemed a long hesitation, they began moving toward it.

"That's it, that's it," Valerie encouraged, dropping more pieces every few feet, smiling even though she was disgusted by the sounds they made fighting over the carnage. At the fence, she unlatched the ivy-covered gate that opened onto Mrs. Rothford's yard and made a trail up to the back porch, where she suddenly thought: what if the door's locked? She tried it; it was. Bad news.

She opened another bag and dumped the contents on the bottom porch step to keep them busy for a while. She had to hurry, though; keep up the enticement or they'd probably go back to her house. For some reason they still seemed very nervous about being out in the open. Wishing she had her crowbar, but knowing it would be dangerous to leave for it, she took the remaining two bags and used them to break the window.

The sound was loud. Valerie held her breath, wondering if the noise had awakened Mrs. Rothford. All she could hear now was the continued slurping of the creatures as they devoured their rancid meat. Then Valerie relaxed, remembering that Mrs. Rothford wouldn't sleep with her hearing aid in, and she was upstairs, so it was highly unlikely she'd heard a thing. Probably wouldn't have if she'd been right there in the kitchen. Careful not to cut herself on the jagged shards of glass left in the window, Valerie slipped her arm through and unlocked the door.

Come my children, come.

They followed her into Mrs. Rothford's kitchen, greedily devouring the chunks of flesh she dropped for them every four or five feet. They were happier now that they were inside. Through the hallway. Up the stairs. Valerie studied the three open doorways. Which one was hers? Then she heard the snoring, and knew. It was the one facing the street, which would be Uncle Herb's old room in her house, where she would soon be writing wonderful children's stories after this madness was under control. To hell with Gavin, she'd write them all by herself.

Mrs. Rothford was snoring away by the window. Valerie's eyes had adjusted to the dark. She could see the shape of the bed, the mound under the sheet on top, which was Mrs. Rothford's body, and her head on the pillow. A light breeze was blowing in through the curtains.

The creatures inched forward in a slithering mass toward the bed, upon which Valerie was carefully placing the last of Gavin, except for his skeleton. Having emptied the remaining bag, she quietly stepped around the slimy throng, slowly, as inconspicuously as possible, until she was back in the hallway. Then she raced for the stairs and nearly fell trying to take them three at a time.

She felt so much better now, standing in her own closed-in porch, breathing the fresh air. But the job wasn't finished yet. She still had to get that clotted skeleton out of the attic and over to Mrs. Rothford's. What she supposed she would do was put it in the bed with whatever was left of Mrs. Rothford by the time she got back, so the things could go ahead and finish Gavin off while they were at it. What a feast they were having tonight.

Upstairs now, and Mary was right, the smell was bad. After she got home again she'd have to take the Lysol up there and spray down the whole attic, and for good measure take all of Vonda's and Grandmother's colognes she could find and sprinkle them over the floor. Valerie pulled the ladder down, silently cursing the squeaky hinges; the sound seemed to fill the whole house. After she got it down and settled into place, she waited. Three minutes, five. Mary didn't appear at the bottom of the steps, asking what in the world. Valerie draped the spare top sheet she'd taken from the linen cabinet over her shoulder and up she went, grimacing with every creak. At the top she switched on the light.

"Covering up your crime, are you?" Aunt Vonda accused from the cracked mirror, her pruney red lips pursed.

"Oh, so I should just leave the skeleton here to stink up the place?" Valerie snapped. "Is that what I should do? First you complain about it being up here, then you get all huffy when I come to take it out."

Vonda's eyebrows rose with indignance. "You're not going to get away with any of this, and if you so much as touch a hair on that child's head—putting her up here with that awful thing, how could you?—well, I'll do something about it, mark my words. Poor child, she'll probably never get over it."

"What about me when I was still just a baby?" Valerie shot back. "Didn't Herb ever tell you what Amanda did to me?"

"Oh, poo. You told him things back then, made up awful stories about Amanda if she didn't let you have your way, and he believed them."

"Hell, Vonda, I wasn't even old enough to talk. You don't know what you're talking about. He even caught her once."

Vonda's wrinkled face darkened. "Well, that's neither here nor there anyway. You did what you did to Elisabeth's little girl, and you ought to be ashamed."

"Well, for your information, it's not just Tamara anymore. Amanda's with her."

"Nonsense." Vonda's features pulled into a bulldog expression. "Who gave you that fool idea?"

"Talk to Herb about it," Valerie said, spreading the sheet over the bones. "I haven't got time to argue with you."

"You're insane," Vonda hissed, fading away. The sound of her voice lingered in the rank air for a few seconds, *aaaane.* . . .

And then there was silence, broken only by the sound of Valerie's heartbeat. When this was over, truly over, she'd ask Uncle Herb to take his wife and leave; she would miss him, but Vonda was intolerable.

She wrapped the last of Gavin's remains tightly in the sheet, tied it with string, and dragged it over to the ladder.

14

The sun was shining through the curtains when Valerie was awakened by a horrendous banging. Tamara was wanting out of her room. She had to go to the bathroom *now*. Valerie dragged herself out of bed, took the key off her dresser and trudged down the hallway, calling to her. "All right, already, I'm coming. Knock off the banging, you'll wake up Mary." She'd hardly gotten a wink of sleep, wondering if the things would return, but she never heard them. They wouldn't venture outside after they'd already materialized, she decided before she finally did fall asleep. Tonight would be the real test, though, to see if they left their bodies for the last place they'd been, or went wherever they damn well pleased, which might be her house again. She had gotten the idea they were really pretty stupid, with minds running on a singular track: feed the hunger, feed the hunger. It gnawed at them constantly; it was all they could think about. Probably they would roam Mrs. Rothford's house in agony for a few nights, not understanding they'd been tricked. They might try someplace else the next time, somewhere they'd been before and had food, but not necessarily next door. Hadn't had any decent flesh there anyway—it would probably be their last choice. Convinced of her reasoning, Valerie felt relieved.

When she opened the door to Tamara's room, she looked down in dismay. Tamara had peed on the carpet. Before Valerie could say anything about it, the girl said willfully, "Told you I had to go. You took too long."

Valerie could buy that, but she still thought Tamara should clean it up. "Go get a towel from the bathroom and soak that up, then I'll have you scrub the carpet with a brush."

Tamara put on an expression that said, not on your life. "You clean it up. It's your fault I did it."

It was obvious that Grandmother was in control again; Tamara wasn't normally such an insolent brat. Valerie grabbed her by both arms. "Tamara, listen to me. Grandma Mandy's doing it to you again, making you misbehave. Now just stop it. Fight her. Assert your own will."

Tamara spat in her face and wrestled free in Valerie's moment of surprise. She was halfway down the stairs in less than two seconds. Valerie wiped the spittle off with her nightgown, her blood boiling with rage. The way she felt that moment, she could have strangled Tamara with her bare hands without blinking an eye. But she reminded herself it was all Grandmother's fault, which diluted her fury to some extent. By the time she was dressed and went downstairs, she would have it under control. That didn't mean Tamara wasn't going to pay. Oh no, she'd pay all right. She apparently needed some incentive to gain strength. But it would take place quietly, later, when Mary was not around to witness.

Mary was whipping up breakfast when Valerie came down, having cleaned up Tamara's mess herself. Tamara was out on the back porch, where she was strictly forbidden to go. Anyone passing by in the alley might see and recognize her in spite of her different hair.

"Good morning," Mary said brightly, flashing her stained dentures. "Hungry?"

"Smells great." Valerie smiled, looking past her at Tamara through the back screen door. "Tamara? Come in now, Mary's almost got breakfast ready." She wanted to go out and yank her back in, but she could do without another scene in front of Mary. "Tamara, did you hear me?"

"She's interested in all those cats," Mary said. "Never seen so many myself. You feed them? I heard them all night."

Cats? Valerie walked to the screen door and looked outside. Indeed, there were quite a few, about fifteen, she guessed, milling about the yard, sniffing the grass. Traces of the meat she'd dropped must have been left behind. At any rate the smell had lingered. Valerie could see over the fence that there were a few cats on Mrs. Rothford's back porch too.

"I want one," Tamara said. "That black one over there. Can I have him? I'm bored."

Valerie considered it. They could use a cat, she supposed, for the mice, and if Tamara had a pet, maybe she would settle down. And of course the cat could always be used as leverage.

"All right, but let me go out and get him for you. You go into the kitchen now and eat your breakfast."

Tamara's arm didn't need to be twisted this time. She went without protest, which Valerie suspected she did because it seemed she'd gotten away with the spitting and was too smart to push her luck. So then, she could control her behavior if she really wanted to, Valerie noted. It was all a matter of will.

The black cat had a pink collar around its neck, someone else's pet. No matter, it was Tamara's now. Valerie carried it into the kitchen and gave it a saucer of milk.

Elisabeth woke that morning to the reality that her daughter was still missing, and went to pieces. She was crying, vowing merciless revenge on Gavin Sheffield, screaming that she was going to go over to Valerie's house and make her tell where Tamara was, all the while tearing clothes out of the closet, throwing things off the dresser and smashing them into the wall, yanking out drawers and scattering the contents, ripping some, tearing at others with her teeth. Jonathan decided she needed to go to the hospital, but when he gently made the suggestion, Elisabeth tore into him, kicking and scratching and pounding on his chest with her fists, screaming that she didn't need to go to the hospital—she needed her daughter back, goddamnit. Why hadn't that stupid Morrison found her yet? What was that imbecile doing? Nothing, nothing, NOTHING! That's what the police were doing! They had other cases to worry about. And what made Jonathan think they could afford to put her in the hospital when their insurance only paid eighty percent? Furthermore, if he did such a thing to her, she would kill herself, so he'd better not even think about it.

Finally, as a last resort, he slapped her, just to snap her out of it. That's what they always did to hysterical women on TV. Only he slapped her a little too hard and knocked her backward, her head hitting the corner of the dresser, and she fell to the floor unconscious.

He took her to the hospital emergency room, where her head was X-rayed. They said it wasn't a severe injury, just a slight concussion, but he ought to have her admitted anyway, since they had been told of the events leading up to the injury. A doctor would interview her when she came around, and might decide she should spend some time in the mental ward for therapy, as further hysterics of this nature could result in self-injury. Jonathan told them what she'd said about killing herself, and the nurse made a note of that on her chart. The doctor would call him after he'd had a chance to talk to Elisabeth.

Jonathan left the hospital with a heavy heart, marveling how easy it was for a family to fall apart at the seams. One day everything was just fine, or at least normal, the next, the whole world came crashing around their shoulders. He needed comfort, but he knew he wouldn't find it in a bottle of Valium or the bottom of a whiskey glass. But he might find it at Valerie's.

Jonathan knew very well how his wife felt about her cousin, but could never understand the basis for her attitude. It seemed to him that she actively looked for reasons to dislike her. On the other hand, Jonathan had been attracted to Valerie, though he'd only been around her a few times. It was the quietness about her, he supposed, her reserved calm, that drew him. She had composure, poise. She didn't seem to get ruffled, like Elisabeth often did, always screaming at one of the kids, bitching about this, that, or the other thing, when all he wanted was peace and quiet. He had witnessed Valerie taking terrible verbal abuse from her grandmother, but she had only smiled, graciously ignoring the senile rantings and talking sweetly to Amanda in return. Since he didn't think it was abnormal or wrong for a married man to fantasize, he'd done some fantasizing about Valerie. Not in a sexual way, but just putting her in Elisabeth's place, imagining how nice it would be to have a wife like that. So after he left the hospital, he headed toward Valerie's house.

Valerie was upstairs with Tamara, who was learning her lesson about spitting in Valerie's face. Valerie had tied her wrists with nylons to the wooden hanger rod in the closet of the spare bedroom, which meant Tamara had to stand on her toes to reach the slanted shoe stand, otherwise the pressure on her wrists was unbearable. Valerie had also stuffed one of Uncle Herb's socks in her mouth to keep her quiet, securing it with one of his ties.

"See you in a week or so," she said to Tamara just before closing the door.

Of course she hadn't really meant that. She only wanted Tamara to think it, so that the hour or so she did spend in there would be all the more meaningful. Valerie also warned that the closet was full of spiders, big hairy ones, for added effect.

She had just sat down behind the typewriter to get some work done when she heard a car pull up in the driveway. At first she feared it might be the detective again, maybe with a search warrant this time. But when she leaned over to peek out the side window, she immediately recognized Jonathan's pickup. What was he doing here? Well, this could be awkward, with Mary around, who was again planted in Valerie's living room watching her television. Valerie had resigned herself to the situation; it was something she would just have to tolerate, she guessed. Best to talk to Jonathan out on the front porch. She rushed downstairs and went out before he could ring the doorbell. He was just coming up the porch steps, looking terribly depressed.

Valerie closed the door behind her. "Jonathan . . . any news yet? Nothing bad, is it?"

"Well, they haven't found that guy yet, or any trace of Tamara, so I don't know yet if that's bad news or good." He sighed, perching himself on the wall where Gavin had sat not long ago, drinking iced tea. "But this morning I had to put Elisabeth in the hospital. She went completely berserk and tore up our bedroom pretty good."

"Tsk, poor cousin Elisabeth," Valerie said, sitting on the swing. "I can't imagine what she must be going through. Well, I would invite you in, but it's so much cooler out here; the house gets unbearable in this heat," she explained. "You don't mind, do you?"

Jonathan didn't mind at all. There was a nice breeze blowing, and in the shade under the eave the heat wasn't so bad. "I didn't plan to stay long anyway. I just needed to talk to someone, I guess. Hope *you* don't mind."

Valerie gritted her teeth behind a smile; what did she look like, a guidance counselor? Of course she minded, she had work to do, which she could finally get done now that a couple of major worries were taken care of. She'd taken care of the smell upstairs, the stench of death was barely even noticeable now, plus she believed the creatures were gone for good. That only left the matter of Gavin and Grandmother being where they shouldn't be, and Gavin wasn't really much of a problem. In fact Valerie was beginning to like him, in spite of his mild obnoxiousness at times, and even if he had purposely set her up to get back at her for killing him. "Of course I don't mind, Jonathan. What would you like to talk about?"

Jonathan looked off down the street, a contemplative expression on his face. His hair had thinned a lot since she'd last seen him, Valerie noticed, and he had also lost some weight, deepening the lines in his face.

"I wonder sometimes," he began softly, "how completely different a person's life would be if one little decision had been made differently. Everything, completely different, if A had been chosen over B or vice versa. Boggles your mind, doesn't it? You choose a course, and off you go. You can only dream about where the other roads might have gone."

Valerie thought about what he said for a few moments, then asked, "Are you regretting your marriage to Elisabeth?"

"I didn't say that," Jonathan said quickly. "I was just—"

Valerie held up her hand. "It's okay, never mind. I know what you meant. Just hard not to wonder, right?"

Jonathan nodded and lowered his head.

Valerie noticed that Mrs. Rothford wasn't out, nor had she picked up her morning paper. It was still attached to her screen door with a rubber band (she tipped the paperboy an extra dollar every month to put the paper on her door). "Well, it's too bad we can't see into the future before we make our decisions, isn't it?"

"Tamara saw into the future a few times," Jonathan said wistfully. "Saw when Herb was going to die about an hour before, you know, and she knew Amanda was going to break her hip. Another time she knew one of the neighborhood kids was going to be diagnosed with muscular dystrophy. Wonder why she didn't see this coming?"

Valerie felt a little nervous about this information. It was the first she'd heard of it. So Tamara was a bit psychic? Might explain why Grandmother had been so interested in eating her. Maybe a psychic's flesh did something special for the cannibalistic vampire-things.

"That's very interesting. Well, maybe she didn't because it wasn't especially bad. For her, I mean. If Gavin has her, he might be taking very good care of her, even spoiling her with gifts and such. She might be laughing at this very moment."

Or screaming behind an old argyle sock, Valerie

thought, imagining big hairy spiders crawling all over her in the dark; but it served the little shit right, after what she'd done.

"I'd like to believe that," Jonathan said, "but Detective Morrison said he was something of a pervert."

"Oh yes, seems he mentioned something to me about Gavin seeing a prostitute . . . is that what he meant?"

Jonathan's jaw muscles tightened. "No, it's worse than that, actually."

"Oh, I see . . . well, would you like some iced tea or anything?"

He shook his head. "No thanks, I really ought to be going pretty soon. Have some calls to make to the women who are watching the kids for us, tell them Elisabeth's in the hospital. They might be watching them awhile yet. And I've got to go to work or I'll go nuts."

Valerie hoped he wasn't hinting for her to take them; what if he asked outright and she couldn't say no? That would be a hell of a circus.

But apparently he wasn't. "I know they don't mind a bit, but I still feel bad about it, for the kids' sakes. They're probably wondering what the hell is going on."

"Don't they know?" Valerie asked, then suddenly jumped. Had she seen a movement in one of Mrs. Rothford's windows?

"Yes, they know Tamara's missing, except for Davie. He's too young, but they don't understand why." His shoulders slumped. "Guess nobody knows that yet, for sure. Except whoever took her."

Valerie watched the curtain in Mrs. Rothford's living room window intently. Surely it wasn't Mrs. Rothford? When Valerie had rolled Gavin's skeleton onto the bed next to the old woman, those things had been all over her. She had seen them.

"Is something wrong?" Jonathan glanced in the direction she was staring.

Valerie looked away and forced up a smile. "Oh no, no, I just thought I noticed my neighbor in that window over there, that's all."

"Well, I guess I'd better be going. I need to be home when the hospital calls, and I've got our bedroom to put back together too. Maybe we'll get good news today. It's about time, I'd say."

"I certainly hope so," Valerie said. "Anytime you need to talk, I'm right here."

Jonathan thanked her and left, feeling better than he had before he'd come. Valerie had that effect on him. He couldn't explain it.

"Who was that?" Mary asked with a smile when Valerie went back into the house.

The remark irked Valerie. She felt like telling Mary it was none of her damn business, and that being too nosy could prove to be a very dangerous occupation.

"Just a friend," she answered.

Mary's smiled widened. "Oh well, I just wondered, after what you told me about that rapist and all. I didn't think that was him anyway, since he didn't have on a suit."

Valerie understood by this that Mary had peeked out the picture window at them. Taking over her living room, and now spying on her. That was pretty bad. Good cooking didn't even begin to make up for spying.

"I was also wondering," Mary went on, now looking a little concerned, "about something I overheard Tamara say yesterday evening. I wasn't meaning to eavesdrop, of course, but she said it so loud I couldn't help but hear. Something about Gavin being dead?"

So on top of everything else, Mary was an inquisitioner. Any little slip and she would be onto it, asking questions, sticking her Roman nose in where it didn't belong, making trouble.

"Gavin is Tamara's father, my ex-husband," Valerie explained with false patience. "He deserted us, but Tamara kept wanting to see him, so I thought it would just be easier to tell her he had died. Only now he's trying to get joint custody, you see. It's all just a big fat mess, and I really don't care to discuss it right now."

Mary clucked sympathetically. "Now isn't that a shame, the things men do?"

"Yes, terrible shame," Valerie agreed. "Anything else you want to know?"

"Oh, guess that's about it, you can go on now with

whatever it was you were doing," Mary answered, patting Valerie's arm.

Valerie tried not to let the indignance show on her face. Oh, so she was dismissed now, was she? Inquiry over for today? Suddenly she didn't like Mary very much. At all.

What do you think of Mary, Gavin? Is twenty-five dollars a week enough for putting up with the likes of her?
    hardly
So, what should I do? Should I ask her to move out?
    i can think of something better
Oh, that reminds me. What was that moving in Mrs. Rothford's window, do you know?
    probably a cat
But Mrs. Rothford doesn't have a cat.
    could have gotten in through the broken window
Oh, that's right, there were a bunch of them in the yard this morning. Didn't think it could have been her. Well, maybe you've got something there, Gavin, about Mary I mean. Maybe I'll teach her not to be so snoopy. You know, I thought about those things going back over there tonight and never finding anything to eat, and what a terrible hunger they suffer . . . don't you feel sorry for your brother?
    he tried to kill me
Well, maybe not him, then, but the others . . . by the way, is that how you got that scar on your face?
    not that its any of your business but yes
I like you, Gavin. You know, I was pretty attracted to you anyway, even with the scar. I even . . . well, it's hard for me to come right out and say this, but I imagined us in bed together. Only we weren't alone, you know, so that kind of ruined it.
    i thought about it too
Valerie blushed deeply, her fingers trembling on the keyboard.
I understand you're something of a pervert. But that's okay, I must admit that's what attracted me to you. I knew it somehow from the start. But you were going to let those things eat me. That's why you moved here.
    yes and i was wondering what was taking them so long

but it was nothing personal thats why i kept my distance you know if id gotten to know you it would have bothered me

Well, that's nice to know. I felt pretty bad about killing you. I'd meant to throw that pudding out, you know. Went to the kitchen that morning to get it but you were already dead.

i know

Although I did kind of think you deserved it, looking to steal food out of my refrigerator, you thief.

Abrasive laughter suddenly filled the room. Valerie's head whipped around, and there was Armand, sitting in Uncle Herb's chair, his face full of mockery. "Are we having fun? Courting yourself now, Valerie? That's a very bad sign, you know."

Valerie glared at him. "I was talking to Gavin. You think I write his answers to myself? Is that what you think, you faggot?"

Armand stopped laughing. "You're completely insane. You've killed two people, you've got your little second cousin hanging in the closet, and you're falling in love with yourself!" He brayed more laughter.

"Maybe I killed Gavin," Valerie said through clenched teeth, "but that was an accident, and I did not kill Mrs. Rothford. Those things did, and you know very well what things. You know what's wrong with Tamara too, don't you? That's what you were talking about in the crypt when you said do it and I'd see. Well, I do see. I see that Grandmother's gone into her, and Tamara has to learn to take control. I can't have her spitting in my face, or worse, trying to kill me. And you can think what you want about Gavin. I really don't care."

Uncle Herb suddenly materialized in the corner and cleared his throat. "Don't mean to interrupt, but I wanted to say good-bye. Seems you've got things pretty well in hand, Valerie."

"But Uncle Herb! What about Grandmother? Aren't you going to take her with you?"

"Not unless you kill Tamara first," Armand sneered. "Go on, do it. Do it! Kill another one so you can feed your slimy little pets next door, which don't even exist except in your warped imagination. Then Mary's next, right? And how many after? You're never going to stop, are you?"

Valerie shot him a go-to-hell look. "Oh, shut up. I'm trying to talk to Uncle Herb."

"Well, he's right," Herb said. "About Tamara, I mean. You decided what to do yet? 'Cause if you're going to get Mandy out, best do it now. Time for me to move on."

"You're still taking Vonda with you, I hope."

Herb sighed. "Yeah, I suppose. Get her out of your hair, anyway. So, what's it going to be?"

Valerie thought about it. Armand kept sniggering. He was so sure he knew every damn thing—what she was going to do, what the future would hold. She'd show him.

"It's all right. Just take Vonda and go. I'll manage. Good luck, Uncle Herb. Thanks for everything."

Herb raised his pipe in salute, his image slowly dissolving into the wallpaper. A few moments later Valerie could hear Vonda pitching a fit in the attic. She didn't want to leave her things, but after a few moments all was quiet. Valerie smiled; things were starting to look a little better.

Armand was gone too, but Valerie doubted it was for good. He'd be hanging around to watch Grandmother win Tamara and use her little cousin to drive her up the wall until she really was insane. Or whatever plot her insidious mind could devise. She turned back to her typewriter.

Gavin?
what
We're alone now.
we are one
I know. We are, aren't we?

15

Valerie decided it was time to let Tamara out of the closet; she'd been in there for almost two hours. Gavin had been saying the most exotic things to her that she'd lost track of the time.

Tamara was hanging limp with her eyes closed. Valerie stroked her face, but she didn't move. "Tamara?"

Slowly her eyes opened and lifted, and with her face still hanging down, she gave the impression of a vulture.

"You can come out now." Valerie smiled, working to untie the nylons. "I think you've probably learned your lesson."

After the gag was removed, Valerie put Tamara on the bed and stroked her hair. "There now, it's all over, and it never needs to happen again, you understand? Would you like to play with your cat now? He's on my bed."

"Mama fell down," Tamara deadpanned.

Valerie's eyebrows raised. "What? Elisabeth fell down?"

Tamara nodded slightly. Her eyes were dry, empty, seeing but unseeing. "Mama fell down like Humpty Dumpty."

Valerie silently rehearsed the nursery rhyme. Humpty

had a great fall. All the king's horses and men couldn't put him back together again. "Did she die?" She'd had a vision, Valerie thought, while she was hanging in the closet. Valerie remembered what Jonathan had said on the porch, about Tamara being psychic. So Elisabeth was going to die. Interesting. Was she going to fall off a high wall? At least Tamara didn't seem too upset about it.

"Well," Valerie said soothingly, "that will only leave me to be your mother then, won't it? I'll go get your cat for you now. What are you going to name it?"

Tamara didn't answer. She was staring up at the ceiling, her facial muscles occasionally twitching as if a spider were crawling along her cheek. Valerie thought maybe she shouldn't have thrown that in about the spiders, but it was too late now. Tamara would be all right in a little while. The cat would snap her out of it.

Valerie had lunch with Mary, having explained that Tamara still wasn't feeling very well and that she would take something up to her later. Mary had said that was too bad, and looked genuinely concerned, but also, Valerie thought, a bit suspicious too. No telling what the wheels were spinning behind those sharp green eyes, which took in everything, every detail, for analysis. She was almost as bad as that detective. She had probably come to no firm conclusions yet, but she was smelling a rat, no doubt about that. The more Valerie thought about it, the more the idea of feeding Mary to the creatures appealed to her. They would be so hungry, and disgusting as they were, that was pitiable. But how to get Mary over there? It wouldn't be so hard, if all she had to do was walk through the house. Valerie could send her over there on some bogus mission, but no one was going to just stand there if something started licking them. The victim had to be sleeping. It would be very hard to convince Mary to sleep over there without sounding suspicious. Mary was pretty sharp, all right.

So then Mary would have to be dead first, but she was a big woman. Valerie couldn't see dragging her all that way, nor did she want to go through the mess of chopping her into more manageable pieces. Gavin was the last time for that nonsense. Which left only one alternative. To kill her over there. Gavin could give her advice on how to do it.

Valerie ate the last of her sandwich and patted her mouth with a napkin. "Mary, I was wondering if you might be interested in helping me this afternoon. My next-door neighbor, Mrs. Rothford, hasn't been getting around too well lately, and I've offered to do her dusting and such, but it's such a big house, like this one, and I really don't have the time to do it all; I'm so behind in my writing. Do you suppose you could do the downstairs? I'll take five dollars off your rent next week."

Mary was quick to accept the bargain. "Oh, no trouble at all, I'll do the whole house if you want me to."

"Oh, I couldn't ask you to do that, Mary, and anyway, Mrs. Rothford doesn't know you, and you know how those old ladies get."

Mary nodded sadly. "Yes, my dear mother got like that. She didn't trust a soul, not even her own children."

"Well, I'll go up and feed Tamara, then, and we'll go."

"Sounds fine with me," Mary said cheerfully.

In spite of the heat, Tamara had fallen asleep, the cat curled next to her. Valerie saw no point in waking her up to eat. After the closet ordeal, she doubted Tamara would have much of an appetite anyway. Valerie left the tray of food on the dresser and quietly slipped out, then went to her study to ask Gavin for advice.

Gavin, how should I do it?
simple hit her over the head with something then tie a cord tight around her neck that should do it
Whatever would I do without you, Gavin?
the same thing
Valerie laughed. She was liking him more all the time.
Oh you. I wish we could be together like we were before, you with your own body and everything. What would you do to me, Gavin? Tell me again.
first i would tie you spread-eagled to the bed
Valerie quivered.

Then?

id take pictures of you

Oh, Gavin, how naughty.

"Yoo-hoo, are we ready to go?" Mary called from downstairs.

We'll have to continue this conversation later, Gavin. It's time to

Valerie was out of room on that sheet of paper, so she removed it. She stuck it in the folder and quickly rolled in another one, calling back, "Just a minute!" and finished her paragraph to Gavin:

kill Mary. I know this is going to sound silly, but I do feel sorry for those things. Maybe not your brother, but it's not right to starve the others because of him.

be sure to hit her hard and wrap the cord tight

I will. Talk to you later.

Valerie sent Mary to wait at Mrs. Rothford's front door while she went around back, so she wouldn't get suspicious about the broken glass in the back door. Mary should have been suspicious about that anyway, and had looked a little confused when Valerie gave the instruction, surely wondering why they didn't just go through the back door together. But any questions she might have had remained behind her lips. There was cat hair stuck to the broken glass; Gavin had been right about what she'd seen in the living room window. Valerie supposed she'd better call the cats out of Mrs. Rothford's house when she left, and get this window replaced before a neighbor across the alley noticed it. For the time being, she could tape it up with some cardboard, so at least it would look like Mrs. Rothford knew about it, and it would keep the cats from getting back in again.

The house was silent as Valerie walked through it, except for the ticking of the grandfather clock in the living room. A gray tabby cat on Mrs. Rothford's pink settee saw her and scrambled for the stairs. Before letting Mary in, Valerie looked around for what she might use. For the heavy object, there was a brass statue of Christ on the mantel. Valerie weighed it in her hands and decided it would do nicely. Then there was Mrs. Rothford's knitting basket next to her doily-covered armchair, containing plenty of yarn, which could be doubled or tripled for strength.

Valerie opened the front door. "Come on in, Mary."

16

Tamara came downstairs while Valerie was on the phone with the newspaper, placing another ad. Tamara had the cat clutched tightly in her arms, too tightly, so that it was struggling to get away. It finally bit her, and she threw it on the floor. It landed on its back, hissing, and tore for the living room, where it squeezed in under the sofa.

Valerie put the phone down and gave Tamara a stern look. "Now, was that very nice?"

"It bit me."

"Well, you were squeezing it. Cats don't like to be squeezed."

Tamara brought up the wound on her wrist and began sucking it. Valerie pulled her arm down. "Don't do that, you'll give yourself a hickey. Is it bleeding?" She looked; there was one puncture, oozing a drop of blood. "We'll have to get an antiseptic on that so it won't get infected. Don't suck on it, your mouth's full of germs."

"It is not," Tamara sulked.

"It is too. Now go upstairs and get the iodine."

Tamara took a step backward. "That stings."

"Only for a second. Go get it."

Tamara looked toward the kitchen drape, which was slightly parted. "Where's Mary?"

Mary was in Mrs. Rothford's living room, laid out beside the coffee table, her hands placed carefully at her sides, her face a deep shade of purple the last Valerie had seen of it. "Mary decided she didn't want to live with us anymore. We'll get someone new."

"I want Mary."

"Well, Mary is gone. Now go get that iodine."

Tamara ran past her to the kitchen and out on the back porch, where she yelled, "Liar! There's her car!"

Valerie stomped through the kitchen after her. "Get back in this house, and stop that yelling."

Mary's car. Damn! She hadn't forgotten about it, she just didn't think there was any hurry. She hadn't yet decided what to do with it. Another trip to Charleston? No, she could sell it to a junkyard. It was an old clunker anyway, and that would bring in a little extra money. The title was sure to be someplace in Mary's room.

"Where is Mary?" Tamara shrieked.

Valerie jerked her back in the house, Tamara kicking and screaming, trying to bite. Valerie was getting extremely upset. She got the kitchen door closed with her foot and dragged the flailing child into the living room, where she forced her down in the rocking chair and stood in front of it so Tamara couldn't get back out.

"She's doing it again, Tamara," Valerie said firmly. "Grandma Mandy's making you misbehave, can't you tell? Don't let her control you like this. You don't have to do what she says."

"Where's Mary?" Tamara demanded with her arms crossed, glaring. "Did you kill her? I didn't tell her anything."

"Oh, just go ahead and kill the kid," Armand challenged from the sofa, his voice ripe with spite. "You've driven her half crazy too. She's never going to straighten up." He was stretched out with his feet up, smirking. Valerie decided to ignore him.

"I told you, Tamara, Mary decided to move out. I think she bought a new car."

"Tell her the truth. Tell her what really happened to Mary," Armand repeated. "You told her about Gavin. What difference would it make? I think she already knows, anyway. Why wouldn't she, after what you threatened?"

Tamara stuck out her lower lip. "I don't believe you. I think you killed her."

"All right, so I killed her," Valerie finally admitted. "Is that what you wanted to hear? I hit her over the head with a Jesus statue, then I wrapped a bunch of yarn around her neck and pulled it real tight, and tied it so she couldn't breathe. Her face turned all purple. So she's dead, next door, and tonight the hungry ones will go there and eat her all up. Feel better now?"

Tamara didn't blink an eye, but her arms did relax during Valerie's account of Mary's murder, and now lay limply in her lap. "You're bad bad bad," she said without emotion.

"She's just crazy," Armand corrected, though Tamara didn't seem to hear him. "Crazy as they come, that Valerie. They're going to put her away forever."

"I'm not bad, Tamara. I just do what I have to do to fix things. Mary was going to cause trouble."

"You're a bitch," Tamara said. "I heard Mama say it once. You're a bitch."

Valerie jerked her off the chair and started pulling her toward the stairs. "All right, young lady, we're going to see about teaching you a lesson you won't so soon forget!"

Tamara began screaming at the top of her lungs.

Valerie gagged Tamara again and put her on the bed, her wrists tied with the nylons to the headposts. Valerie didn't know what else to do yet, what might make a firm enough impression, but she was certain that Gavin would come up with something.

She sat at the typewriter.

What now, Gavin? I'm about at the end of my rope with that kid. She simply refuses to learn. What should I do?

why did you kill me

I told you, Gavin, it was an accident; you ate the tapioca before I could get rid of it. And the only reason I made it in the first place was because Uncle Herb said it was the only way.

this is mary

Valerie bit her lip. "Oh, no."

why did you kill me

Hell, what was this? Now Mary was in her too? Damn, what did she look like, a ghost hotel? Valerie felt like screaming as she typed her answer:

You shouldn't have been so nosy, Mary, for one thing, and for another, I didn't like the way you were taking over my house.

dont hurt tamara

Mind your own business, would you? Gavin, is this going to happen every damn time I kill somebody?

Gavin?

Jonathan had gotten most of the mess in the bedroom cleaned up when the telephone rang in the kitchen. His gut tightened. It could be Morrison. Or it could be bad news about Tamara, her body found somewhere, mutilated. At least, then, he wouldn't have to spend the rest of his life wondering what was happening to her.

But it wasn't Morrison. It was a hospital official, a man with a very grave voice who identified himself as Dr. Chadwick. After confirming that he was speaking to the correct party, he told Jonathan that he needed to come to the hospital. It was about his wife.

"Is she all right?" Jonathan asked, alarmed.

"Just please come to the hospital, Mr. Wade. I'll be waiting for you at the reception desk."

Jonathan gripped the phone, a dark awareness settling in. Elisabeth wasn't all right. "Is my wife dead?"

A sigh. "I'm afraid so, Mr. Wade. I didn't want to have to tell you over the phone. I'm terribly sorry."

Jonathan could hardly find his voice. "How did it happen? Was it because of her head injury?" He didn't think he could live with something like that, having killed his wife, even accidentally, on top of losing Tamara.

"Just come to the hospital, please, I'll give you the details then," Chadwick said.

What had happened was that Elisabeth had awakened in a semiprivate room. There was another patient with her, a Mrs. Darling. Elisabeth asked Mrs. Darling where she was, and Mrs. Darling told her she was in the psycho ward of Doctors General.

Elisabeth said nothing more for a long time, according to Mrs. Darling. All she did was lay there, staring into space. A nurse came in, welcomed Elisabeth back to the world, checked her blood pressure and pulse, and told her that Dr. Foudray would be in to see her soon. A few minutes after that Elisabeth shut herself in the bathroom and hung herself with her underwear, one leg hole around her neck, the other gathered around the clothing hook on the back of the door.

Jonathan stared at his wife's body in the hospital morgue for a long time, not knowing how it could really be true. She'd told him she would kill herself if he took her to a hospital. So he wouldn't have taken her if she hadn't hit her head—if the fall hadn't knocked her out. He'd been afraid not to, then. So, was he still to blame? Probably not, but he felt an overwhelming sense of guilt anyway.

She lay there under a crisp white sheet pulled down to her collarbone, her face mottled, eyes bulged out, tongue swollen. They'd warned him it wouldn't be a pleasant sight, and they were right. What determination she must have had, to hang there against the door, when at any moment she could have pushed up with her feet and saved herself. Perhaps it hadn't taken long. Her lips were purplish-blue, like the rest of her face, only the lips were much darker. She had been in the bathroom fifteen minutes before Dr. Foudray had come in to talk to her. By that time it was obvious that any attempt to resuscitate her would be futile.

Why, Elisabeth? Jonathan asked her silently. She had deserted the whole family in their time of greatest need. Had she thought she was the only one suffering? How were the children to do without a mother? He without a wife? How could all this be happening?

It seemed the administrator, Dr. Chadwick, was worried about Jonathan bringing up a lawsuit. Chadwick dared not say the word, just in case it wouldn't otherwise cross Jonathan's mind, but Jonathan could tell by Chadwick's overly solicitous manner that was exactly what was on his mind. They would handle the funeral arrangements. No bill would be sent (that was a dead giveaway), and if there was anything, anything else at all they could possibly do, he had but to let them know. Jonathan told him there was one thing. He couldn't bear to tell Elisabeth's mother, Sadie. Chadwick told him the hospital would certainly do that for him.

Jonathan wasn't going to sue. What would be the point? So what if he had explained to them that Elisabeth threatened to kill herself if he took her to the hospital, and because of that they should have taken extra precautions with her? But who would even think about someone hanging herself with her underwear? They couldn't be blamed either, really. If that was what Elisabeth had decided to do, she would have found a way regardless.

Jonathan decided it was time to get drunk.

Gavin and Mary were having an argument.

i dont care whats good or bad and its none of your business anyway i say valerie should make tamara eat a dead mouse she wouldnt forget that for a long time

youre both absolute monsters monsters no decent person would ever dream of doing that to a child ever no i wont let you do it i wont

I ate one once. Valerie typed for herself, somewhat entertained by all this. **Didn't do any permanent damage.**

She had finally remembered a fragment of that long-ago scene—Grandmother forcing those mouse entrails down her throat. Just a flash, lasting less than a second, but she saw it all. She even remembered Uncle Herb slapping Grandmother afterward, slapping her hard.

Yes, Gavin, I think that's a good idea. There might be one down in the pantry now. I haven't looked yet.

no i beg you dont do that i will make her behave i will i will go in her instead and i wont let amanda take control of her anymore

What do you think, Gavin? Would that work? If she really wants to leave, she can.

make tamara eat the mouse

Now Gavin, there's no point in being mean to her just for meanness' sake. It's not been Tamara's fault, really. She's just weak. Maybe Mary could keep Grandmother in line.

whatever you say

Valerie had to put in a new sheet of paper; the two had been arguing back and forth for some time.

All right, Mary, we'll do this on a trial basis. But if Tamara acts up one more time, she eats the mouse.

i promise she wont act up anymore i will make her be good i am very strong tamara will be a good girl now i promise

well there she goes

That would be Gavin. Valerie sighed with relief.

That's good. Having both of you at once was a bit much. Well then, maybe all our problems are solved? Except for the room. I need to get it rented again, and this time I'm going to make it clear from the start that the rest of the house, besides the kitchen and downstairs bathroom, is off limits. What if another man calls, Gavin? Would you be jealous?

no

No? Not even a little? Not even if I went to bed with him?

i would watch

Valerie quivered.

Jonathan called an hour later. Valerie could immediately tell he was drunk. When she answered, he said flatly, "Elisabeth is dead. She hung herself."

"What a terrible thing," Valerie replied, marveling at the accuracy of Tamara's vision, except for the part about falling like Humpty Dumpty. "You must be very upset."

"Do you mind if I come over?"

Valerie hesitated. She still had Mary's things to get rid of, and her car. The sooner done the better. The personal things could go in the attic, of course. Some day she could have quite a yard sale. But the car, that had to be driven to the salvage yard, and she could take a cab home. "Well, I don't mind, of course, but I have an errand to run. How about three o'clock? And are you sure you can drive all right?"

"I'll see you at three," Jonathan said.

Valerie hung up, smiling. Elisabeth was so stupid. She went back upstairs to Tamara's room. Tamara languidly watched her enter.

"Well," Valerie said, removing the gag, "let's see how this is working out." Sitting on the edge of the bed, she rubbed Tamara's chin. "Guess what, I've got some good news for you. Mary is inside you too, now, and she's going to keep Grandmother from causing trouble. Isn't that nice of her?"

Tamara only looked at her.

"Well, I've got to run out to the salvage yard. Hope that title is handy. Anyway, I think it best to leave you tied up, until we know for sure. I'll be back soon, and if you're good, we'll take a nice long drive up in the mountains this evening. I think we both need to get out of the house for a while, don't you?"

Tamara numbly watched her leave. She'd been certain Valerie had carried her back upstairs to kill her as she had Mary, and on top of the other horrors she'd been subjected to, it had simply been too much. She'd slipped into a state of shock.

Jonathan arrived at ten after three, more or less sober. Valerie led him into the living room and sat beside him on the sofa. "Poor Jonathan, you've suffered so much lately. Are you going to be all right?"

He had already rehearsed a speech. This would no doubt take Valerie by surprise, but he was a desperate man with three other children. He had to keep what was left of his family, and himself, glued together.

"Valerie, I'm going to say something, and I know it'll be a shock to you, but I'm standing on a sinking ship.

Now, I don't know how you feel about me, and that's not important now, but I need you, really need you. The kids need some stability. I can't be there for them all the time, and I can't let them stay separated at neighbors' houses like this. It's just too much all at once, and I'll be lucky if I can just handle my job at this point. We've already got some enormous adjustments to make, and I just don't see how we can make them with the whole world up in the air like this. I know it's asking for a big adjustment on your part, but at least I can make it up to you financially. It would be worth every penny I make to see that my children have what they need to grow up well-adjusted."

"What are you saying, Jonathan?" Valerie asked, nonplussed. "You want to move in here with the kids? What on earth would people think, Elisabeth not even in her grave yet?"

"I would hope they'd understand it was for the children's sakes. I know they'll wonder why I didn't turn to Elisabeth's mother, and I did consider her first, but . . . Sadie's lived alone for so long and she's terribly set in her ways. She and I never really got along that well, either. So what do you say, Valerie? I could rent my house out to make the mortgage payments, and let you have what I earn from my job, which after taxes comes to about fifteen hundred a month. I might as well admit while I'm at it that I've been . . . attracted to you for some time. Of course, I'm not asking for an emotional commitment, not for me, but you might keep that in mind for the future."

Fifteen hundred a month! Wow! Valerie started thinking. Jonathan could have the dining room, and Uncle Herb's old room, her office now, could be converted back into a bedroom for the boys, and Jennifer could share the other bedroom with Tamara. But this was definitely an awkward situation. How was Tamara to be explained? Well, that could be worried about later. The writing desk and typewriter would fit in her bedroom and she could work in there, or chat with Gavin, in her spare time, which would be at night, when Jonathan was there to watch the children. There was really only one drawback.

How would the creatures be fed, if she couldn't run ads for the room anymore? Then suddenly she knew. Ha, it would be so simple, and certainly less troublesome than the ad business. Hitchhikers. Derelicts. Drunks. No possessions to get rid of, no way to be traced.

"I think we can probably work something out, Jonathan," Valerie smiled, patting his knee. Fifteen hundred a month! "When would you and the children like to move in?"

After Jonathan left, Valerie went back upstairs to tell Tamara the good news. "Guess what, Precious, your daddy and your brothers and sister are moving in with us after your mother's funeral on Saturday . . . What's today, Thursday? That's just two more days after today. Oh, I forgot to tell you, you were right about your mama dying, but she didn't fall, she hung herself. Anyway, won't that be nice?"

Tamara said nothing, did nothing.

Valerie frowned. "You have nothing to say about it? I was thinking of you when I agreed to this, you know, how much happier you would be. Don't I even get thanked?"

Tamara opened her mouth, then closed it again.

Valerie shrugged. "Well, this will be much better anyway. I won't have to worry about someone seeing you anymore, although I do need to come up with a good explanation for your being here when they come on Saturday. I know! I'll say Gavin brought you back. I could call that stupid detective and even report it tomorrow. I could say I got back from the grocery store and here you were sitting on my porch swing, safe and sound. You wouldn't tell them otherwise, would you?"

Tamara only blinked.

"I'll tell you what to say," Valerie continued, accepting Tamara's silence as consent. It was miraculous, the change Mary had made. "You'll say Gavin took you somewhere, you don't know where, but he was very nice to you, and when you told him you wanted to go home, he brought you to my house. Can you remember that?"

Tamara still said nothing.

"Oh my God," a voice cried, "what have you done to my baby?"

Valerie jumped off the bed and scanned the room, but she could see no one. She recognized the voice, though. It was Elisabeth's. For crying out loud. "Where are you, Elisabeth? I can't see you."

Elisabeth slowly materialized before her, a shimmering apparition with a purple face.

"You look terrible," Valerie said.

"Look at my Tamara, she just lies there not saying a word, not moving a muscle," Elisabeth wailed. "You bitch, what did you do to her? You took her, didn't you?"

"She damn sure did," Armand said, stepping out of Tamara's closet. "I'll tell you everything she did."

"You stay out of this," Valerie warned.

"Tell me," Elisabeth pleaded with him. "What terrible things has she done to my baby?"

"Put her up in the attic with a dead body, for beginners."

"Shut up, Armand."

"Filled her head with all this craziness of hers. Shut Tamara up in the closet for two hours after telling her it was crawling with big hairy spiders . . ."

Elisabeth swooned against him. "Oh stop, stop, I can't bear to hear any more. I knew if I died I would be able to find her, and I expected her to be depressed, but look at her! She's a vegetable!"

"She's just fine," Valerie snapped at her cousin. "Mary's just keeping her calm."

Armand snorted. "Yeah, so Valerie won't make her eat a dead mouse."

Elisabeth turned to her, stricken. "You wouldn't."

"It was Gavin's idea," Valerie said defensively.

Tamara lay wondering who Valerie was talking to. It was a dull curiosity; she really didn't care. For the most part her mind had retreated to a deep inner sanctuary.

Staring at the window, she had a vision of herself climbing through it. On the outer sill she became a bird and flew away.

"Yeah, Gavin, her imaginary lover. She killed Gavin,

plus a couple of others so far. There's nothing she wouldn't do. Nothing!"

"He is not imaginary!" Valerie bellowed. "And I don't have to take any of this!"

Valerie stalked out of Tamara's room into the front bedroom and plopped behind the typewriter, feeling an immense headache coming on.

Can you believe it, Gavin? Now I have to put up with Elisabeth too.

looks that way

What do you think about Jonathan and the other kids moving in? We're going to have a houseful.

the more the merrier

Valerie's waking concern the next morning was to check on Tamara, for she hadn't uttered a single word the whole previous evening, even during their car ride up in the mountains. She wouldn't play with her cat (who had crapped behind the couch, so Valerie tossed it out later, when she discovered the source of the smell), and wouldn't eat either. She wouldn't do anything but go to the bathroom when Valerie took her in. A well-behaved child was one thing, but Tamara had become a zombie. Valerie didn't like it at all. She got out of bed, put on her robe, and took the key to Tamara's room off the dresser. Maybe this morning, after a good night's sleep, she would be better.

She was gone.

Valerie stared at the empty bed in disbelief. The nylons were still dangling from the headposts, but Tamara was nowhere to be seen. Valerie checked under the bed, then in the closet. She even pulled out the dresser drawers. Tamara was gone. This was terrible. Had someone kidnapped her? Or even worse, had the creatures come back here and eaten her? Oozed themselves through the cracks around her door to get at her? Terrible, terrible. Valerie sat on the bed, deeply depressed.

"What's the matter, your little prisoner get away?"

Armand again. He came in and perched himself on the dresser, eyes gleaming with triumph.

"Leave me alone," Valerie mumbled. "I'm grieving."

He laughed. "You, grieve? You haven't got a heart to grieve with."

"What do you want, buckets of tears? I was getting very attached to her. Now I think they've gone and eaten her, and after all that trouble I went through to give them Mary. I suppose she's over there just going to waste."

"Maybe you killed Tamara in your sleep."

Valerie glared at him, her features twisted in rage. "I most certainly did not. I had no reason to."

"You don't need a reason, you can just make one up. You like to kill and torment. You enjoy it. Look at all those things you did to Mandy. You were having fun. Oh, I know how it is, believe me. You know there aren't any slimy vampire-things showing up to eat people in their sleep. Come on. If you told that to a thousand people, how many do you think would believe it? I'll tell you how many, none. Not one. You're crazy, it's as simple as that."

Valerie started to cry. "I am not. You just go over there and look. Mrs. Rothford's body will be gone, and so will Gavin's skeleton. Have you seen Mrs. Rothford out on her front porch lately? No. Because she's not there anymore. They ate her."

"Oh, Mrs. Rothford is dead all right. She had a heart attack when she put on her glasses that next morning and saw what was in bed with her. She was a little confused before that, thinking her husband had come back somehow. Quite a shock she had coming. Her old ticker just went right into arrest."

Valerie had managed to compose herself. "I know that's a lie. I saw those things on her. I know what they do."

"Really, now. Well, why don't you send the police over there, then? If there are no bodies to be found? See what they say."

"Mary might still be there."

"So, they would tell you, 'There's a dead body in that house.' Not, 'There are three dead bodies in that house.'"

He was so stupid. "Oh sure, and then I'd be getting asked a lot of questions. No thanks."

"Wonder what you did with Tamara's body? Same thing you did with those two bags of Gavin you hallucinated the monsters eating, that you put down the garbage disposal so your fantasy wouldn't be disturbed? Or maybe she's next door too, lying beside Mary, a treat for your slimy pets. In that case, the police would say there are four dead."

"I'm not calling the police and I didn't do a thing to Tamara," Valerie said stonily, rising to her feet. "And there was nothing left in those bags to put down the garbage disposal. I was just sleepwalking, like I was the night this whole ugly mess got started. I know what you're trying to do, and it's not going to work. You're on Grandmother's side. You want to help her get revenge on me for what I did to her, but she deserved it all, and more. I'm sure there's nothing you two would like more than to see me rot in an insane asylum, but I know what I see. There's not a damn thing wrong with my mind. Now if you'll excuse me, I have a lot to do today."

Jonathan called shortly after ten, jubilant. "I just got a call from Detective Morrison. They've found Tamara!"

Valerie didn't know if this was good news or bad. At least she'd been wrong about the things coming back to her house; they had gone next door, where they'd had their last meal, and there had been Mary, all ready for them. They were probably very grateful. So Tamara must have loosened the nylons somehow, maybe Elisabeth had coached her, and crawled out her window to the lower roof, from where she could easily get down to the back porch roof, which was low, and from there to the ground. Valerie was glad Tamara was alive, very glad, but had she remembered what to say? Valerie had planned to rehearse with her at least a couple more times before calling the police station today, to report that Tamara had showed up on her porch swing.

"Is she all right? Was she with Gavin?"

"No, all by herself, wandering along some street near

your house, Morrison said. That's all I know so far. I'm still at the job site. I was just on my way to pick her up. I have to take her to get a physical, you know, to see if he . . . well, I was just wanting to know if you'd like to go with me to the police station. Morrison's going to go with us to the hospital."

Valerie felt she had no choice. "Of course. Pick me up. I'll be ready when you get here."

17

Morrison had Tamara in a private interrogation room of the police station. The walls were pea green, the floor scuffed hardwood, the only furniture a table and two chairs. An officer took Jonathan and Valerie to it and admitted them. There was a pop can on the table in front of Tamara, and a bag of potato chips which she had apparently not yet touched. Jonathan was a little shocked at first by his daughter's appearance, but he rushed over to her and put his arms around her. Tamara didn't respond. Morrison relinquished the other chair and offered it to Valerie. She told him she preferred to stand.

"She's apparently been badly traumatized," Morrison said to Jonathan in soft tones. "Can't get a word out of her. Probably get our explanation for that at the hospital."

That wasn't so bad, Valerie thought, considering what the child could say. All the way over to the police station, she'd pictured Morrison waiting for her with a pair of handcuffs.

"You should probably get her psychiatric help as soon as possible," Morrison added, then turned to Valerie. "A patrol officer spotted her in your neighborhood, almost didn't recognize her because of what Sheffield—or whoever took her—did to her hair."

The way he said "whoever took her," Valerie thought he might as well have said *you.*

"I hardly recognize her myself," she said, not the least bit nervous now. Let Morrison suspect all he wanted. If Tamara hadn't said a word against her by now, she never would. "But thank goodness that officer did. I'll have to take her to the beauty shop and see what they can do about changing the color back. I think blond suits her much better."

"Honey, it's your old dad," Jonathan was saying to his still-silent daughter. "Don't you recognize me? It's okay now, Tamara, you'll be going home soon, you're safe. We're going to be moving into cousin Valerie's nice big house, all of us . . ." His voice trailed off. She was already traumatized; he couldn't tell her about her mother yet.

Morrison shoved his hands in his pockets. Jonathan had told him about his wife's death over the phone. How ironic it was, Jonathan had said, that if Elisabeth had just held on for one more day, there would have been no reason for her to die. Jonathan had not told him, however, that he was planning to move the rest of his family into Valerie Scott's house, and now that Morrison knew it, he had a very uneasy feeling. He had his suspicions, his gut feeling, but the kid wouldn't talk, so what could he do? Maybe she would, though, after some therapy.

"If you need to get back to work, why don't you just leave Tamara with me after we get through at the hospital?" Valerie suggested to Jonathan as they followed Morrison's car to Saint Mary's, Tamara sitting in the front seat of the pickup between them. "I'll take care of her until . . . well, you know, Saturday, and then of course you'll all be there. By the way, do you need any help packing?"

She marveled at how well everything had worked out, even better than she'd planned.

Jonathan was sad, thankful as he was to have Tamara

back, but her state of mind frightened the hell out of him. "No, I think I can manage with the packing, and yes, I'd very much appreciate it if you could keep Tamara for me. I know I should stay with her, but I just can't . . . deal with this right now. She acts like she doesn't even know me." Tears formed in the corners of his eyes. "See if you can find a good psychiatrist for her. Looks like she's going to need one. God, what did that bastard do to her? I've never seen her like this, never."

"Oh, she doesn't need a psychiatrist," Valerie countered mildly, thinking of the cost. Besides, what might happen if a doctor put her under hypnosis or something? "She just needs lots of TLC. She'll snap out of it."

Jonathan wiped his eyes with the back of his hand and glanced soulfully at his silent daughter. "Well, I don't know . . . I guess we could give it a few days and see."

Well Gavin, how do you like that? Isn't it incredible how well things work out sometimes?

Valerie's fingertips flitted lightly over the keys, waiting for his reply. She was falling in love with him, she realized. How nice it would be if he could go into Jonathan's body. Then they could be together like regular lovers, without having to use the typewriter to communicate, and be able to touch each other and do things they would never mention.

Gavin, are you asleep?

no are you

Very funny. Well, everything's working out just great, don't you think? Except for Elisabeth and Armand, I'd say things were just perfect. Fifteen hundred dollars a month, can you imagine? I won't have to worry about getting published, I can just write for the fun of it.

almost perfect

Valerie blushed; he'd read her mind, thinking about him going into Jonathan and the things they would do behind closed doors.

You read my mind, didn't you? My idea about Jonathan?

you want me to go into him

Well, how about it?

no

No? Why on earth not? Isn't that what we both want, separate bodies? That we can do things to each other with?

jonathan is ugly

So okay, I admit he's no Romeo, but that wouldn't matter to me. You should have seen Doug.

i dont know

It would be very handy, since he'll be living here anyway. Just don't look in the mirrors.

can we feed the children to the vampires

Of course not, Gavin. What's the matter? Don't you like kids?

not real ones

Well, forget that idea. I thought I could pick up hitch-hikers or bums for them. People no one would miss. As a matter of fact, I'd better go out and look for one now, for their dinner tonight. Please think about it, Gavin. It would be lovely, us together with the kids. You could learn to like them. We'd be a big, happy family.

He was walking near the mouth of a downtown alley in a grimy muscle T-shirt, baggy gray pants covered with filth, wearing an unmatched pair of shoes. She would be doing him a favor. He stopped to rummage through a trash bin in the alley. Valerie pulled the Datsun up to the curb and rolled down the passenger window, a little nervous. She had never spoken to such a person before. "Excuse me, sir?"

He turned slowly to look at her, shoulders stooped with the burden of a thousand sorrows, eyes bloodshot, his face—what she could see of it through the scraggly beard—etched with deep creases.

"Whaddya want?" he scowled, showing a mouthful of rotting teeth.

"Well, I've got a proposition for you," she answered, thinking how that sounded, but he didn't start to leer or anything, just stared at her, waiting for the rest. "Would you like to earn fifty dollars?"

His attitude changed immediately. He straightened, his eyes brightening. "Sure I'd like fifty dollars. Whaddya want? I can paint, do good paint work." He stepped up and leaned on the window, driving Valerie back with his stench. She suspected he was remembering the past. He probably couldn't hold a brush steady enough to paint a barn anymore.

"I don't need you to paint, just to sleep. A friend of mine is gone on vacation, you see, and she asked me to stay at her house, only I can't stay tonight, so I have to find someone else. It's very easy. All you have to do is sleep there."

That sounded easy enough for him. There would be food too, not just garbage, and then of course the fifty dollars, which would buy more pints of Scotch than he could count. "Sure missy, I'll do it. Sure will, anytime." There would be a bed too, not just a dirty, lice-infested mattress under a cardboard box in the alley. Had he died and gone to heaven?

"All right." Valerie smiled. "You be waiting for me in front of the library at nine-thirty. I'll come pick you up."

The old beggar nodded enthusiastically. "Nine-thirty, I'll be there. Front of the library."

Jonathan came by after work to check on Tamara's progress, of which there was none, except that she'd eaten, and Valerie had taken her to get her hair bleached out and cut better, throughout which Tamara had said nothing. But the fact that she had eaten was an encouraging sign, Valerie assured Jonathan, and he left feeling a little better. He had been relieved to be told at the hospital that Tamara had not been sexually molested, that much the doctor could tell, but questions still nagged him. What the hell had happened to her that would make her act this way? And Morrison's reaction to the news had been puzzling. Something had apparently clicked into place for him. Jonathan had seen it on his face, but when he asked him about it, Morrison just said he'd remembered something he had forgotten to do.

Jonathan was on his way now to visit his other kids for a while, to gather them from the neighbors and somehow find the words to tell them their mother was gone. But they would make it. They still had each other, and a new life was awaiting them. It would be hard, but cousin

Valerie was going to make it a little easier. Though she could never replace their mother, of course, she would be there for them, and gradually the shattered pieces of their lives would be pulled back together.

"You bitch!" Elisabeth shrieked from the staircase. "First you steal my child, then you steal my husband!"

"You're the one who committed suicide." Valerie shrugged. "Looks to me like he's up for grabs, and I could sure use that fifteen hundred a month he brings home. Besides, he came to me."

"But oh, just wait until he finds out the truth about you," Elisabeth hissed, floating down the stairs. "You think he'll be understanding? I wouldn't bet on it. He thinks you're some kind of angel." She laughed bitterly. "When he finds out what you really are, he's going to nail you to the wall."

Valerie, sitting in the rocking chair, smiled. "And what am I really, Elisabeth? A bitch?"

"You give the word *bitch* a bad name. There isn't a word that describes the evil depths in which you're sunk. You make the devil look like Mary Poppins."

"Thank you."

Elisabeth hovered near the bottom step, her bulging eyes gleaming with hate. "Proud of it, aren't you?"

"No, I'm just trying to make you mad, and I think it's working. I'm not a bad person," Valerie said, glancing at her watch. Seven-thirty, two more hours until she had to pick up the bum. "If you take something that's of no use and give it to the poor, would you be doing something wrong? And what about self-defense? If it's a choice between you and them, it's going to be them, right? Unless you're just plain stupid, and I think you are, for hanging yourself like that. And just what is it you find so outrageous?"

"Armand told me you were killing people all over the place! I'd say that's pretty outrageous!"

Valerie rolled her eyes. "Only two. Gavin, which was an accident, and Mary, and that's all I'm going to do."

Elisabeth gripped the banister, her purple hue darkening, her transparent, sheet-draped body swimming in and out of focus. "That's *all?* Oh well, I just murdered two human beings, no big deal. What's two when there are so many?" she sputtered sarcastically.

"And to think I wanted to make friends with you," Valerie responded with a shake of her head. "You're so judgmental. You know, Jonathan sort of slipped the other night and basically told me he was sorry he married you. I can certainly see why."

"You lying bitch! Jonathan worshiped the ground I walked on."

"Must have been a short service," Valerie quipped, "as fast as he came running to me."

At that Elisabeth screamed at the height of her voice as she faded completely away, the sound trailing her into the beyond. Valerie rocked a few more minutes, half expecting Elisabeth to reappear, since it was hard to imagine she would let her have the last word, but she didn't, so Valerie went upstairs to check on Tamara again. Valerie had given her some dolls to play with, some of Aunt Vonda's antique dolls that Gavin had seen in the chest. Vonda had collected them, and they had been her prize possessions, probably what she'd wanted to take with her so badly. All of them were beautifully dressed; Vonda had made some of the clothes herself.

Tamara had picked out two of them, the bride in her white lace and satin, and the duchess in a red velvet Empire gown with fake diamonds around the bodice. Valerie was pleased. "Ah, I see you're finally coming around. Having fun?"

The bride said yes. The duchess said no. Tamara placed each doll in front of her face to speak for them. Valerie thought that was amusing.

"So why aren't you having fun, Duchess?" she inquired of the doll, playing along. Tamara put the duchess doll back up to her face.

"Because I have to be here with a witch like you."

The game was no longer amusing. "That's a very rude thing to say, Duchess. I demand an apology this instant."

Tamara put the bride doll up. "I'm sorry, you're not a witch. You're very nice. Would you like some tea?"

Valerie wondered what was going on. Was Tamara just

playing? Or was she hearing the voices of Amanda and Mary? Or had Tamara's mind just snapped? Jonathan wasn't going to like this at all. "Tamara, say something to me without the dolls."

Tamara had nothing to say without the dolls.

Valerie picked up the princess, decked out in royal blue velvet with a fake diamond tiara on her head and handed it to Tamara. "What does the princess have to say?" Tamara just looked at it. Valerie, losing patience, put the doll up to Tamara's face. "Make the princess talk."

Still nothing.

Well then, if that's the way it was, all she had to do was take away the duchess doll. Take them all away except the bride. Tamara watched her gather them up under one arm, then reach out with the other hand, snapping her fingers. "Give me the duchess."

Tamara put the duchess doll in front of her face and retorted, "Go eat shit."

Valerie tore the doll loose from her grasp, expecting Tamara to pitch a fit, but she only looked startled, and made no effort to get the doll back. Instead, she put the bride doll to her face and said, "Oh thank you for taking away the evil duchess. Better lock her away."

Valerie knew just the place—the chest in the attic from which the dolls had come. There was a key around someplace; she would lock it. Jonathan still wasn't going to like this much, but at least with the duchess doll locked away, Tamara would be pleasant all the time. A little bizarre, perhaps, but everyone had their quirks.

It was time to head for the library. When Valerie explained to Tamara that she had to leave for a little while, to get some groceries (not exactly a lie), Tamara held the bride up and said sweetly, "Okay, Mother, don't worry, I'll be good." Valerie had no doubt about that. It was nice not having to worry about Tamara's behavior anymore.

The derelict was there, shuffling his feet on the sidewalk in front of the library, now wearing a tattered, greasy jacket over the T-shirt. Valerie noticed he had combed what was left of his hair, though, and had even shaved. When he got in the car, he smelled strongly of Old Spice.

"When do I get my fifty dollars?" he asked anxiously as she pulled away from the curb.

"In the morning, of course, after the job is done," she replied. "If I gave it to you now, how would I know you'd stay?"

"Morning be fine," he said quickly, not daring to offend her.

"This is how it's going to work," Valerie said, all businesslike. "In the morning I'll come to pick you up, and then I'll pay you your fifty dollars."

The bum nodded up and down. "That's fine, fine. My name's Louis," he said, offering his hand.

Valerie shook it briefly. "Pleased to meet you, Louis. You can call me Val."

"Val." He repeated the name with a nod.

"The door's unlocked," she told him when she pulled up to the curb in front of Mrs. Rothford's dark house a few minutes later. "Just go on in. Have a good evening, sleep tight."

"Will do," Louis said, opening the door, still unbelieving of his good fortune. "Nice house, very nice house."

Valerie watched him shuffle up the walk as if he were entering Paradise, open the door and go in. When the door shut behind him, she pulled up in front of her own house, parked, and went up her own walk, humming softly to herself.

As soon as Louis flipped on the light, his eyes nearly popped out of their sockets. He stood statue-still for several moments, trying to convince himself he was just having an hallucination, that he really wasn't staring at a purple-faced corpse stretched out on the living room floor, but the image didn't dissolve under his horrified stare. The woman's body was really there.

He should have known this was too good to be true. Looked like Val was trying to set him up. Then again, maybe she didn't know about this. It wouldn't make sense for her to leave the body out in plain sight if she was wanting him to put his fingerprints all over the place.

One thing was sure. He wasn't about to spend the night with that thing, so there went his fifty bucks. But what might he find if he poked around a bit? Some nice jewelry, perhaps? A cache of money under the mattress? Perhaps the poor woman had already been robbed, but surely he could find something of value. He felt he could afford the risk, since he had nothing left to lose. To look at the bright side, he would get three squares a day in prison.

Moving toward the staircase, Louis noticed a dark, lumpy object on the carpet. At first he thought it was a sock, but on closer inspection he discovered it was a coiled rope of sausage, partly chewed, and it had long since gone bad.

Wearing an appropriate expression of disgust, he rose from his haunches and noticed another foul object on one of the steps. Peering through the banister supports, he decided it was calf liver, also rancid, also partially eaten. A few steps up he could see something that looked like a rotten banana.

What the hell?

Careful of where he stepped, he climbed the staircase to the second floor, where he noticed that the nauseating trail led to the front bedroom. Shaking somewhat from the need for a drink, he followed it. At the doorway he reached in and flipped on the light.

The sight that greeted him sent a siren scream through his brain. An old woman was slumped over the side of the bed, eyes forever open in an expression of horror. Next to her, propped up on a fluffy pillow, was the definition of grotesque, the remains of a human being so savaged it was beyond comprehension. Rotting clumps of flesh and internal organs were scattered all around it.

Louis stumbled from the room, gagging, his mind reeling in shock. He had but one thought, and that was to get the hell out of the house as fast as possible.

Rushing back down the staircase in blind panic, his right foot slipped on what he'd thought was a rotten banana, tumbling him forward. He somersaulted the rest of the way down, breaking his neck on the last stair.

Five minutes later he was dead.

18

With Tamara tucked away, her bride doll snuggled next to her on the pillow, Valerie took a cool, relaxing bubble bath by candlelight and afterward sat at the typewriter to have a word with Gavin before going to bed. It was humid, so she turned on the window fan. The soft hum and caressing wind made her feel drowsy. It had been quite a day, but she wanted to know if Gavin had reached a decision. The sheet in the typewriter was pretty full, so she put it in the folder with the others, rolled in a clean sheet and typed:

Gavin? Have you decided about Jonathan yet?
yes
And the answer is?
if
What do you mean, if? If what?
if you can get him in bed
You devil. Well, he said he's been attracted to me for some time, so I don't think that will be a problem. Anyway, I'm tired, Gavin. I think I'll call it a night. It's been a rough day. Wonder if old Louis is asleep yet? Poor hungry things, I hope they don't have to wait long.
youre such a soft touch

Thank you, Gavin, it's nice to hear something like that once in a while, instead of being cursed up one side and down the other, or told that I'm crazy, or what a bitch I am. Well, good night.

good night my love

My love. The words were like music to Valerie's ears. Even though they hadn't been said with a voice, she could imagine Gavin saying them, and she heard them echoed over and over until at last she fell asleep.

Going to sleep with Gavin on her mind like that, Valerie was surprised to find herself dreaming about Doug. Doug was the ultimate male chauvinist pig. He held the old double standard that women should be chaste and men could be alley cats. He'd put her through some emotional trauma when she admitted she'd had some experience before he came along, bad experience actually, but that didn't matter to him. In his eyes she was defiled, and he made her feel it. He eventually got over it, supposedly, but on occasion he would dredge it up again, in different ways. He'd make accusations if she went somewhere and was gone too long (he thought), or licked her lips when Dennis was around, or if she paid too much attention to a handsome passerby on the street.

In the dream, she first went through a succession of all the bad memories of her life with him, wanting as she had then to attack and strangle him. But the opportunity never presented itself, which, in a dream, it should have. He had just found out about Gavin, and decided to mess things up for her by telling Jonathan all about her, so he would reject her. Jonathan didn't know what to think, so there was a trial, she of course being the defendant. Doug was the main prosecutor, Armand was his assistant. At the defense table, sitting on either side of her, was Gavin and Uncle Herb. On the spectators' benches sat the high school boys who'd raped her under the bleachers, and Steve Whitman from the reunion, whom Doug planned to call as witnesses. Elisabeth and Vonda sat in the front row on either side of Tamara, who was playing with her dolls, the bride and the duchess. Valerie was very upset to see the duchess doll, which she knew good and well she had locked in the chest in the attic. And of course Jonathan was there, seated near the back, chatting with Detective Morrison. A bailiff came out and said loudly, "All rise!"

Valerie held her breath as she waited for the judge to appear. Who would it be? And when she saw, her heart sank. It was Grandmother. Amanda sat behind the bench in her black robe, then everyone else sat back down, and court was now in session. The bailiff read the charges so everyone could hear. "State of West Virginia versus Valerie Scott, who is hereby charged with murder in the first degree."

Valerie gasped. Murder! She'd been tricked! This was supposed to be a sex trial. Doug had accused her of being a whore. How did murder get into this? And then she knew. Grandmother! She was smiling at her from the bench with malicious glee. Valerie knew she was going to be railroaded, no doubt about it. She looked desperately at Uncle Herb, who only patted her hand consolingly and told her not to worry, then got up and approached the jury box, which was filled with thirteen black-hooded figures whose faces were hidden. Thirteen? Valerie thought there were only supposed to be twelve jurors, but no one else seemed to notice.

Uncle Herb began his opening statement. "Ladies and gentlemen of the jury, Valerie Scott is not a murderess—"

Armand sprang up from the prosecutor's table. "I object, Your Honor!"

Valerie balked. He couldn't do that. He wasn't supposed to say anything during the defense attorney's opening statement, but Amanda said, "Sustained."

Uncle Herb shook his head and went on. "She is only a victim whose fragile mind was twisted in youth by acts of violence perpetrated upon her person by someone in this very courtroom." He stared openly at his sister behind the bench.

"You're in contempt of court!" Amanda bellowed, banging the gavel. "Any more remarks like that and I'll have you taken from this courtroom and placed under custody!"

Behind Valerie, Elisabeth was snickering. Tamara's dolls were having a fight.

Uncle Herb saw how it was going to be and gave up. Turning back to the jury, he said, "Thank you, ladies and gentlemen of the jury, for I know you will find that my client is innocent." He shuffled back to the defense table, sat down in his chair and lit his pipe.

"What kind of appeal was that?" Valerie whispered harshly, incensed that he should give up so easily. He only looked at her and winked. Valerie didn't understand. What did he know that she didn't?

Doug and Armand were in conference for a few minutes, after which Doug got up and faced the jury. "Ladies and gentlemen of the jury, there is nothing innocent about Valerie Scott. She is evil through and through."

Elisabeth and Vonda burst into applause. Judge Amanda allowed the disturbance. Doug went on, "She's the spawn of the devil, that's right, ladies and gentlemen, spawn of the devil himself. Charles Scott was not her real father. Valerie Scott's mother had lain with the Prince of Darkness, and now I ask you, no, I demand that you find her guilty, and sentence her to death. Thank you."

"That lying bastard," Valerie hissed under her breath. "Armand told him to say that. It's a lie."

"Of course it's a lie," Herb agreed. "But don't worry, the jury didn't buy it."

"How do you know?"

"Mr. Prosecutor, call your first witness," Amanda said.

Doug called Mary to the stand. Valerie hadn't even known she was there; a surprise witness. That was it, it was all over. She closed her eyes and covered her ears and daydreamed she was on a plane headed for France. The next thing she knew, Uncle Herb was saying to Amanda, "The defense rests."

Valerie looked around. "It's already over?"

"Almost." He smiled. "Jury's got to make their decision." They were filing out now.

"How did it go?" Valerie asked Gavin, squeezing his

hand. It was then she noticed how he looked, a skeleton with pieces of flesh hanging from it, hideous.

"It went pretty bad for you," he admitted, "just the way things looked, you know. But I think the jury will acquit you anyway. You'll walk out of here."

Valerie couldn't stand to look at him anymore, and cast her eyes downward. "Then we can be together, like we planned?"

"Yes, my love."

"You won't look like this, will you? I mean, you're still going to take over Jonathan's body, right?"

"What's the matter, Valerie? I thought looks didn't count."

"Well good grief, to a certain extent they do."

"I was just kidding," Gavin said.

The jury was already filing back in. "That was quick," Valerie said, apprehensive. "Guess they'd reached their decision before they even left."

"Not only that," Uncle Herb said, leaning back in his chair, "but their minds were made up before they even came to court. In your favor, I might add."

Valerie didn't believe him; how could that be? She'd seen Mary up there on the witness stand, and she had murdered Mary. She'd even admitted it. For good reasons, of course, but nonetheless . . . "Why would they be in my favor?"

Herb smiled. "Because you fed them."

Then Valerie understood, and she too smiled. No wonder Uncle Herb hadn't been worried. Valerie turned to look at Elisabeth and Vonda, looking so smug, so self-righteous. Tamara was between them, whispering something through her bride doll.

"Oh no," Valerie said. "Not Tamara too?"

"Might be for the best," Herb advised.

Valerie shook her head. "No, not her, she's all right. I'll just get rid of that duchess doll once and for all. Not Tamara, no."

Herb shrugged. The bailiff asked the jury if they had reached their decision. One on the end rose, holding up a piece of paper. The bailiff announced that the court would now hear the verdict.

"We the jury find the people in this courtroom guilty of bearing false witness against the accused. The penalty is death."

Loud protests filled the room. The two high school boys and Steve rushed for the back doors, but they were locked. It was then Valerie noticed that Jonathan and Morrison were gone. Amanda was banging away with the gavel, shouting, "Order in the court!" but her command was ignored. Doug and Armand were yelling at the jury spokesman, who was Gavin's twin brother. Elisabeth and Vonda were yelling too, wanting to know what was going on. The jury couldn't accuse them of anything. Then the jury began to disrobe.

Here they were visible, no longer transparent but no less slimy. Valerie wondered where the extra ones had come from; she thought she only had five. More had joined, she supposed. That meant more flesh would have to be provided.

They did have human facial features, but they were more like caricatures, exaggerated rather obscenely, covered with festering sores. Their slobbering, toothless mouths opened and closed, opened and closed like gills, nostrils flaring at the scent of fresh human meat. Everyone screamed in horror, except for Gavin, Valerie, Herb, and Tamara. The rest were trying desperately to get out now, even Amanda, but there was no escape. The jury began to move together, their bodies in constant, sticky touch, their feet slapping wetly on the hard floor, and they fell upon their victims one by one. The sounds were horrible.

"Shall we go, my love?" Gavin asked. "Or perhaps you would prefer to stay and watch."

"I have to go," Valerie said. "There's someone at the door."

There really was someone at the door. The bell was ringing, followed by insistent knocking. Valerie opened her eyes and saw that it was morning. Filled with apprehension, she pushed back the covers and slipped out of bed. After the dream she'd just had, she was almost afraid to answer the door; what if it was the police? But no, all of her accusers were dead, she had nothing to worry about. She put on her robe and went down.

When Valerie opened the door and saw who it was, she was stunned, even a little disoriented for a moment, imagining she was only dreaming this too. There stood Doug, smiling.

She thought it would sound stupid to ask if it was really him, so she asked instead, not returning his smile, "What do you want?"

"Is that any way to treat someone you haven't seen for three years?" he asked, obviously offended. "I came all this way just to see you."

Valerie eyed him suspiciously. "You're out of a job again, aren't you?"

"That's not why I'm here," he said coldly, but she could see she'd hit the nail right on the head. "Couple of days ago some detective called asking questions about you, and I realized how much I missed you. Aren't you even going to invite me in?"

She's the spawn of the devil, that's right, ladies and gentlemen . . .

"What about it, Valerie? Aren't you glad to see me?"

Valerie Scott's mother had lain with the Prince of Darkness . . .

"Or maybe you've already got company, huh, is that it?"

I demand that you find her guilty and sentence her to death.

"Of course I'm glad to see you." Valerie smiled. "Please do come in."

He sat at the kitchen table while she made some Kool-Aid, asking her what all that was about, the detective and all. Had she done something? (As if she would tell him.) Was she in trouble of some kind? As if he hoped.

"It was about one of my second cousins," Valerie answered stiffly, thinking about the cyanide she hadn't yet thrown away. "She got kidnapped, but the police found her yesterday. She's here now. I'm taking care of her."

Doug seemed disappointed. "Oh. Well, he was asking a lot of questions about you, like he suspected you did it or something."

"What sort of questions?" Valerie casually moved to the cabinet below the sink and picked up the bottle, concealing it with the sleeve of her robe. Doug might suspect a sweetener with a skull and crossbones on it.

Doug cocked his head. "Oh, just a bunch of personal questions. Did I know of any trouble you'd ever been in, had you ever seen a psychiatrist, what did you think of kids, what was your attitude about sex, that kind of thing. If you'd ever exhibited odd behavior."

"And what did you say?"

"Nothing bad," he said defensively. "Told him you were a regular girl, you know, stayed home most of the time. That's all."

And so, it went without saying, she owed him a favor. "Who knew you were coming?"

"Well, I told Dennis. Why?"

"Just wondered." Valerie tapped a spoonful of the deadly poison into one of the glasses. "How is Dennis these days, anyway?"

"Oh, the same, I guess." He studied her a few moments, forming his next question. "Tell me, now that it's over between us . . . you really did have a thing for him, didn't you?"

Valerie added Kool-Aid and ice to both glasses and stirred, using separate spoons. "Actually yes, I did."

A barely concealed look of contempt settled on Doug's face. "I knew it. So did you ever make it with him? He never said, but of course he wouldn't, knowing I would have punched his lights out. Did you? Ever go to bed with him?"

"I only wished." Valerie smiled, carrying the glasses to the table, thinking, Doug gets the one in my left hand, *left, left, left.* "How I wished and dreamed. You were really so dull, Doug. Incredibly dull." If he had anywhere to go, she knew, this would be his cue to get up and storm out of the house, cursing her all the way to get the last words said, calling her a bitch and a whore. But he was a long way from home, so he had no choice but to stand his ground.

"You weren't exactly exciting yourself," he retorted angrily, his face all red. "Most of the time you just used to lie there like a sack of cement."

Before Valerie could think of a snappy comeback, Tamara appeared in the kitchen with her bride doll. Not very good timing.

"There's Tamara now," Valerie said, putting the verbal war on hold. "Tamara, this is Doug, an old friend of mine. Can you say hello?"

Tamara lifted the doll to her face. "Hello."

"Well hello," he said back, seizing the opportunity to give Valerie the cold shoulder. "That sure is a pretty doll you have. What's her name?"

"Mary."

Not now, Valerie thought. Wait until he drinks his Kool-Aid.

"That's a nice name. Well, I heard you got kidnapped."

That was Doug and his usual diplomacy. "What a thing to say, Doug," Valerie snapped. "She was severely traumatized."

He tossed her a frosty look but turned back to Tamara and said, "I'm sorry. Maybe it's something we shouldn't talk about. Want to tell me some more about Mary?"

Unfortunately, Tamara did. "She's dead."

Doug was somewhat taken aback by this. He looked at Valerie again, this time in bewilderment. Valerie gave him a terse smile and explained to Tamara that her doll wasn't dead because it had never been alive to begin with. "Go watch television or something," Valerie instructed. "Doug and I are trying to talk."

Tamara put the doll back up. "Yes, Mother, I'll go watch television." And she turned, disappearing through the drape in a little march. Valerie sighed. Doug still looked bewildered.

"Why did she call you Mother?"

"Because on top of everything else, her real mother just died." Valerie lifted her glass and drank thirstily, hoping to encourage Doug to do the same. "I told her to call me that, since I'll be raising her now, and her brothers and sister. They're moving in tomorrow."

This wasn't good news for Doug. "Oh. So what about the father? He still around or what?"

"He'll be moving in too," Valerie replied lightly. "So it's a good thing you didn't come up because you were out of a job, right?"

Doug frowned. "I am out of a job, and spent the last of my money coming up here. I drove straight through because I couldn't even afford a motel room."

"Well, you can't stay here, there wouldn't be room," Valerie said. "But the house next door is vacant. There's furniture and everything, but no one's living there. I've got a key. I could let you stay there while you find a temporary job; make enough money to get back home and on your feet."

A lecherous half-smile appeared on his face. "Next door, huh? Could we maybe get together sometime for old times' sake? I'll show you some action, baby."

"Sounds tempting."

"How about now?"

"Drink your Kool-Aid." Valerie winked. She would see some real action then, all right.

He took a healthy swallow—which wasn't really so healthy, he would soon realize—and another, and Valerie smiled, drinking her own, wondering how long it would take. She was telling him about all the hell she'd gone through taking care of Grandmother, all the verbal abuse she'd had to take, and how she had started thinking about killing her, maybe with poison, something like cyanide, which she just happened to have a supply of.

Doug started looking at his empty Kool-Aid glass very nervously, very nervously indeed, probably thinking about her asking him who knew he'd come up, but oh God, surely she wouldn't, she wouldn't really, she was just a regular girl who stayed home most of the time. She was only trying to scare him, and doing a damn fine job of it, and he really didn't mean that, about her just lying there like a sack of cement.

Valerie watched as the symptoms crept up on him within five minutes of his first swallow: the rubbing of his hands together because they were getting clammy, and suddenly he couldn't breathe so well. He started gasping, his tongue sticking out as he retched, a look of horror seizing his face, because now he knew.

She *really would.*

He fell to the floor and started to convulse. He kicked over his chair, tearing at his mouth, making a vain attempt to suck in air, making a horrible sound, chronic emphysema amplified, his skin turning blue. It was over in about thirty seconds. Quick, that cyanide. Couldn't beat it for killing mice. Or rats.

Having heard the commotion, Tamara came back into the kitchen. She stared at the body for several seconds, her expression blank. Finally, hidden behind the bride, she asked, "Is he dead?"

"Quite," Valerie answered. "Now you're not to mention this to anyone, you understand? Not even Daddy. And please, don't say Mary is dead either; you have to learn, people get funny thoughts when you say things like that. They'll think you're strange, and they might even put you away, lock you up in a room with nothing to do for the rest of your life. You wouldn't want that to happen, would you?"

"No, Mother."

"Well then, I suppose we have another car to get rid of, don't we? And it's probably loaded with everything he owns. The nerve of that guy, thinking he could come up here and start using me again and that it's all right, because I'm a 'fallen woman.' What a jerk. He deserved to die, don't you think?"

"Yes, Mother."

"And besides, I've got to get another body over there today. There's thirteen of them now, you know. Just like our street number, thirteen."

"Thirteen," the bride repeated.

Valerie drummed the tabletop with her fingertips, thinking. Dennis would probably never even call, but if he did, she would tell him that yes, Doug came up, but because of her new situation, she couldn't let him stay, so he left. The sort Doug was, Dennis would never become alarmed. Doug would just become "someone he used to know." The only trouble Valerie could foresee was if Doug should start talking to her on her typewriter. That would really be trouble, him in there with Gavin. She would never have a moment's peace.

Doug's car, she decided, she would park at a local motel. When the police were called to investigate, they would find out who owned it, and that he had never been registered. They would then assume he'd met someone who had been registered at a bar or something. (But who? All those registrations, and if she picked the right motel they wouldn't even know for sure which day the car showed up.) So, A: Doug had left behind everything he owned to traipse off into the sunset with that person to live happily ever after, or B: that person had murdered him and taken the body somewhere else. There would, of course, be other possible scenarios, but none of that would matter without a missing person's report. Which Doug's parents might file, and maybe the police would end up knowing he'd come to see her, and drop by to ask a few questions. If they did, she would tell them the same story she had ready for Dennis. He came, he went. They wouldn't be able to prove otherwise.

Damn, but she was clever!

"What are we going to do with him?" the bride asked.

Valerie sighed. Doug was pretty big; she was going to have a hell of a time dragging him over to Mrs. Rothford's. "Take him next door, like I said, so the monsters will have something to eat. Now I only have to get one more."

"Who?"

Valerie got up and kissed her on the cheek. "Don't worry, I'll find someone. I'm going to get dressed now, unless you want your breakfast. Hungry?"

Tamara shook her head, still fascinated by the dead body.

Valerie really didn't want to ask, but she had to know.
Gavin, Doug isn't in there with you, is he?
does a rocking horse have a hickory dick

You don't have to get sarcastic. What's he thinking?
he is pretty pissed
Valerie smiled. Wasn't that just too bad?
Doug? Sorry about that, but I think you deserved it.
Now get out, go to hell or wherever it is you're supposed to go. Gavin and I would like some privacy.
i bet you would whore
Chauvinist pig. Gavin, hit him.
with what
Valerie tore the sheet out and stuffed it in her folder. She would have thrown it away, but it had some good stuff from Gavin on it. This was ridiculous; how could she stand it? She should have just sent Doug over there. He would have gone on his own two feet, and now she had to drag his body through the backyards and into Mrs. Rothford's kitchen. Besides that she had his damn soul to put up with. What had she been thinking? But she knew. In spite of the risk and the extra trouble, she'd wanted to do the honors herself. It was her privilege, after the way he'd treated her for two years. So the only question that remained was, had it been worth it? The answer didn't look like yes so far, that was for sure.

Armand was standing in her closet when she opened it, giving her a start. "Piling up over there, aren't they?" he asked accusingly. "So when are you going over to pay the old wino? He's waiting, you know."

"He's gone," Valerie muttered, reaching through him to get the sundress she wanted to wear.

Armand stepped through her into the room. "That's what you think. He's got a few questions to ask you too, about those three bodies in the house. But you probably won't have to worry about him going to the police; he's seen the inside of a jail too many times, doesn't much like cops, and would probably be afraid they would accuse him of the crimes. When he sees you're not going to show up, he'll stuff his pockets with whatever valuables he can find, maybe a couple of pillowcases too, for food. Then he'll just quietly slip out the back way."

Valerie wasn't even bothered by Armand's lies anymore. She knew exactly where he was coming from, so it was stupid to let him upset her. "Oh, I'm sure you're right, Armand. I'm just crazy as a loon. I've made up those things in my mind for an excuse to kill people. You've got it. Pretty smart, aren't you?"

"You're just being sarcastic," he complained.

Valerie dressed in front of him, supposing he'd seen her nude plenty of times before when she didn't know it. "Me, sarcastic? Why on earth would I want to be sarcastic? I'm just saying you're absolutely right. I'm criminally insane. I love to kill people! So what?"

"So you should be locked up, that's what! Like I was!"

"Are you saying you killed people too? Is that why they locked you up, Armand? Jealous that I'm getting away with it?"

Armand's face pinched in anger. "You think you're so smart. Well, you'll get caught, all right. You're not as smart as you think."

"We'll see. But that's it, isn't it? You're jealous. I get to have all the fun. How many did you do in, Armand, before they caught you? How many?"

"Two," he mumbled, eyes downcast.

"Only two. So I'm already two up on you, three if you want to include Grandmother, but she would have died pretty soon anyway, even if I hadn't cheated her on her heart medicine. Why don't you go away and leave me alone? I've got enough to worry about without you popping up every time I turn around. And take Elisabeth with you."

"She won't go. She wants to see how many people come to her funeral."

"Well, hang around until tomorrow, then. I'd really like her out of here."

"I won't make her go if she doesn't want to," Armand argued. "Maybe she wants to stay and give you a hard time for stealing her family."

Valerie was ready to drive Doug's car to the motel. "Armand, I did not steal Elisabeth's family. She's the one who hung herself, so it's none of her business anymore. Well, I have to get rid of that car. Evidence, Armand. You have to get rid of the evidence. Maybe that never occurred to you?" Smiling, she turned on her heel and stalked out.

19

When Jonathan came by that evening after work to see Tamara, Detective Morrison was with him. Valerie was a little nervous about it because Doug's body was out on the back porch wrapped in a sheet. She couldn't drag it over to Mrs. Rothford's until it was dark. But she was no longer worried about Tamara saying something she shouldn't. She understood now about what sort of things were all right to say and which were not, so when Morrison asked if Valerie wouldn't mind giving him and Jonathan a little time alone with the girl, Valerie went to the kitchen without hesitation.

Tamara was in the rocking chair with her mouthpiece, the bride doll. Jonathan spoke to her first. "How are you feeling, honey? Better?"

"I feel very well, thank you," Tamara answered behind the doll.

"I can't see you very well with that doll up in front of your face like that." Jonathan smiled. "Want to put it down so we can look at each other while we talk?"

"No."

Jonathan looked at Morrison and shrugged. Morrison bent over to meet Tamara's eye level, hands resting above his knees. "Hi, Tamara. Remember me? Alex?"

"I remember."

"Mind if I ask you a few questions?"

Tamara hesitated. "No . . ."

Morrison felt encouraged. "Okay, I was wondering if you could tell me anything about what happened to you. Do you remember who it was that took you away from your parents' house?"

"Yes."

Morrison smiled. "Who was it, Tamara? Who took you? Did you know them?"

"It was Gavin."

The smile fell flat. "Gavin. Okay, now let me ask you this. Was there anyone else besides Gavin? Was it just the two of you, or was there someone else?"

Tamara started rocking the chair and began to recite what Valerie had taught her to say. "Just me and Gavin. He took me somewhere but I don't know where, and he was real nice to me and when I told him I wanted to go home he brought me here but I didn't know where I was so I started trying to find my own way home."

Morrison knew a rehearsed speech when he heard one, so now he was certain, and every damn bit as helpless to do anything about it. "All right, Tamara, now let me ask you this." Surely Valerie Scott couldn't have covered all the bases, not with a seven-year-old. "Do you know where Gavin is now? Can you remember any numbers on a house or street?"

"Gavin is gone."

"Gone where, honey?" Jonathan prodded. "Did he tell you where he was going?"

Tamara turned the bride to face him. "The monsters ate him."

Jonathan and Morrison exchanged confused glances. "Monsters?" Morrison asked. "What kind of monsters?"

"Hungry ones."

Morrison pulled Jonathan aside and whispered, "She ever talk about monsters before?"

Jonathan turned his back so his daughter couldn't read his lips and muttered softly, "The night before she disappeared, she thought she saw one in her closet, but Elisabeth explained it was only headlights shining on the knobs, and I've had to explain several times about TV monsters being actors with makeup jobs. But she never talked about seeing them eat anyone. You think she could be talking about dogs or something?"

Morrison went back over to the rocking chair and squatted. "Can you describe the monsters for me, Tamara? Do you remember what they looked like?"

"I didn't see them."

Morrison rubbed his forehead. It seemed unlikely Miss Scott would have advised Tamara to talk about monsters eating Sheffield; she certainly could have come up with something better than that. "If you didn't see them, Tamara, how did you know they ate Gavin?"

"Valerie said."

Morrison glanced toward the kitchen drape. Now maybe he was finally getting somewhere. Lowering his voice, he asked, "Valerie told you the monsters ate Gavin? Did she see them?"

"She just told me that so I wouldn't be scared of him coming to get me anymore."

"I guess that was Valerie's way of helping her cope," Jonathan said. "Looks like it helped. She's come a long way just since yesterday. I'm amazed, myself."

Morrison was furious, but he kept it hidden. "Well, it was nice talking to you, Tamara. You be a good girl, now."

"I have to," the bride answered.

Morrison bet she did. Valerie Scott was apparently a master at brainwashing; only a psychiatrist could dig the truth out of the kid now. But the girl's father was "amazed" at what he interpreted to be signs of recovery. He probably couldn't be persuaded otherwise. Morrison couldn't argue without telling him exactly what he believed, but since he didn't have a shred of evidence to support his theory that Tamara had been here all along, he strongly doubted he could convince Jonathan that his daughter needed a psychiatrist more than ever. After learning what he had at the hospital, Morrison began to doubt that Sheffield had even been involved. Valerie Scott had gone to a lot of trouble to make it seem as though he had been, though. So Sheffield was more than likely dead, and as meticulous as Valerie was, the body would probably never be found. Morrison just hated to see people get away with things like kidnapping and murder.

Before leaving, he stepped into the kitchen to speak to Valerie, who was standing at the stove stirring a pot of spaghetti sauce. "I'll be on my way now," he said, noticing the faint look of alarm on her face when she saw him. He'd only startled her, he supposed. People like her didn't suffer from guilty consciences. "Kid seems to be coming along. That idea of yours about the monsters got her talking again, even if it is behind a doll. What do you make of that?"

Valerie cleared her throat. "I just gave her the doll to play with. I didn't tell her what to do with it. Now what was it you said about monsters?"

"The ones you told her ate Sheffield, so she wouldn't be scared of him coming to get her anymore."

"Oh, those monsters." Valerie nodded. "Well, that made it simple for her. I wanted to tell you, we certainly appreciate everything you've done. Can you see yourself out? Hate to be rude, but I'm sort of busy."

"That's fine, I don't need courtesies; I'm a cop, remember?"

Five minutes after Jonathan left, the telephone rang, a throaty female voice inquiring about the room. Valerie was about to tell her it was no longer available, but then stopped herself. Why waste the opportunity? It would save her having to go driving around looking for another bum or a hitchhiker. She could invite the woman over for an interview. Yes, an interview.

The doorbell sounded a half hour later. Tamara was still eating her supper in the kitchen. Valerie opened the door to find a very attractive young woman, probably mid-twenties or a little older, with shoulder-length red hair and wide green eyes, flawless complexion, dimples in both cheeks, and a suitcase in her hand. She introduced herself as Jade Green, and laughed, saying, "Cute, huh? My mother apparently thought it was."

Valerie led her into the living room, apologizing for the heat.

"Oh, heat doesn't bother me at all," Jade said as she took a seat on the sofa. Valerie took in the expensive look of her clothes, silk clam diggers and oversized matching top, and the heavy gold bracelets around her tanned wrists. Everything about her looked expensive. Someone who would probably be missed. From a rich family which would spend its last dime finding out what had happened to her. She'd come in a cab. The driver might remember. A woman like this, yes, he would remember. Why on earth was she wanting to rent a room?

Jade gave Valerie a dazzling smile. "It seems I'm in a bit of a fix. I came up here about six weeks ago to live with a man and, well, it hasn't worked out." She laughed. "That's an understatement. He took me, cleaned me out, at least of the money I'd managed to draw out of my account before Mother closed it. She didn't approve of Steve and swore she'd disinherit me if I left with him. But I was in love, right? Well, turns out she was right about him, and so she has to say 'I told you so' by refusing to send me any money to get home." She paused, catching her breath. "The long and short of it is, my father will wire me plenty, but he's out of town right now and I can't get hold of him for three days. Do you think you could . . . trust me for the money until then? Motels won't, I assure you. I've already tried six of them. I just need a place to stay until I get it."

No one knew where she was except the cab driver. But what if a picture of her was pasted on the front page of the paper? No, too risky.

"I don't mean to offend you," Valerie said, "but I don't trust anyone for anything. Sorry." There was something suspicious about all this. If she was broke, how had she paid the cab driver? Let him cop a feel up her blouse?

Jade cleared her throat, hanging her head slightly. "That wasn't exactly the truth, but if I told you why I really came here, you'd think I was crazy."

Valerie lowered herself into the rocking chair, extremely curious. "Try me."

Jade cleared her throat again, wringing her hands. "Well, it started a few nights ago. Steve had gone to a party without me, and as it turned out, he didn't come home until the next morning."

Valerie knew how that went. "Go on."

"Anyway," Jade continued after taking a deep breath, "I was lying in bed almost asleep when I heard something like a . . . well, kind of like a lip-smacking sound, and when I opened my eyes I saw a pair of yellow eyes near the foot of my bed. I know I wasn't imagining it, and this is going to sound even stranger, but I had the strongest impression that the thing, whatever it was, was wanting to eat me. I hurried to turn on the light, and when I did, it vanished. Naturally I couldn't go back to sleep."

Valerie hid her amazement. This woman knew about the vampire-things; probably one of the few, like herself, who knew and lived to tell! Suddenly Valerie felt an affinity for her, the intimacy of a shared secret. Jade was the friend she had always longed for. Tamara was pleasant company lately, but she was only a child, could only speak on a child's level. But why had this woman come to her? How had she known?

"I believe what you're saying is true," Valerie said carefully. "I know what they are. What I'm wondering now, though, is how you came to me? You saw my ad, obviously, but I get the impression you knew I'd believe your story. How? How did you know?"

"Actually this is the craziest part." Jade laughed nervously, tossing back her thick red hair. "You know I had to get out of that apartment after two more nights without sleep because I could hear those smacking noises. I'd pretty well had it with Steve anyway, so I looked in the paper for a room to rent. Just to get some sleep, really, is all I wanted, about all I could think about, but something about motel rooms . . . I don't know, I just never feel comfortable in them. But frankly, I'm so exhausted now I could probably sleep in a boxcar." Her eyelids drooped as if to prove it. "Anyway, it was like your phone number just jumped off the page at me, and I knew—at least I had this overpowering feeling—that whoever placed that ad could help me understand this. And maybe allow me to get some sleep."

"There's a nice comfortable bed just beyond those doors." Valerie smiled, pointing toward the dining room. "Sleep away. We'll talk more when you're feeling better."

Valerie put Tamara to bed early so she wouldn't disturb their special guest. The bride asked Valerie if she was going to feed the special guest to the monsters for dessert.

"No, not this one," Valerie told her. "She knows about them. She's special like us. But be a good girl and go to sleep now. I have to get Doug's body next door before she wakes up. It would probably be better if I explained things to her first, before she knows about that."

It took Valerie almost half an hour to get the job done, but finally, sweat and toil spent, Doug's body was in front of Mrs. Rothford's refrigerator. She didn't bother looking around the house, having assumed the vampire-things had already polished off the derelict. Valerie spoke into the darkness, "Dinner time, children. Sorry it's only one."

When she stepped back into her own rear porch, Jade was standing just on the other side of the screen door, no telling for how long.

"What were you dragging?" she asked.

Long enough. Wasn't she supposed to be exhausted enough to sleep in a boxcar?

Valerie joined her in the kitchen. "Care for some iced tea? This is going to be sort of a long story. I can tell you about it out on the front porch. We'll be cooler."

Jade was quite shocked to learn Valerie had considered feeding her to the things, and looked ready for a moment to bolt from the swing and run away screaming. Yet Valerie carefully explained the creatures' plight, and Jade gradually became sympathetic.

"Well, I certainly never imagined it was human. I guess that's a little different. Too bad we can't find out who they were, so we could set them free like you did your grandmother."

Valerie agreed, then went on to make Jade an offer.

"I'm going to have a full house after tomorrow, but we can figure something out . . . the attic could make a nice bedroom, if you wouldn't mind. There's a lot of junk up there right now, but I can get rid of it. But I guess I'm getting ahead of things, aren't I? I haven't even asked if you wanted to stay. You can, as long as you like. But I suppose you have better places to be."

"Actually, I don't, and thank you, I would like to stay, at least for a while. But you wouldn't expect me to help you get people over to that house, would you? I don't think I could do that."

That was exactly what Valerie expected. Since Jade shared the secret, she should also share the responsibility, and she would eventually adjust to the idea.

"I'd really appreciate it if you could just help me with the house and kids. I've already got one . . . you know, body for tonight. That's what you saw me dragging over there. But there's more of them than there used to be, at least I think there are, so I really should give them two. Oh well, they'll just have to make do with one tonight, I guess. I just feel like taking a cool bath and going to bed."

"I could use some more sleep myself." Jade yawned, stretching. "Good night, Valerie."

"Good night, Jade. Sleep tight. Don't let the monsters bite."

Jade gave her a sidelong glance. "Did anyone ever tell you you have a weird sense of humor?"

A few minutes later, sitting on the couch in the dining room, Jade took a deep breath and smiled. Valerie had swallowed the whole enchilada. It had been so easy; all that worrying she'd done had been for nothing.

God, but she was still nervous. The things Valerie had confided to her were horrifying to say the least. She would have to be very careful.

Very careful indeed.

20

Saturday morning at ten o'clock Jonathan arrived with Todd and Jennifer. Lynn's mother was keeping Davie and Lisa, her granddaughter, so Lynn and her husband could attend the funeral.

"Are you ready?" Jonathan asked Valerie when she opened the door. "I left the kids in the station wagon. I can bring them in if you're not. I guess you think it's all right for Tamara to go? You don't think it would upset her more?"

"I decided it would be best to leave her here, actually. Jade will watch her."

"Jade?"

Valerie told him on the way to the car that Jade was a cousin from her mother's side who had come to help her with the kids. Jonathan said that was nice, it was quite a job, and Tamara needed a lot of extra attention right now.

There were not many people at the funeral, Valerie was pleased to note; Elisabeth would really be upset. Only her widowed mother and younger sister, best friends and their husbands, and a woman Valerie didn't recognize. Armand was there too, sitting in the back row. Valerie nodded at him as she passed.

Soft music was playing, the standard organ dirge. All the others were sniffling, except for the men, at least until Valerie and Jonathan took their seats in one of the front rows with Todd and Jennifer between them. It became very quiet after that, except for the music. Eyes questioned, suspicions rose, hatred bloomed. Valerie didn't care. She studied the white coffin surrounded by funeral wreaths, wondering if the mortician had been able to straighten Elisabeth out enough to allow viewing.

"You bitch," a voice hissed in her ear. Valerie jumped and looked over her shoulder. Elisabeth was leaning over from the next pew back, and she did look remarkably better, except for the hateful expression on her face.

"What's wrong?" Jonathan whispered over the children's heads.

Valerie turned back around. "Oh, nothing."

"Nothing for you!" Elisabeth screamed loudly. "You bitch, I could kill you! Stay away from my husband!"

"Lovely coffin," Valerie murmured to Jonathan. "And flowers too."

"Bitch! I meant to come back! I thought they would revive me!"

Valerie sighed. "So tragic, to die so young. And for nothing, that's the worst thing. All for nothing."

"I'll haunt you until the day you die!"

"So when are they going to start?" Valerie asked Jonathan, sliding her arm across the back of the pew to rest her hand on his shoulder. It was a bold move for her, but she knew how furious it would make Elisabeth. "Doesn't look like any more's going to show up. Guess poor Elisabeth didn't have that many friends."

Elisabeth screamed throughout the whole service.

After the burial, Jonathan took Valerie and the kids back to her house. "I'm only bringing our clothes, mostly, and the kids' toys, of course," he explained as they walked through the front door. "And the food. Maybe a few other odds and ends we might need."

Valerie waved at Tamara and Jade, who were still on the sofa watching television, and said to him, "We'll need an extra bed, though. Jade's going to use the one in the attic that used to be Uncle Herb's, and it's only a single anyway. The boys will need something bigger. But I suppose Davie still uses a crib?"

"All right, I'll bring over the crib, and Todd's single, in the pickup. The rest I'm going to sell, then I'll put the house up for rent. Unless we'll need more linens and towels, just tell me what we need. I'm not very good at these things."

"I believe I've got everything else covered," Valerie said.

Jonathan turned to Tamara and smiled. "Hi, hon. How are you getting along?" His smile passed to Jade. "I'm Jonathan. I assume you're Val's cousin Jade. Thanks for watching Tamara."

Jade looked questioningly at Valerie. "My pleasure, Jonathan. She's quite a little girl."

"Been through a lot these past few days."

Todd and Jennifer asked if they could go out in the back yard.

"Not in those good clothes," Jonathan told them. "Go get that suitcase out of the car. It's got some playclothes in it. But don't you want to spend some time with your sister? You haven't seen her in a while."

Jennifer timidly approached the sofa. Tamara was a novelty now that she had been kidnapped. Jennifer would have asked about her haircut, but her attention was captured by the doll in Tamara's arms. "Where'd you get the pretty doll, Tamara? Can I play with it sometime?"

"No."

"I've got lots of dolls like that. You can have your pick," Valerie said quickly. Todd insisted that he wanted to play outside, and too drained to argue, Jonathan gave his consent. Todd rushed back out the front door to get the suitcase out of the back of the station wagon, and Jennifer was now staring expectantly at Valerie.

"Can I have it now?"

"Certainly," Valerie smiled. "Come with me. They're in the attic."

When Valerie unlocked and opened the chest, Jennifer gasped with delight and immediately seized the duchess. "I want her!"

Valerie cursed herself for not having more foresight. "Any one except that one, Jennifer. That one has to stay locked in the chest."

"But why?" Jennifer pouted. "You said I could have my pick. You said!"

"Just not that one, it's special."

"That's why I want it!" the five-year-old wailed. "She's the prettiest one, even prettier than Tamara's."

Valerie sighed in resignation; this was no way to start off. "All right, Jennifer, I'll let you have it, but you have to promise me something. Don't ever, ever ever let Tamara play with your doll. Understand? Not even if she wants to trade for a little while. Promise?"

Jennifer nodded happily, her arms wrapped possessively around the doll with the red velvet dress. "I promise."

Jonathan had gone to get the clothes, toys, bed, and crib. Jade was downstairs with the children. Valerie was in Uncle Herb's old room, which soon would be the boys' bedroom, trying to communicate with Gavin, but Doug was making it very difficult. Sometimes she couldn't tell which one was talking to her, but mostly she could, since Doug nearly always called her a bitch first thing. Gavin was trying to tell her something that sounded important.

look out

yeah look out for me bitch i am going to make you pay jade is

a fox thats what makes you look like a sack of shit valerie i bet jonathan will be humping her before long he will forget all about you

Shut the hell up, Doug, I want to hear what Gavin has to say. Jade is what? Am I supposed to look out for her?

shes crazy like you shes going to kill you bitch

Gavin, can't you make him shut up? What about Jade? What's going on?

dont trust her dont trust her

Valerie gasped. Jade knew everything, absolutely

everything. Why couldn't she be trusted? What was she up to?

Tell me, Gavin, is she just pretending to believe in the creatures? To make me trust her? But how would she know about the yellow eyes and their lips smacking, and that the one she supposedly saw was wanting to eat her?

maybe shes been here before and read our conversations dont trust her

Valerie sat back in the chair, trying to think. She was almost always at home, never gone for very long, never at night, when it would be most likely for someone to get in, except for when she had taken Tamara from her home and when she'd picked up the bum at the library. And there were no conversations to be read that first time, and the second she'd only been gone for about ten minutes.

Then she knew. The long drive she and Tamara had taken in the mountains the other evening. Jade must have come then. But why? She was a total stranger, knew nothing about her. So then she must have picked the house at random. A thief? No, she hadn't taken anything. She would have taken the silver if she'd been a thief. So then what? She'd read the papers in her folder, about the creatures, what they sounded like. Valerie must have mentioned something about their lip-smacking, about the yellow eyes. Yes, she remembered now. About killing Mary too, and Gavin.

Valerie bolted forward in her chair and flipped open the folder. Thank goodness the papers were still there. She relaxed a little. Maybe Jade was a blackmailer. The Steve she mentioned could be her partner. Get into people's houses, look for information. Not nearly as risky as burglary, if they found what they were looking for, personal Polaroids maybe, torrid love letters, things like that . . . things people would pay to keep secret. But these papers in her folder, anyone could have typed them. They could have done it themselves. It wasn't like the conversations were in Valerie's own handwriting. If that were the case, that would certainly be useful—very incriminating. So they knew. Jade and her partner Steve knew, but they had no real proof . . . not yet. That was what Jade was here to get. Pretending to be her friend. It just happened that Valerie had run an ad in the paper. Jade might have used the phone to call Steve and tell him what she had found the first time she was here and noticed the number. It was an easy one to remember. Then she ran across it by accident in the paper—a perfect way to infiltrate. The bitch.

Valerie put her hands on the keyboard.

I think I've figured it out, Gavin. She's a blackmailer. What should I do? What I was planning to do with her in the first place? But how would I explain to Jonathan? And she's got that partner Steve, somewhere. He knows she's here. If she disappeared, he would make trouble.

you just want to kill her because youre jealous

Shut up, Doug, I'm not talking to you. Gavin, what should I do?

jealous jealous jealous

Valerie angrily switched off the typewriter, tore the sheet out of the roller and stuck it in the folder with the others, then wondered where to hide it. She didn't want to burn her conversations with Gavin. They meant a great deal to her. Where? Under her mattress. They would be safe there.

She hurried into her bedroom, wondering what the hell to do. Jade might have a little tape recorder . . . blackmailers loved tape recordings. They could call the person up and play it back to them each time they wanted a payment. Valerie would have to be very careful about what she said from now on . . . but what if Jade had already taped everything? No, then she wouldn't still be here. Wasn't that smart. Oh damn, this was trouble deluxe!

The plot began to thicken when Jade's accomplice called an hour later to see if she was there. He probably wanted to know if she had found anything useful yet. Jade had a guardian and so couldn't be killed. Unless Steve could also be killed, lured to the house. They were both criminals, and criminals had no friends, no family who would claim them. They wouldn't be missed.

Valerie went into the kitchen after handing Jade the

phone, but she stayed just on the other side of the drape, listening.

"No Steve, I'm not coming back to you."

Valerie translated Jade's answer. This meant no, she had not found anything yet besides the papers. Jade thought she knew where some bodies were, but they couldn't blackmail Valerie about bodies. She would just get rid of them—as if there were really any to get rid of. If and when she did find viable evidence, Jade would say something like, "Well, I'll think about it, maybe we can get together a little later to talk this out." He would know then they had a way to get every penny of Valerie's inheritance which she had gone through three years of hell to get.

"Leave me alone, Steve, it's over." Then Jade's voice dropped to a low whisper. Valerie couldn't tell what she was saying, because in addition to the fact Jade was whispering, a loud commotion began in the living room. It sounded like Jennifer and Tamara were having an argument. When Valerie stepped through the drape to see what was going on, Jade abruptly slammed down the receiver.

"They're always so sorry when they're losing you. Promise to change, they'll do anything if you'll just come back." She put on a look of determination. "Not this time. I've heard those promises before."

Valerie was sure she had; how long had they been doing this together?

"Yes, it's so hard to find a good man, isn't it," she answered, not the least bit fooled anymore. "Well, I have to see what's going on with the girls."

Tamara was crouched in the corner next to the sofa, behind the standing lamp, with both the bride and duchess clutched tightly in her arms. When Jennifer saw Valerie, she wailed, "She took my doll and won't give it back!"

Valerie's face darkened. She strode over to the corner. "Tamara, give the duchess doll back to Jennifer. It's hers now."

Tamara put the duchess doll in front of her face. "I don't have to mind you, you ugly old witch! Killer!"

Jennifer gasped and stared at her sister in open shock. She'd never heard her talk to an adult that way before. Killer?

Valerie knew it would be useless to stand there and argue, and the duchess had said too much already; now Jennifer was going to have to be reasoned with. What she had just heard could never be repeated, of course. So Valerie bent over and tore the duchess from Tamara's grasp. This doll was simply too dangerous; it would have to be destroyed. Jennifer held out her hands, expecting to get it back, but Valerie shook her head.

"You promised me you wouldn't let Tamara play with it, and you broke your promise, so you can't have it anymore."

Jennifer started to cry. "I want my doll I want my doll . . ."

Jade was watching the scene, so enraptured that Valerie was surprised she didn't take out a notebook and start taking notes. The lying bitch.

"You can choose another one, Jennifer. How about the princess doll? She's much prettier than the duchess."

"I want that one!" Jennifer tried to take the doll away from Valerie, so she held it out of her reach and said sternly, "Now Jennifer, you stop acting like a baby this instant. I mean it. You cannot have this doll back, so just forget about it. They're all pretty much the same."

Jennifer collapsed on the floor, sobbing.

"Kids," Valerie muttered. She wondered if Jade had put two and two together, as they say. She'd already asked why Tamara always talked with the bride doll in front of her face, which that stupid detective had also been curious about. Valerie told her about the kidnapping (the official version, and now she was very glad about her discretion in that matter) and that the doll probably represented in Tamara's mind the little girl she'd been before Gavin had taken her, which didn't make much sense, but it was the only thing Valerie could think of, aside from the truth, that it was Mary's voice. Now she would have to convince her that the duchess doll represented the little girl Tamara had been while she was with Gavin. He'd encouraged her to be a spoiled brat. He'd taught her to say nasty, mean things, because he thought it was amusing or something. Behind the two dolls was the little girl Tamara was now that she was back, and once the conflicts were resolved, she wouldn't need the dolls to speak anymore. It wouldn't do at all for Jade to realize that Tamara with the duchess was all that was necessary in the evidence department.

"See if you can calm Jennifer down. I can't stand tantrums," Valerie said to Jade. "I'll go up and get her another doll."

Valerie went upstairs, first to her bedroom, and stuffed the duchess in a dresser drawer beneath her undergarments. Later tonight she would take it out to the alley and burn it. She also had to do something else tonight. It wouldn't be very prudent of her to keep supplying victims next door with a blackmailer watching her every move. The hungry ones would have to be moved to a place where there would always be an abundance of food, and Valerie knew just the place: the penitentiary. Tonight she would coax them into her car and drive them out there. They would have no trouble getting in. They would never be hungry again, if they didn't make absolute gluttons of themselves. In a way, she was going to miss them, but it was just too risky to keep feeding them with Jade around. And it was safer to get rid of them than Jade. Even if Valerie simply asked her to leave, that could start trouble. Blackmailers didn't like to be outwitted, especially the stupid ones, because then they had their own incompetence to face.

When Valerie was in the attic getting the princess doll for Jennifer, Elisabeth showed up in the mirror. "I know what you're planning to do with that duchess doll, and it's not going to work, you know. Tamara's going to figure it out. I'm going to help her. And when she does understand she doesn't need the dolls to tell her which way to behave, you're really going to be sorry. She's going to kill you. She's going to cut your throat in your sleep, and Jonathan will wake up with your blood all over him. Count on it, bitch. I'll help her get you one way or another, and you can't touch her now. You'd get caught for sure."

Valerie laughed. "You only hope."

"I *know,*" Elisabeth stressed, "because I'm going to go inside her too. That'll be two against one, Amanda and me against that Mary. You just wait and see."

Valerie stared tensely at the vindictive expression on Elisabeth's pasty, transparent face, afraid she might be telling the truth. On the other hand, it could just be a trick, to keep her from destroying the duchess. Elisabeth was right, Valerie would just have to wait and see, but just to play it safe, she'd burn the doll anyway, like she'd planned. Damn, just when she thought everything was working out, things like this had to come up, threats to keep her worried, too preoccupied to get any writing done. She wanted to get a book started and finished. All these distractions were most frustrating.

Elisabeth had vanished without further ado, apparently satisfied that her parting words, "You just wait and see," were sufficient. And they certainly rang of confidence. Valerie felt so alone, conspired against on every side. All she had, really, was Gavin and her creatures, one inside her who could hardly get a word past Doug now, the others sleeping in their rotting corpses, only to come out at night, only to feed.

Taking the princess with her into Uncle Herb's old room, she sat behind the typewriter, hoping Doug would be decent enough to let her talk to Gavin when she was feeling so depressed. She rolled in a fresh sheet of paper.

I wonder why I don't just end it, Gavin? Better to do it myself than have my throat sliced open by Tamara. What if Elisabeth was telling the truth? Jonathan will be around at night. He would never go for having Tamara tied up in the closet.

sure he would

Gavin, is that you?

bitch is that you

Alright, Doug, enough. I'll make you a deal. You think Jade is pretty, right? Well, suppose I get her partner Steve over here somehow. You could go into him, and then you would have Jade. You could make her go away with you. How about it? Steve is probably a lot better-looking than you were.

how stupid do you think i am youre planning to kill them both

How stupid do you think I am, Doug? You think I want Steve and Jade in me along with you? I should have learned my lesson about that by now, wouldn't you suppose? Just think about Jade, all the things she'll do to you. And you'll have money too, all you could ever want. People will pay a lot to keep their secrets hidden. How about it, Doug? You and Jade, you in Steve's beautiful body, rich. You would be stupid not to. Now may I please speak to Gavin? I'm depressed.

so what

Listen, Doug, I'm not in the mood for this. Just butt out, will you? Gavin?

yes my love

Oh Gavin, I'm in such a mess. I wish you could put your arms around me and hold me awhile. I'm really getting tired of all these problems cropping up left and right. What was that you said about Jonathan? He wouldn't mind if I tied Tamara in the closet, or to the bed at night? I'm going to have to do something about her or she'll kill me first chance she gets.

i didnt say anything about jonathan just get jade up in the attic and knock her out like you did mary only just tie her hands and feet and the next time steve calls you tell him jade is sick and wants him to come over then you take him up in the attic and do the same thing to him

Then what? Just leave them up there? Let them starve to death?

come on youre more creative than that

valerie creative thats a laugh

But I really do want to get rid of Doug. Don't you like my idea about him going into Steve? He'd never go for it if I had Steve tied up in the attic.

damn right you bitch

dont worry about doug you know his type

she damn well better worry about me asshole

you know his type he wont be able to stand it watching us in bed together

dont make me puke

what a sweating slut you become with me

shes a slut all right
Oh Gavin. Tell me again, all the things you're going to do.

Since Doug wouldn't let Gavin say two words in a row, Valerie went ahead and took the princess down to Jennifer. Jade was rocking her, telling her the story of Goldilocks and the Three Bears. Tamara was nowhere in sight.

"Look here, Jennifer," Valerie said. "You can have the princess doll. Didn't I tell you she was much prettier than the duchess?"

Jennifer gave her a sulky look and didn't answer. Valerie asked Jade, "Where did Tamara go?"

"Out in the back yard to play with Todd."

Valerie thought that was probably all right. She laid the princess doll on Jennifer's lap. "There, take it or leave it. If you don't want her, then you just won't have a doll."

Jennifer picked up the princess and embraced it. So at least that matter was settled.

"Jade," Valerie said, "I'd like you to come upstairs with me for a private chat. And I have something to show you."

Jade nodded, gave Jennifer a parting squeeze and slipped out from under her. "I'll finish telling you the story when I get back," she promised.

"I already know what happens," Jennifer said. "Mama told me the story before."

Jade smiled, her eyes full of sympathy. "Well, I'll try to think of a new one, then. Be good now."

If she were ever to leave the attic alive, Valerie thought on the way upstairs, Jade would certainly have a new story to tell, with a moral at the end: don't mess with Valerie!

Jade watched her curiously as Valerie pulled down the attic ladder. "We're going up in the attic?"

"I have something to show you," Valerie replied. "Some pictures I took."

"Pictures of what?"

"You'll see." She started to climb. "I also wanted to explain about Tamara when she gets hold of the duchess doll. You see, the duchess represents the little girl Tamara was when she was with Gavin . . ."

Jade was sitting on the chest by the time Valerie finished, looking a little apprehensive. She shook her head. "I don't know, I guess that makes sense. But what have you told her? Have you told her about the . . . the things and all that?"

Valerie knew what she was thinking. Witness. Pay up or I'll turn the cops onto the little girl, and if anything happens to her, I'll tell the father. I can make him believe. I know about those papers. I'll show them to him, show him how they were done on your typewriter. He'd kill you.

"She already knew about them," Valerie said. "She saw one in her bedroom, just like you did, with big yellow eyes. I explained what it was, of course. Would you tell her she was only imagining things?"

"She saw one too?"

What, couldn't Jade understand plain English? Valerie knew what Jade was thinking, that the creatures existed only in her mind, so how could Tamara have seen one? Maybe Jade was now considering that it might be true. Too late.

"I also wanted to tell you my idea." Valerie smiled. "I've figured out a good way to take care of them without taking any more personal risks, and do society a favor at the same time. Tonight I'm going to get them in my car and drive them out to the prison."

Jade seemed impressed, or at least very interested, despite the fact this had to be disappointing news for her. "That is a good idea. Guess we'll be hearing about a lot of escapes, then."

"It will get too embarrassing pretty soon," Valerie predicted. "They'll start hushing it up, before the whole county goes into panic, thinking all those escaped convicts are on the loose."

"So what was it you wanted to show me? Pictures, you said?"

"In that chest you're sitting on," Valerie answered, pointing.

Jade got off the chest, looking intrigued, and turned to lift the lid. Valerie stooped to pick up a heavy lamp base which had once been on Uncle Herb's nightstand.

Jade looked in the chest and saw only dolls. Thinking maybe the pictures Valerie wanted her to see were under them, she started digging through the pile of elaborate materials and real human hair when an explosion suddenly occurred in the back of her skull and all went black.

Valerie stared down at the limp body slumped into the chest, at the lovely red hair beginning to show wet crimson. Perhaps she'd struck too hard and killed her. Not another one. If Jade got inside her too, Doug would never leave, or maybe they would both leave together; that would be nice. She bent over to check for a pulse. Seemed a little erratic, maybe a little weak, but it was there. Jade was still alive. Valerie went to Vonda's old sewing basket and found some wide ribbons. One blackmailer down, one to go. She hoped Steve would call again soon. It would be nice to have this all taken care of before Jonathan got back. Then there would just be Tamara to worry about.

As Valerie tied Jade's hands and feet with the ribbon, it occurred to her that it wouldn't be entirely necessary to lead the creatures away now, except for the sake of convenience, which she supposed was reason enough. With the children all out of school for the summer, plus the baby, it would be difficult to take care of them too.

After she finished tying Jade up, Valerie found another of Uncle Herb's socks to use for a gag, and another ribbon to hold it in place. By the time she had it secured, Jade was starting to come around. Her eyes barely opened at first, struggled into focus, then opened wide as realization hit.

"Well, what did you think of the pictures?" Valerie asked tauntingly. "Were they what you expected to see, or should I say hoped to see, like maybe ones I'd taken of Gavin and Mary and Doug after I killed them? Think I'm that stupid? Not smart enough to figure out what you were up to? I know you looked at my papers, how you pretended to believe so you could get in and figure out a way to blackmail me. Isn't that so?"

Jade shook her head adamantly from side to side and made noises behind the sock. Protests, Valerie assumed. Denials. But the gig was up.

Valerie touched Jade's cheek. "No? Refuse to confess? Don't think I can be persuasive? What, are you impervious to pain? Well, I guess we'll find out. You'll confess, all right. And if not, surely Steve will, after he sees what I've done to you. Men are really such babies when it comes to pain, aren't they? I'd like to see them put up with monthly cramps. Well, you think about it for a while. When I come back, we'll see what your answer is."

21

Tamara was sitting on the back porch watching Todd, near the rose bushes, catch bumblebees in a fruit jar he'd taken from the porch. Valerie warned him to be careful, to which he replied that he knew they could sting, so he was being careful anyway. Valerie didn't much care for the sound of his response, but decided to let it go. After all, he had gone to his mother's funeral today, and here his dad was moving right in with her cousin. Had to be confusing for a boy of nine, understandable if he was a little resentful at first. But he would come around. She saw how quick he was, there were already four bees in the jar, and felt a touch of pride. He was her son now. They were all hers now.

Valerie sat down beside Tamara on the porch. She noticed the absence of the bride doll, and tensed, remembering Elisabeth's warning. Tamara hadn't parted once with that doll since Valerie had given it to her, until now. Coincidence?

"Where is your bride doll, Tamara?"

The girl's head turned slowly and looked up at her. "I buried her."

Valerie's tension increased. "Well, I suppose you can do anything you want to her, she's your doll. Anyway,

I'm glad to see you don't need her to talk through anymore. That doesn't mean you're a bad girl now, does it?"

Tamara's eyes twinkled. "Bad like the duchess?"

"Yes, exactly."

"No."

Well, that was nice to know. Elisabeth had just been bluffing. "I'm certainly glad to hear that. So what would you like to do?"

Tamara turned her attention back to her brother's activity. "Watch Todd catch bees."

"I'm afraid that isn't much entertainment for me," Valerie said as she rose, wondering why Elisabeth wouldn't have made good her threat. Maybe it wasn't possible to go into a body from the outside. Maybe you had to be in a body to pass to another body. Who knows? Maybe she could find the answer in those library books, if she ever got time to look at them. She went back into the house to see if Jennifer would like to hear the story of the Monster in the Bedroom. If Jennifer liked it, Valerie could type it up, have her first children's book written in less than a day.

"Where's Jade?" Jennifer asked when Valerie reappeared in the living room. "Isn't she coming down?"

Valerie knelt in front of the rocking chair. "What's the matter, don't you like me? Don't you think I can tell good stories too? I'm going to be a writer, you know. I'll make up stories you never heard before. But you won't know if they're really made up or not, will you?"

"I want Jade to tell me a story."

Valerie frowned. "Well, that's too bad, because Jade left and she isn't coming back."

Jennifer's eyes darted toward the staircase. "She did not leave! She's still upstairs."

"You just didn't see her leave," Valerie insisted, grabbing Jennifer by the cheeks. "You must have been too busy playing with your new doll. She left about five minutes ago. She said she didn't like us. Especially you, since you're such a crybaby. And while I have your attention, I wanted to explain what Tamara said about me being a killer. She just said that because I killed a mouse, but everyone kills mice because they're nasty, so just forget about it."

Tears formed in Jennifer's eyes. "Jade did not say she didn't like me. She told me she likes me."

"Are you calling me a liar, Jennifer? I know what she said. She was only pretending to like you, pretending to like all of us because she's really a two-faced bitch. Now, do you want to hear a story or not?" Valerie removed her hand from the child's face and smoothed her fine white-blond hair. "How about it, huh? It's a spooky one. You like spooky stories?"

Jennifer's mouth pulled down. "No. I want to go upstairs and find Jade."

Valerie smiled thinly and took firm hold of Jennifer's hand. "All right, if you insist. Let's go up together, shall we? You'll see she's not there. And then you're going to listen to my story whether you like it or not."

"I don't like scary stories!" Jennifer cried, trying in vain to pull her hand away.

"What about Little Red Riding Hood? Did your mother ever tell you that story?"

"Yes . . ."

"Well, that's a scary story. The big bad wolf went and gobbled up Little Red Riding Hood's grandmother, and he was going to eat Red too, with his big sharp teeth. That's pretty scary, isn't it?"

"But the woodman comes and chops him up."

"That's right. And that doesn't bother you, does it? What about Jack and the Beanstalk? The giant wanted to eat Jack. Fe fi fo fum, he smelled the blood of an Englishman. What about that? Does that scare you?"

Jennifer nestled her doll up against her cheek for comfort. What was scaring her was Valerie. "The giant falls down the beanstalk."

"Right again. Snaps his neck probably, huh? Breaks his back? Maybe a lot of blood comes out of his mouth. Did you ever think about that? That's what happens to people when they fall from a high place."

Jennifer looked on the verge of tears again. "I wanna go see Jade."

Valerie yanked her from the chair. "All right, you little brat, let's just go upstairs and have a look."

Valerie stood at the head of the stairs while Jennifer made a careful search of the second-floor rooms, perhaps thinking Jade was playing hide and seek with her. She went over them twice. Valerie began to smile in amusement. The girl never once looked up at the attic door. "What's the matter, Jennifer, can't you find her? Is she hiding from you? Maybe she's a magic genie and she can shrink herself tiny enough to hide in a drawer. Did you check the drawers? I told you she left. She's gone, isn't she?"

Jennifer shuffled dejectedly out of the front bedroom, sniffling. "Where did she go?"

"Home, wherever that is. Now come in here, Jennifer. This is going to be yours and Tamara's bedroom. Come in here and listen to my story."

Jennifer looked down the stairs. "I wanna go outside."

"'Wanna go outside,'" Valerie mimicked her. "Too bad, Jennifer, but around here you do what I say. Now get in there."

"I want my daddy!"

Valerie grabbed her up and took her into the room, backing against the door to shut it before letting go. Jennifer fell to the floor, kicking and crying now for her mama. That damned Elisabeth.

Valerie got down on her hands and knees and pinned Jennifer down, hissing in her face, "You know where your precious mama is, Jennifer? Didn't you see what they did with her? She's in a dark, narrow box six feet under the ground with the worms, all covered up with dirt. You want your mama, well, we'll just have to pretend. I'm going to put you in that bottom dresser drawer, and it'll be just like being in Mama's casket. You can pretend your mama's body is right there beside you, with worms all over her face, like there really are. You don't get to hear my story now. You've made me mad."

She released Jennifer's wrists to pull out the empty drawer, then took the princess doll away and snapped off its head, sending Jennifer into near hysterics. Valerie clamped a hand over her mouth, disgusted by the snot from Jennifer's nose, mingled with tears, touching her skin. "See how I took off that doll's head, Jennifer? If you ever tell anyone, anyone at all about me putting you in this drawer, that's what I'll do to you. I'll just snap off your head. Remember that, because I mean it. Now you'd better do as I say or I'll snap it off right now, and you'll bleed to death. Now get in the drawer and you keep your mouth shut. Remember when you get in there, it's your precious mama's casket, and people in caskets can't talk. It'll be dark, like in the grave, under the ground. Think of the worms crawling all over her, see how much you like her then. Think about having to stay in there with her forever and ever and ever."

Jennifer would think twice about ever mentioning Elisabeth again.

Eyes round with terror, Jennifer stepped meekly into the drawer and lay down, drawing up her knees to fit in completely. She was trembling almost convulsively, afraid that when the drawer was shut, worms would start crawling all over her.

Valerie began pushing her into the dresser. Jennifer watched in horror as the space above her closed. She opened her mouth to cry out, then remembered what Valerie had done to the princess doll. Biting down on a fist, she kept her silence, completely convinced that Valerie would have no qualms about doing the same thing to her.

Just before the darkness enveloped her, she saw through the crack that Valerie was smiling.

The moment Valerie stepped out of the room, something whizzed by her face making a familiar loud hum, a sound that warned to stay away. Bumblebee. Todd. If he'd emptied that jar in the house . . .

He had. They seemed to be everywhere, huge, menacing, black and yellow missiles darting angrily from corner to corner, diving at Valerie as she hurried through the foyer to the kitchen, frantically waving them away. There were none in the kitchen. He'd deliberately set them loose in the main part of the house! She slammed back the screen door leading to the back porch and went out, furious, scanning the long narrow yard bordered with ivy and roses, looking for Todd, who would soon be obliged to catch every damn one of those bees with his bare hands. The yard was empty, porch steps bare. He had taken off somewhere, and so had Tamara. Had she been in with him on this? Seething with anger, Valerie went into the yard and looked on both sides of the house, up and down the alley. No sign of them.

Valerie started thinking that maybe motherhood wasn't all it was cranked up to be. Did she really need this? Whining crybabies who wanted their dead mama, a nine-year-old terror who thought it would be funny to set a swarm of bumblebees loose in the house, a girl who may or may not try to cut her throat, a baby still in diapers? Oh yes, the diapers, shades of Grandmother after she broke her hip. Valerie hadn't considered that when she'd pushed her down the stairs, but Grandmother had called her a bitch just one too many times that day.

You've been sneaking men in the house after I go to bed, haven't you? You think I'm deaf? I hear what you're doing down there. You're like a dog in heat, aren't you?

Grandmother, you can't hear what I'm saying if I'm just halfway across the room. What makes you think you can hear anything downstairs? You're just imagining it, because that's what you want to hear. I'm not even interested in sex. I think it's disgusting, actually, boring at best. Like you did.

Don't you talk that way to me, you foul-mouthed bitch!

Valerie stormed back into the house to get the bug killer. Couldn't leave the bees for Todd. She might get stung.

She was going to go to bed with Jonathan tonight. And the next morning, she and Gavin would discuss the best way to get rid of the children.

22

There was only one bumblebee left, which had found its way into her bedroom and gotten trapped behind the curtain. Valerie had an idea. She ran downstairs to get an empty jelly jar from the back porch. Still no sign of Todd and Tamara. No matter, they would have to come back sooner or later. What Valerie thought she would do was tell Jonathan what Todd had done, and demand that he take appropriate action with Uncle Herb's razor strop. It was in his shaving kit in the attic. And if it was determined that Tamara was an accomplice, Valerie would deal with her later. She knew what that razor strop could do.

She went back up to her room and captured the bee, then took it out in the hallway. From the other side of the girls' bedroom door, she heard quiet sobbing. What? Wasn't Jennifer enjoying her visit with Mama?

Valerie unwound the cord from its hook and pulled down the attic door, unfolding the ladder. Holding the jar carefully, she started up.

"Jade, I've got a surprise for you."

Jonathan returned at four o'clock with the back of the pickup loaded. By then Valerie had Todd and Tamara sitting on the sofa, Todd having been told his father was going to let him have it with the razor strop for what he'd done, even if Tamara had originally made the suggestion, as he claimed. Tamara denied it, but Valerie wasn't convinced.

Jonathan came in carrying Davie, and handed him over to Valerie, then noticed the solemn looks on the faces of his older children. He asked Valerie if anything was wrong.

Before she could tell him what Todd had done, the boy blurted, "Tamara told me to! It's half her fault!"

"Told you to do what?" Jonathan asked, placing his hands on his hips.

"He set a jarful of bumblebees loose in the house," Valerie said. "I think he needs a sound whipping with a razor strop. It's waiting on the bed in the next room. Pull his pants down when you do it."

Jonathan looked at her, shocked. "I've never laid a hand on my kids. Elisabeth used to spank them sometimes, but just with her hand, and she never pulled their clothes down. I always thought grounding was a lot more effective."

He could hardly believe what Valerie had told him to do. It was the last thing he would have expected. He also had trouble believing Todd would set bumblebees loose in the house—that certainly wasn't like him, but he had admitted it . . . what the devil had gotten into him? Obviously he should be punished, then, but a razor strop on his bare bottom? Had Elisabeth been right about Valerie after all?

"Pain is the greatest teacher," Valerie said, her eyes challenging. "If you won't take the strop to him, I will. I could have been severely stung. In my book what he did was a major offense."

Jonathan sighed. He supposed she was right, though the thought of administering such a punishment sickened him. The very day of Elisabeth's funeral too, which made it seem like something of a crime. He wouldn't pull down the pants, but he would do it. Valerie was angry and might go overboard if he left her to do it.

"I'll do it. Come on, son, let's go in the next room."

Todd looked terrified. "But Dad!"

"No buts! Let's go."

"But what about Tamara? She told me to!" His freckled face was growing red, his Cupid's-bow mouth arched upside down in protest.

Jonathan was tired and short on patience, and he still had a lot of work to do. He wanted to get this over with as soon as possible and try to forget it ever happened. "What if she told you to jump off a tall building, would you do that too? That's no excuse, Todd. Now into the other room. Let's go."

The boy pushed himself off the sofa, extremely sullen, hazel eyes glowering at Valerie, his true enemy, on his way to the dining room.

Shoulders slumped, Jonathan followed him through the double doors.

Valerie put Davie down on the floor and turned to Tamara. "Still deny you told him to do it?"

"Yes. He always does that. He tries to blame everything on me."

"Then I guess I'll have to believe you. Now come with me to the kitchen. You're going to help me make dinner." Valerie supposed Davie would be all right by himself; there was nothing in the living room he could hurt himself on.

Tamara glanced at the closed dining room doors. "I want to hear Todd get spanked."

"Come now," Valerie insisted, holding out her hand. "That's a terrible thing to say. You shouldn't enjoy it when other people suffer."

Tamara's face suddenly began to look hazy, like a reflection on a rippling pond, her features enlarging slightly, re-forming, becoming less rounded. Valerie blinked, and found herself looking at Elisabeth, who said, "Aren't you one to talk, with what you just did to that girl you've got tied up in the attic, putting that bee in her blouse. You didn't enjoy that? You didn't thrive on the horror in her eyes when you told her what you were going to do? You can't lie to me. I know what's inside you. I know what you are."

"She wouldn't confess."

"Because she's not a blackmailer. Did it ever occur to you she might be a cop? Or a cop's girlfriend? That maybe Detective Morrison sent her over here to find out more about you? Maybe the night he came over with Jonathan he went upstairs before he left and saw what you'd written, all that about killing those people and all that craziness about the vampire-things. It proves how insane you are, but you're supposed to be a writer, so what can he say? Maybe she called him while you were at the funeral and told him you'd confessed to everything, told him she'd stay here to protect the kids while he got a warrant for your arrest. Maybe he's on his way over here right now to take you to jail . . ."

Valerie squeezed her eyes shut and covered her ears. *"No!"*

"I wasn't doing anything," Tamara said. "Who wouldn't confess?"

There was a thin whack in the next room followed by a cry of pain. Another. Another. No more. Just three whacks, and Valerie could tell they hadn't been delivered on bare skin. That was Jonathan's idea of a spanking?

"Never mind," Valerie muttered. "Well, you heard it, now come help me fix dinner."

Wearing a hint of a smile, Tamara rose from the sofa and followed her.

Jonathan came into the kitchen a minute later looking ten years older. "I don't think he'll be setting any more bees loose in the house. Where's Jennifer?"

"Taking a nap upstairs," Valerie said. "She wasn't feeling well, so try not to disturb her when you move those beds up to the boys' bedroom; just move what's in there now into my room, it should all fit. Incidentally, Jade decided she wasn't interested in helping out after all, so she left."

Jonathan rubbed his face; it was neither here nor there to him. "Hope Jenny's not coming down with that virus Tamara had."

Valerie handed Tamara the potato peeler and set her to

work at the sink. "I hope not too. I know Tamara was just miserable the day I went over to sit with her."

"Well, I'd better get to work. The truck's not going to unload itself, unfortunately."

"I need to go out a little while around nine," Valerie said. "You didn't have any plans for tonight, did you?"

"Oh no," he answered, running his hands through his thinning crop of hair. "Soon as I get things in order here, I just plan to watch some television, try to pull myself together. I still feel dazed by all that's happened lately."

"I know just what you mean," Valerie said. "Well, there's one bit of good news. Tamara's given up her doll. I told you she wouldn't need a psychiatrist."

Jonathan went over to give Tamara a hug and kiss on the cheek, thankful for the one ray of sunshine on such a gloomy day.

Davie started crying in the living room. Valerie sent Tamara to see what he wanted, and she came back carrying him by the wrists, her nose wrinkled. "He dirtied his diaper. He always cries when he does that."

Valerie looked at the baby with disgust. "He should be potty trained by now. He's old enough."

Tamara deposited her wailing baby brother on the kitchen floor and shrugged. "I don't know. He's just a baby. Change him, he stinks."

"You change him. I'm busy, and I can't stand that crying."

Tamara balked. "It's not my job

Valerie suddenly heard Elisabeth's voice:

"Not my job anymore. Like you said, I killed myself. It's no longer any of my business. It's your family now. Davie is your baby now, so you should change his diaper, and kiss his velvety little cheeks and tell him what a good baby he is. A good mother would do those things. You are a good mother, aren't you?"

"Tell your father to change it, then," Valerie snapped, turning back to the fried chicken. Damn that Elisabeth.

A few moments later Jonathan appeared through the drape. "I was moving that desk out when I thought I heard Jennifer crying in her room, but the door's locked. Have you got a key?"

Valerie wiped her hands on a dish towel hanging from the oven door. "I'll go check on Jennifer. You change Davie's diaper."

Davie was howling at the top of his lungs now, and she couldn't take another second of it. "Tamara, watch the chicken. Don't let it burn."

Jennifer blinked when Valerie pulled out the drawer. "All right, you can come out now," she said, pulling on one of Jennifer's cramped arms. "Did you enjoy your visit with Mama?"

Jennifer choked on a sob. "No."

"Then you'll never mention her to me again, you understand? And remember the doll. If you ever tell anybody, I'll pull off your head, right off your neck. Now go wash your face and get downstairs. Supper's almost ready. You tell your daddy you were feeling sick so you took a nap, but now you feel all better. Got that, Jennifer?"

She nodded, drawing in a ragged breath.

Valerie was pleased with herself. The children wouldn't live much longer, but as long as they did, they were going to behave. She knew how to discipline. Good mothers knew how to control.

Before leaving, Valerie gave Davie a bottle of milk and put him in his crib, which he did not protest. He looked up at her with big round blue eyes, suckling his nipple as she stroked his velvety cheek, murmuring softly for him to sleep, sleep. She'd turned on the fan so he wouldn't get too hot. Babies cried when they were too hot, or too cold, or for a hundred other reasons they couldn't explain. How did women stand it? But babies' cries were terrible, impossible to ignore; whoever said they were helpless? Their cries were their power, a very strong power. It would get them whatever they needed, or get them hurt. Or killed.

"Precious baby," Valerie cooed. "If you'd only been mute."

Then she realized he could be. It would be something to consider. Soft, velvety skin. Big round blue eyes. So darling, really.

What was she thinking? They were constant work. She'd never get any writing done.

Valerie explained to Jonathan that she had to go next door before she left, to check on Mrs. Rothford. She hadn't seen her lately and her newspapers hadn't been taken in. Jonathan asked if she wanted him to go with her. She told him no, that was all right, and left through the back door. Night had fallen and they had awakened, come to awareness of the gnawing hunger—the ache of rotting. Valerie walked casually over to Mrs. Rothford's back yard and went up the porch steps. Would they come without a bribe? They had to come, she would carefully explain. Of course they would want to go to a prison, would have gone to one on their own, probably, but they were blind, drawn by the scent of human flesh which didn't reach far, so they counted on their memories. Apparently none of these had been in a prison, so they didn't know how to find one.

Valerie stepped into the dark kitchen, listening. "Are you here? Come, gather around me, I have some wonderful news for you."

They were there all right, and they had already gathered around her. She could suddenly feel them pressing in, wet and sticky against her skin, and for a moment she panicked; were they going to eat her? But then she realized they were only kissing her; perhaps they already knew it was good-bye. Valerie closed her eyes, relaxing, even enjoying, no longer repulsed by the slimy feel or the stench of their ethereal bodies. She realized this was how their living victims felt as they were being devoured, why they didn't awaken; the creatures had the power to impart a numbing sense of pleasure in mortal minds. She let them do it for a few minutes, then moved back toward the door to tell them the news. She felt they understood, and they trusted her now; in fact they loved her now, so they willingly followed her to her car, five of them. The eight others she'd only imagined in her dream.

* * *

On the way back home Valerie was hoping Jonathan had the other kids tucked in bed by the time she got there, so she could begin her seduction. She felt so empty now that the creatures were gone. She didn't think they could smell the flesh of convicts from the place she'd parked to let them out, but she'd pointed the way and listened as they began tentatively moving in that direction. Farewell, children of the night. She'd even shed a tear.

But when Valerie stepped into the living room at a quarter to ten, all three of the older children were still up, huddled close to their father on the couch, watching an old movie on TV.

"Jonathan, it's almost ten o'clock. Shouldn't the kids be in bed?"

"The movie will be over at ten," he said tiredly, "then I'll put them to bed." As they started to protest, he shook his head. "No arguments. We've got to get up early and go to church tomorrow."

She's the spawn of the devil, that's right, ladies and gentlemen, spawn of the devil himself. Charles Scott was not her real father. Valerie's mother had lain with the Prince of Darkness.

"That's right. Tomorrow's Sunday," Valerie said. "So as soon as the movie's over, off you go to bed." She went upstairs, desperately needing to talk to Gavin. Jonathan had moved the desk, typewriter, and Uncle Herb's chair into her bedroom, which made it cramped for space, but she didn't mind since it was only temporary. She shut and locked the door.

Gavin, what was that Elisabeth said about Detective Morrison sneaking up here and looking at my papers? Is that true? Is Jade a woman police officer or Morrison's girlfriend?

i think elisabeth was only trying to scare you go ahead and kill jade i think i know how you can keep her out

hey bitch get ready to go to jail

Shut up, Doug. Really, Gavin? How?

think black

217

theyll put you in a cell with some big black dykes all
right

I told you to shut up, Doug. I'm talking to Gavin. That's
all? Just think black?

try it

youll probably love it too wont you bitch

Gavin dear, you could have told me that before I killed
Doug, you know. Why didn't you?

Valerie decided to just ignore Doug's comments,
which would undoubtedly make him madder than anything she could say.

you didnt tell me you were going to do it

hey val gonna stick out your tongue when they sit on
your face

You knew I was going to kill Mary, though. Why didn't
you say anything then?

i didnt know she would come

think of the diseases

Well, it doesn't matter now. Think black. That sounds
simple. Just might fool them, huh? Oh, I hope our
creatures find their way to the prison all right and don't
get lost. I don't think they will. I pointed them right at it.
Some idea I had, wasn't it? Why didn't you ever think of
doing that?

syphillis gonorreah

guess im not as smart as you

Don't say things like that, Gavin. You've helped me a lot
when I didn't know what to do. I can't wait to be with you.
I'm going to seduce Jonathan tonight, and then you'll be in
him, right?

herpes

i dont know

What? What do you mean you don't know? This is it.
Everything is set up. He makes good money too, only you
won't have to do the work. You can let him be in control in
the daytime. But I want you in control in the nighttime.

i will be my love

genital warts

Oh Gavin, I can hardly wait.

* * *

Jonathan put his children to bed. Valerie joined him downstairs after getting the whispering hushed in the girls' room. She wondered if they were exchanging testimonies of their experiences. Tamara's in the attic and closet, Jennifer's in the drawer. All kids did that, backstabbed their parents, complained how mean and unfair they were, how cruel. They were born with the impression that the world was a fantasyland in which their every desire should be gratified. Parents were supposed to be some sort of recreation directors, filling their days with fun, their Christmas stockings with lots of presents. They grew up thinking others would carry on the tradition, that bosses would hand them undeserved raises, that everything they wanted would just come to them, like magic, and they would always be protected from the bad things. In other words, totally unprepared for the true ugliness of life. Death and disease, poverty, abundant crimes, creatures that feed upon them in the night. A parent who prepared them for reality might seem cruel, but actually had the true well-being of the children at heart. And the parents who killed them to spare them from it loved most of all. Valerie didn't ask Tamara and Jennifer what they were whispering about.

Jonathan had switched off the television, and sat rubbing his eyes, obviously exhausted. Too exhausted for love? Valerie wondered. She hadn't sat very close to him. This wasn't like her, to boldly seduce a man. She supposed some women could be brass enough to move right over and climb into his lap, begin to kiss him passionately. She would have to be pretty drunk first, like she'd been at that reunion. But she'd been nervous, hadn't really wanted to go in the first place . . . what, to see if all the people who hadn't wanted to be her friend back then had changed their minds after ten years? Yes, that was exactly what she'd thought. Steve had been the only one to speak to her, and look what he'd done, bending her over the trunk of that car like a piece of meat.

Jonathan was looking at her now, as if trying to decide whether or not all this was a dream. A nightmare for some, Valerie would admit, including herself. She wanted to wake to freedom, a quiet house, her lover Gavin by her side. No, she didn't need to be drunk. Desperate people did desperate things, and Valerie was getting quite desperate.

"Jonathan, would you like to make love to me?" she blurted out.

She might as well have slapped him in the face, as shocked as he looked. For several moments he couldn't seem to find his voice. He had the look of a trapped animal.

"Valerie, I just buried my wife today," he finally said quietly.

She felt the sting of rejection, of reproof, and she was reminded of Doug and the way he made her feel so many times. "I know that. I was at the funeral, remember? I thought you were attracted to me. I thought you wanted me. Isn't that why you moved in here?"

His mouth opened and closed; his hands opened and closed. He started to sweat. "I said that, yes, and I meant it, but I wasn't talking about sex. I hadn't been thinking of you that way. The reason I moved in like this, so quickly, was for the kids. To give them some stability, otherwise I just would have started taking you out, you know, so we could get to know each other better. So we could build a relationship based first on friendship, which can still happen, but I don't think we can make it overnight by jumping into bed, Valerie. I just can't, certainly not the day of Elisabeth's funeral, and not for a while, probably. I still haven't quite gotten it in my head yet that I'm not a married man anymore. I'm sorry, I couldn't even think about it."

Valerie smiled tersely. "Well, in that case, I think I'll go upstairs now. Good night."

Doesn't that take the cake, Gavin? He as much as tells me he regretted marrying Elisabeth in the first place, and now he can't touch me because he's thinking of her! So, can't you just go into him anyway? He's such a drip! He and Elisabeth deserved each other.

he isnt the right one

What does that mean? You can change him. You can take over. I know you're very strong.

just trust me

You're confusing me, Gavin. Who else is there? What do you want me to do, start hanging out in bars? Jonathan is living here. It would be much more convenient if you'd go into him.

just wait youre so impatient

Damn right I'm impatient! I've been under too much stress for too long, and I'm ready for things to settle down. I've still got to kill Jade tomorrow, and try to get my hands on that Steve ... by the way, I notice we haven't been interrupted by Doug lately. Is he still in there with you?

no

No? Well, that's certainly a piece of good news. He just left, then? Didn't even say where he was going?

he said he had better things to do like haunt the playboy mansion

I suppose he thinks that will make me jealous? Ha! Well, I can't believe he didn't hang around to cuss me out some more, but I'm relieved to hear that he's gone. So now I just have to kill Jade, and wait for Steve to call. I'll tell him she wants him to come over, and when he does, it's good-bye Steve. All right, I won't worry about anything else for now. I'll just try to relax.

dont worry about being the devils daughter either youre not

So why do I keep thinking that? I dreamed about it too. It was awful. How did I get an idea like that in my head?

remember

Remember what?

remember the mantel

Valerie closed her eyes and delved tentatively into the dark recesses of her mind.

The mantel.

Yes.

Grandmother had sat her up on the mantel, way up there, it seemed to her. She was afraid of falling, afraid Grandmother wouldn't catch her if she did fall because Grandmother had a mean look on her face.

"You know what's inside you, Valerie Scott? A demon,

*that's what. A demon, because your real father is the devil.
You don't understand what I'm saying now, but someday
you will. You're a devil child. You're a bad, bad little girl.
You should never have been born.*

**Oh Gavin, what did she do to me? Am I really evil? Did
she make me evil?**

yes but thats okay im evil too

The church was packed. Everyone was in their Sunday
best, the choir in their shiny blue robes, seated now. The
singing was over and it was time for the sermon. The
bald, skinny preacher gripped both sides of the pulpit,
his spectacled eyes sweeping over the congregation,
satisfied the collection plates would be filled. "Brothers
and sisters, I know you came here this morning to be
uplifted, but it's not an uplifting message the Lord has
laid on my heart, no it isn't." The preacher's voice was
deep and resounding; it filled the room without benefit of
a microphone.

Squeezed in the back pew between Jonathan and some
fat woman wearing too much perfume, Valerie began to
feel uncomfortable. It was too hot in there, with all those
bodies burning their calories and lungs breathing the
same air. The stained-glass windows lining both sides of
the small single-aisled chapel glowed surrealistically with
bright greens, blues, yellows, reds, and purples, but
Valerie was thinking black.

The preacher shook his head sorrowfully. "There is an
evil that walks among us, right in our very midst, an evil
so great that it is as incomprehensible as the grace of
God. As evil, brothers and sisters, in the guise of human
flesh, as the very devil himself, and the name of this evil
is Valerie Scott."

Whispers flew. Who was Valerie Scott? Do we know
her? Is she here? Valerie grabbed Jonathan's arm. "Let's
get out of here. I don't have to sit here and take this."

"It's either church or the insane asylum," Jonathan
said. "Which is it? Are you truly evil or just insane?"

The preacher was pointing at her. "There she is! The
spawn of the devil! The Antichrist! Queen of the Flesh
Eaters! Murderer of young children!"

Valerie paled. "Jonathan, I thought you understood. I mean Gavin is inside you now, and we agreed it would be for the best. Have you seen their pretty little graves in the back yard? How I outlined them with pretty rocks and planted flowers? They look just like gardens. It was for the best, we agreed, for both them and us. Gavin? Aren't you in there?"

"My name is Jonathan, and I didn't agree to kill my children."

Everyone had turned to stare at her now. She was an abomination in their sight, and it showed on their faces. Child killer. Murderess. The preacher was droning on about all of her wicked acts.

Jonathan sighed. "There is no Gavin, Valerie, because you killed him, the same way you killed Mary and Doug and all the rest. It's only been you, don't you understand? Only you. So, are you going to get baptized or not? If not, I'm just going to have to take you to the insane asylum. Evil can be overcome, but insanity . . ."

What kind of choice was this? She had to publicly admit she was either evil or crazy?

They were all waiting. The preacher was waving her up. Come, confess, witch. Valerie knew what would happen. He would put her under the water and hold her down until she had drowned.

"All right, all right," Valerie sighed in resignation. "Take me to the insane asylum. It wasn't my fault. I wasn't born evil, it was her. It was Grandmother and all those things she did to me. She made me this way. I couldn't help it. You can see that, can't you? You can see I'm not to blame?"

You can come out of the closet now, Valerie. I guess the monsters weren't hungry today or they would have eaten you up. But I bet they will next time. Maybe tonight they'll come to your house and gather around your bed. You won't see them except for their big yellow eyes glowing in the dark, but you'll be able to hear them, their lips smacking, their bodies slithering like worms. You'll feel them start to eat you. It'll burn, like acid. Maybe tonight, Valerie. You never know. . . .

* * *

"Valerie?" Someone was knocking lightly on her bed-room door. Valerie opened her eyes, wincing at the sunlight. Jonathan's voice. "Valerie, are you awake? Are you coming to church with us?"

Was he kidding? "No."

"Well . . . all right, but we don't have to leave for another forty-five minutes, in case you change your mind."

Valerie sighed and said nothing more. Soon she heard him go back downstairs.

She lay there very quietly, looking at the ceiling. Had she imagined it all? Maybe Gavin had never really come to her house to rent a room, nor Mary. Maybe Doug didn't really come to see her. Maybe she had only daydreamed about tying Tamara up in the closet and shutting Jennifer up in the drawer. Maybe Jonathan wasn't here now either. He might be at his house with Elisabeth, who was still alive and well, and they were getting their children ready for church. Maybe none of it had really happened for real but only in her mind.

She waited until she heard the front door open and close (or at least thought she did because she was expecting it to), then slipped out of bed. She stared for a few moments at her silent typewriter on the desk, on which she'd written two- and sometimes three-way con-versations, giving voices to the people she'd imagined she had killed. What would she find in the attic this morning? If she told herself Jade wasn't really there, would the attic be empty except for all the junk? If she thought she saw Jade but stared at her hard enough, would she disappear, evaporate like the ghosts in her imagination?

Valerie put on her robe and went up to find out.

23

Jade lifted her head from the dusty floor and watched with terror-filled eyes as Valerie approached. Valerie stared down at her for a long time. Jade didn't disappear. But maybe when a person was thoroughly and completely insane, there was simply no control over such things, none at all, never any way to tell the difference between real and unreal. All the senses were called into play. Uncle Herb's cherry tobacco. The creatures' wet kisses. Faces melting into other faces.

Finally she knelt down and untied the ribbon holding Uncle Herb's sock in the woman's mouth, and pulled it out to see what this hallucination would say.

"Are you going to let me go?"

Valerie sat cross-legged and rested her elbows on her knees, her face in her palms.

"Would it matter? Does anything matter that you do in your mind? It's not that I really hurt anyone. I just think I do, see, so tell me, is it anyone else's business? Everyone does it, they do terrible things in their minds, things they would never admit to anyone. They kill, I know they do. They get very angry and they kill. But they know the difference. I'm afraid I don't, but still, I don't think that's any reason to put me away, do you?"

Tears slid down Jade's dirty temples. "You are mad. Steve warned me that you might be, but of course that's why I came. You remember Steve, don't you? Steve Whitman? Last time you saw him was at your tenth high school reunion. He's my brother."

This was certainly confusing, but it couldn't be real. She was telling herself these things. Her brain was exceptionally good with imagination.

"You were drunk that night, he said, very drunk, but you said some things to him alcohol couldn't account for, about these things that eat people in their sleep, like you really believed it. He'd always thought you were rather strange anyway, but when you started talking about these things, you scared the hell out of him. I guess this was after what happened in the parking lot. He told me about that too. He'd taken you to sit in his car because he thought you were getting sick. I'm working on my doctoral thesis on paranoid schizophrenia, but I want to study the uninstitutionalized, and they're pretty hard to find. Steve found out from your parents where you were, gave me your address and phone number, and I flew up, then looked for a room to rent until I could figure out how to approach you, and there was your ad." She laughed sardonically. "You don't even know that I'm real, do you? Are you planning to kill me?"

Valerie was thinking. If this was an hallucination, it certainly was a clever one, but Valerie *was* very clever. She'd always known that.

"Yes, I'm going to kill you, not that it matters."

"Listen to me Valerie," Jade implored. "While you were gone to the funeral yesterday I did some snooping around, and I found a package of letters your grandmother had written to somebody named Armand. I guess they never got mailed, but she confessed in them to doing terrible things to you. She was paranoid schizophrenic too, and thought you were a child of the devil. She hallucinated all kinds of things, like you do. You know it's a hereditary disease, but commonly skips a generation. So you see, you really are her granddaughter, or were, I should say, and I think I can help you. You don't have to kill me. I'm not your enemy. I'm not going to do anything to hurt you."

"I don't want to talk to you anymore," Valerie said, rubbing her temples. "I don't like the things you say." It was becoming very difficult for her to maintain the belief that Jade was only a figment of her imagination. Valerie felt a little dizzy.

Which is it? Are you truly evil or just insane?

"All right, all right, we don't have to talk about that. We can talk about whatever you like."

Valerie stopped rubbing her temples, staring hard at Jade, a sneer on her lips. "Oh right, you want to hear about all my hallucinations, don't you, so you can write them in your little notebook. Case history number 666, Valerie Scott. And you'll publish this paper about me and tell the whole world how crazy I am, the things I've done. Well, I can't let you do that. I've been very careful. I'm *always* very careful. I usually don't make stupid mistakes, but I sure made one when I believed you and let you into my house. I thought you were my friend. I only have one. I only have Gavin. If he's real to me he's real, right?"

Panic was beginning to show on Jade's face. She knew she was in deep, deep trouble. "Of course Gavin is real, Valerie. I believe that, I really do. You want to tell me about him?"

Valerie thought about it for a few minutes, finally coming to the conclusion that this woman would say anything to save her life. Jade didn't believe. She was lying again, buying time until she could figure out a way to escape.

"Tell me this much. Is my cousin Elisabeth really dead? Did she really hang herself? Are Jonathan and the children really living here? Don't lie to me. I can tell when you're lying. Don't think I can't. I know you don't believe in Gavin."

Jade was white as a sheet. "I'm sorry, Valerie. I'm just scared. Can't you understand why I would be? Yes, yes, your cousin is really dead and Jonathan and the children moved in yesterday. You see, that's how I can help you. I can tell you what's real and what's not. Eventually you'll learn the difference and be able to function outside an institution."

Valerie smiled. "I've been functioning quite well, thank you. I don't need your help. Gavin helps me. But you've answered my question. If Elisabeth is really dead and Jonathan and the children are really here, then it's all been real. I haven't imagined a thing."

"I saw your conversations with Gavin, Valerie." Jade's voice was quivering now. "He tells you to do terrible things. You don't really want to do those terrible things, do you?"

"I haven't done anything so terrible," Valerie said defensively. "I killed Gavin by accident, but even if I'd done it on purpose, Uncle Herb told me to do it. He said it was the only way. He meant I would have something to feed them so they wouldn't eat me, and why not Gavin? He brought them here to eat me in the first place, all but one of them anyway.

"And then Tamara. I had to take her so I could protect her. You would call it a crime, but I did a good thing for her. I can't help it if her parents freaked out. They wouldn't have understood. And the things I did to her. I had to teach her how to behave. I was never mean to her for no reason. It was always because she did something bad to deserve it.

"And Mary. Mary was going to get me in trouble, though it was none of her business. People should mind their own business, I think, and she was getting old anyway. What did she ever do but sit in my living room and watch my television? She was useless, so I made her useful. You don't understand their pain, how terrible it is when they don't have their flesh. I thought they were horrible at first, but I came to understand them. I pitied them. So I helped them, and at the same time gave Doug his just desserts, the bastard! And that bum, living out of trash cans, you think he wanted to live? So here you are now. They're gone, I've taken care of them, but you know everything . . . everything there is to know."

Valerie turned and reached into Vonda's sewing basket, her fingers closing around the cool steel handle of a letter opener. "So of course there's no way I can let you live."

She plunged the letter opener into Jade's chest. Jade screamed and Valerie watched the blood, bright red, oozing through the white blouse. She plunged again and again and again until the screaming stopped, thinking about the color black.

Unfortunately Valerie couldn't wait for the luxury of darkness in which to do her deed. Steve could call at any time, and if he got no answer, or was told Jade was no longer there, or sick and couldn't come to the phone, he would surely call the police in Huntington and ask them to investigate. It had to be done now, before Jonathan and the children got home from church.

She wrapped Jade's body in the same sheet she'd used for Doug and dropped it out of the attic, followed by the suitcase Jade had brought. It fell open, scattering the contents, and Valerie noticed a notebook, probably full of things about her, so of course it would have to be destroyed. Thank goodness she'd seen it before she threw the suitcase into a Dumpster. She wouldn't have thought to look otherwise. And it was a mistake like that which could be her undoing. She climbed down the ladder and put it back up, then wrapped the cord around its hook and picked up the notebook. Should make for interesting reading later. No time now. She hurried into her bedroom and put it in the drawer with the duchess, then returned to the hallway to get the body downstairs when she suddenly realized she was about to go off doing what she had to do in her nightgown and robe. That would certainly draw some attention. She went back in her room and dressed quickly.

Fifteen minutes later she had the body and the suitcase on the back porch. All she had to do was pull the car up in the driveway, past where it ended at the sidewalk leading to the back porch, and park it so that the trunk of the car would be right in front of her. The ivy-covered fence on one side and her house on the other would hide two directions, and if she looked the other ways first, saw no one and moved very quickly, she could get the body and suitcase in the trunk without being seen.

In five minutes it was done. Valerie jumped behind the wheel and backed up to the street, then headed for the cemetery.

Of course there would have to be mourners there today, two couples about thirty graves apart, one old and one middle-aged, staring at the headstones of their beloved dead. Valerie got out of the car and pretended to visit the grave of Vernon Addams, who'd died in 1981. She knelt before the headstone. "Are you one of them, Vernon? Do you wake at night hungry for human flesh?"

She could hear the voice, from far under the ground, tones smothered with earth, an echo at the end of a mile-long tunnel.

"Yessss . . ."

"Would you like me to set you free? Drive a silver stake through your brain to sever the cord?"

"Yessss . . ."

Valerie patted the ground. "It's terrible, isn't it, what you have to do. I know. Look at the things I have to do. I know you can't help it, and I would set you free, but you're buried in the ground, and I'd have to dig in the daylight, because you have to be in there when I do it, and it's likely I'd get caught and put away. I can't take the risk, I'm sorry. You do understand, don't you, Vernon? But it needn't be so bad. Just find your way to a prison. At least there you'll have a constant source of food."

Valerie stood and looked around. The couples had placed their flowers and were walking back to their cars. She waited until they had driven from the cemetery, then went back to the trunk and opened it. "We're here, Jade, your new home. You and Grandmother can keep each other company."

She dragged the body out of the trunk and into the crypt, then went back to get the crowbar. Today was the day she would get rid of all of her problems. There were plenty of drawers in here, one for Jonathan too. It would be stupid to bury them in her backyard and pretend their graves were flower gardens. Their stench would arise from the ground to accuse her . . . call out to her neighbors across the alley, "We are buried here, she murdered us." Only in a dream would she do something that stupid.

With the crowbar, she pried off the plate over Amanda's drawer, catching it so it wouldn't make such a loud noise, then rolled out the casket, remembering what a horrible sight she'd seen the last time she'd opened it. But there wasn't the stench, as before, so probably the maggots would be gone, because Amanda was no longer one of those creatures.

Valerie opened the lid and looked. Sure enough, there was Grandmother, looking very much the same way she had the day of her funeral, except for the mold and the butter knife lodged in her left eye socket.

Valerie heaved Jade's body, still wrapped in the bloodstained sheet, on top of her grandmother's body, and shut the lid. After replacing the brass plate, she headed downtown to find a Dumpster for the suitcase.

The phone was ringing when Valerie stepped through the front door. She walked calmly to the small built-in table and picked up the receiver. A man asked to speak to Jade Green. Jade must have made up the last name Green, as well as the little joke about her mother naming her that because she thought it was cute, so Valerie wouldn't know the Steve she was talking about was Steve Whitman, her old high school heartthrob, who was now waiting for her reply. Now that she thought about it, his voice had sounded vaguely familiar yesterday when he called. If she had been on her toes, she could have put it all together right then and there.

"Well hello, Steve, this is Valerie. Your sister left yesterday, I caught her snooping around in my things and told her to get out."

There was a long pause, then: "I wonder why she hasn't called me, then, or come back."

"I wonder too," Valerie snapped, "but it's not my problem, is it? Maybe she went to spy on someone else." She slammed the receiver down. Good-bye Steve Whitman, and all who are like you. May some big round yellow eyes appear in your bedroom one night while you're sleeping.

The house was quiet. Too quiet, suddenly. Valerie wondered if Steve would call the police. Of course he would. Jade might have told him all kinds of things over the phone, but probably hadn't said that much, with Tamara around. She could have called him while they were at the funeral, after she'd done her snooping. But Jade would not be testifying, and hearsay could not convict. And who would think to look in Grandmother's coffin?

Just then Jonathan came in the door, alone.

Valerie turned to him. "Where are the children?"

"I took them over to Lynn's," he said heavily, leaning against the banister with his hands in the pockets of his suit pants. In a suit he looked a little handsome, Valerie thought. But something was wrong, he wouldn't look at her. Had Jennifer told? Had Tamara? No. If they had, he would have come with the police. For sure he would have.

"I guess it's just not going to work," Jonathan said. "I'm sorry, Valerie. It's not me, it's the kids, and as I said, I was mainly doing this for their sakes. But they literally begged me not to bring them back here. Jennifer even started crying. I guess it was just too much too soon. I don't know. I thought this would help them adjust. I was just doing what I thought was best at the time, but it looks like I'm going to have to work something else out. Todd threatened to run away, and Tamara . . ." He shook his head. "Tamara actually said she would kill you. I guess they think I'm trying to replace their mother, and I understand how they feel. I should have known. Please don't take it personally, I know you wanted to help. I'll come get our things later this afternoon."

Valerie patted his shoulder. "I understand, Jonathan. Don't worry about it. I hope everything works out for you."

He gave her a quick peck on the cheek and left.

So that was that.

Valerie walked slowly into the living room and sat on the padded seat of the rocking chair, leaned back against the blue and gold afghan and began to rock herself, thinking. That was that. Simple. No mess, no fuss. Much simpler than killing them all and hauling them out to the crypt.

She needed to place another ad for the room—fifteen hundred dollars a month had just walked out the door. A nice gentleman, good-looking, tall and dark. Gavin would like that. And they would be all alone, all alone, to do whatever they liked. Yes.

There would be no more problems then, nothing at all to worry about, except the girls talking, especially Tamara, but they were only kids. Kids were great about making up wild stories about people they didn't like, people they thought were trying to replace their dead mother. No problem, no problem at all. Nothing to worry about at all. What a feeling of peace.

The house was so very silent. You could hear a pin drop. There was just the quiet creak-creak of the rocker as she went back and forth. Very nice. They were all gone. Herb and Vonda and Grandmother, who would probably never leave Tamara—Grandmother had certainly been attracted to that psychic energy. Elisabeth would leave, though, when Jonathan started dating someone she approved of, then she would transfer into her and have him back. Fine with Valerie; Jonathan was certainly no prize. Mary and Jade, Jonathan and the kids, Armand and Doug, and the creatures she had grown to love, all gone.

All gone except for her, and the one inside her who could only speak through her typewriter. She got off the rocker and went upstairs to see what Gavin had to say to her now.

Well, we're alone now, Gavin, completely alone, and everything is taken care of. Peace at last . . . I can hardly believe it. I thought the nightmare would never end. But I'm going to run another ad for the room, and I'll wait until just the right one comes along. You'll tell me which one, but I hope it doesn't take too long. We need the money, you know. How did you know Jonathan wasn't the right one? See, you're a lot smarter than you think.

the right one is coming my love

Oh, I'm so glad to hear that. Do you mean now? You don't mean right now, do you?

yes

Who is it? Someone I know?

yes

Well, don't play games with me, tell me. Who?

youll see

Oh, all right, be that way. I'm going to lie down for a while now. I suddenly feel very tired. Too much excitement.

Valerie kissed her fingertip and touched it to the sheet of paper, then moved over to the bed to lie down. Relax. It had been a while since she could do that. Nothing to worry about, nothing at all. She began to feel happy, and wondered who it was that could be coming. She didn't know anyone in this town.

Gavin must be mistaken.

Suddenly there was a scratching noise in her dresser drawer, a frantic scratching. Valerie bolted upright, her heart pounding. Had a mouse gotten in there, or . . . ?

Trembling, she got off the bed and slowly approached the dresser. No one but herself appeared in the mirror. She was all alone, except for Gavin, but something was definitely making noise in that dresser drawer. Valerie jerked it open and jumped back.

Her underthings were moving, rising. Valerie blinked and stared hard. Nothing changed, the pile was still growing; something beneath it was pushing it up. Valerie held her breath as a half-slip fell away and unveiled the duchess. She was sitting up, staring at Valerie with her china-blue eyes.

"You didn't think I would give up, did you? After what you did to me?"

A high-pitched squeal escaped Valerie's throat as she backed farther away, eyes round with terror. "I'm not seeing this. I'm not! You're not real!"

The duchess stood up. "I'm real enough to kill you."

"You can't. You can't really move. You're just a doll! If Jade was here she would tell me I'm not seeing any doll standing up in my dresser drawer, talking to me. You're not really there. I'll just relax, lie back down and take a nap. Nothing here can hurt me. Maybe I shouldn't have killed her. Maybe I could have trusted her after all."

"That's right, Valerie," the duchess said, smiling. "She would tell you that, and you should . . . you should lie back down and take your nap so I can cut your throat open with a razor blade."

The duchess stepped out of the drawer onto the dresser top and pivoted in front of the mirror. "Such a lovely dress, so red, red like the blood that's going to gush from your throat." Then she leaped to the floor and ran into the hallway.

Valerie stood motionless for several seconds, completely stunned. Dolls didn't move on their own for sure, nor could they talk, or run away, or take a razor blade and cut someone's throat. They absolutely could not. The duchess doll was still in the drawer where Valerie had put it, inanimate, lifeless, powerless. Amanda was in Tamara.

At least she had been.

Valerie timidly stepped up to the open drawer, not wanting to stick in her hand, but she had to know. She reached in quickly and pulled everything out, the bras, the panties, the slips, the hosiery, dropping the pile immediately to the floor. She stepped on the pile, flattening it. There was nothing else, and nothing else in the drawer but Jade's notebook.

If she had to take the house apart, she vowed, she would do it until she found that damn doll. When she did, she would snap off its head like she'd done to the princess, and that would be that.

Valerie rushed out into the hallway and looked both ways. It was empty. Had it gone in one of the other upstairs rooms, or downstairs? It was a big house. Quiet again. Deadly quiet.

24

The doorbell rang. Valerie had searched every square inch of the second floor, finally becoming convinced it had gone downstairs, probably by sliding down the banister. Not it. *Grandmother*. The duchess was Grandmother now.

Valerie left the kitchen, where she had been going through all the cabinets and drawers when the doorbell rang. Jonathan, probably, coming to collect his possessions. What a waste of time that had been, getting all moved in, then right back out again.

But it wasn't Jonathan. It was Detective Morrison. So Steve had called the police, as she'd known he would.

"Sorry to disturb you," Morrison said politely, "but I got a phone call about a missing person, and this was the last place she was known to be. Mind if I come in?"

Valerie minded very much, but she stepped back and gestured for him to enter. "You must be talking about Jade Green, or rather, Jade Whitman. She lied to me about her name. I talked to her brother Steve just a while ago. I knew him in high school."

Morrison nodded, looking around. "Yes, that's who I spoke with. So she was here then, is that right?"

"Briefly," Valerie answered curtly. "She was here to

spy on me. I caught her snooping through my things, so I threw her out."

"I see." Hands clasped behind his back, Morrison sauntered into the living room. "Well, I promised her brother I would have a look around. He seemed pretty upset. Would that be all right with you?"

"Go right ahead."

She followed him into the dining room. In there he asked, "So why was she spying on you?" Although he knew very well the answer to that question already, he was curious as to what she would say.

It was a game, Valerie decided. Steve had sung him the whole song—what he knew of it anyway. Morrison just wanted to see if she would lie.

Getting on her hands and knees to look under the bed, she said, "She admitted she was doing a doctoral thesis on paranoid schizophrenia, which she supposed I had a problem with because of some crap Steve told her, things I'd said to Steve when I was drunk at our high school reunion. I knew very well what I was saying, though. I was only joking. He should have known."

Morrison looked at her curiously. "What are you doing?"

"Looking for a doll I lost."

His curiosity getting the best of him, Morrison crouched and took a look for himself; he just about had to, in case Valerie was trying to trick him into not looking because she had Jade Whitman's body under there. He very much believed Jade Whitman was dead.

There was nothing under the bed, so they both rose to their feet. "So, is everyone settled in?" Morrison asked her. "Jonathan and the kids?"

"They were, but they're moving out," Valerie said, checking under the couch cushions. Nothing under there but those three library books.

"Oh?" Jesus, Morrison prayed, not them too. He'd definitely have to check that out.

"Seems the kids were a bit resentful toward me, thinking I was trying to take their mother's place. It was Jonathan's idea to begin with, I really don't care one way or the other." She leaned over to check behind the couch.

Morrison started moving toward the kitchen. "All they've been through lately, I guess it's understandable. Kids' minds are pretty fragile. By the way, how is Tamara coming along?"

That was an obvious jab, but Valerie decided to ignore it. So maybe he knew some things—or thought he knew. What could he prove? "She seemed much better, about normal, I'd say. Damn, where could she have gone?"

Morrison turned. "Jade Whitman?"

"No, the doll. I've got to find that duchess doll. It has on a red velvet dress. If you see it, please let me know."

She followed him into the kitchen, standing by the refrigerator as he looked around the back porch, then inside the pantry. No doubt when he left he'd have a walk around her yard, looking for broken patches of dirt. He said as he preceded her through the kitchen drape into the foyer, "So, I take it there's no history of mental illness in your family?"

He stopped near the base of the staircase to await her reply, his eyes boring into hers brazenly. He didn't care if she knew he suspected, she thought; in fact he seemed to enjoy making her feel uncomfortable. She wouldn't let him get to her, though. That would really piss him off.

"Well, I do believe one of my grandmother's uncles was in a mental institution. What of it?"

He shrugged and started up the stairs. "Just wondering."

In her bedroom he walked up to her desk and started to read what was in the typewriter. Valerie yanked it out and slapped it facedown on the desk. "I do believe I'm entitled to some privacy here, unless you're arresting me for something. For having a great-great-uncle in a looney bin, perhaps?"

Somehow, Morrison thought, he would get ahold of those papers he'd heard about. With or without Jade Whitman's body, they would probably be sufficient to put this crazy bitch away for good. "Excuse me, didn't mean to be too nosy, but I can't help it, I'm a cop."

Maybe tomorrow, Monday, he could have a talk with Judge Rivers and explain things. Rivers was a personal friend, and he might issue a search and seizure warrant without his having to produce the standard probable-cause evidence.

He checked the other two bedrooms and found nothing—not that he'd expected to. In the hallway again he looked up at the attic door. "Guess I'd better check in the attic, so I can tell Mr. Whitman I looked everywhere."

The blood! Valerie hadn't remembered to clean it up. The phone call had distracted her, then the business with that damn doll . . . but the blood should be dark by now. The attic was hot, maybe the blood was already black . . . it could be any sort of stain, actually. Tar, maybe. Valerie unwrapped the cord and pulled the ladder down for him. "Be my guest."

This time she didn't follow him. There was no point, really, because the doll couldn't have gotten up there, for sure. And if he saw the blood and knew what it was, it wouldn't matter if she was standing there or not. There would be nothing she could do short of killing him too, if she could, and even so, that would only make matters worse. Morrison would not have come over here without making sure someone else knew. So if he saw the blood, he would bend down right in front of her and scrape some off into a little plastic bag, and go have it analyzed, comparing the type with Jade's. And when it matched, what then? All that meant, she would explain, was that Jade had accidentally cut herself while snooping around in the attic, cut herself very badly, it looked like. She did remember a bandage on Jade's foot, now that she thought about it. At least she'd thought to wipe the letter opener clean on Jade's pants and put it back in the sewing basket, down in the bottom. Morrison wouldn't waste his time looking all around the attic for the murder weapon, would he? Through all that junk? No, more than likely, he would get his blood sample and pretend she was off the hook so she wouldn't worry about getting rid of anything. And when he got that blood report, he'd get a search warrant, quick as lightning, and come back to search at his leisure, probably with a whole team.

But she would get rid of the letter opener, damn sure would, and hide it where it would never be found. But she would wipe her fingerprints off anyway, just in case. So really, there was still nothing to worry about. It wasn't as if she had lied and said Jade had never been in the house.

Morrison reappeared a few minutes later and climbed back down. "Well, sorry I wasted so much of your time. I guess I've done my duty."

That didn't mean he hadn't seen the blood, collected some with a pocketknife and now had it in one of his pockets.

"No trouble at all." Valerie smiled. "I was pretty angry with Jade when I found out what she was doing, but I hope nothing bad happened to her."

Morrison put up the ladder and closed the attic door. "Never know. There were three escapes from the prison last night, pretty bad characters. If she ran into one of them, she could be in trouble."

Morrison knew Jade Whitman hadn't run into any convicts. What she'd run into was Valerie Scott. Jade would have been safer with the convicts.

"Oh, really? I hadn't heard about that."

"Well, it's not in the papers yet. It was just discovered this morning. You can probably catch the story on the radio, though. By the way, I noticed a bunch of newspapers on your neighbor's porch. You know if she's all right? Old people sometimes, if they're all alone, can die in their beds and no one knows about it for weeks, until someone starts noticing the smell."

Valerie looked toward the window on the lower landing, through which she could see the side of Mrs. Rothford's house. Jade had known what was going on over there, or what she thought was going on over there . . . had she mentioned anything about that to Steve? Not that it was anything for her to worry about. There was nothing over there for Morrison to find, not even a drop of blood. With Tamara there, probably listening, more than likely Jade would have talked as briefly as possible and said as little as possible, in case Tamara should repeat it to Valerie. Maybe Jade had talked in code, but there couldn't have been a previously planned code for "she's putting dead bodies in the house next door." Jade had planned to return to Savannah alive, where she would fill Steve in on all the nitty-gritty. Jade had said something about the papers, though, as curious as Morrison was about what was in her typewriter. Generalities. Saw some papers that would curl your hair.

"Mrs. Rothford knew she was nearing the end," Valerie sighed heavily, "so she went to stay with one of her sons in Tennessee. Guess she forgot to stop the paper. I'll take care of it."

Morrison didn't suppose she would be lying about that. If Valerie had done something to her neighbor, she wouldn't be stupid enough to let the newspapers pile up, begging for investigation. Not this one, not a mistake like that. "Well, too bad, but I guess we all have to go sometime. Good that she can be with family, seemed like a pretty sweet old lady."

"Yes, she was. I feel a little bad now, talking about what a motormouth she was."

Morrison grunted. Valerie Scott feel guilty about something? That would be the day. If not a paranoid schizophrenic, she was a complete sociopath . . . psychopath. He started down the steps, then stopped, looking up at her. "You busy tonight? I've got a bottle of wine at home in my refrigerator and no one to share it with."

The question startled her, but she quickly got the message. He wanted to get her drunk so maybe she would pass out and he could come upstairs and get her papers. Maybe she would even pretend to pass out, just so she could catch him in the act. That might be fun.

"That sounds wonderful. Tell you what, I'll even broil some steaks and we can make it a dinner date. Seven o'clock?"

The doll, the doll, where was it? Valerie had searched everywhere, from top to bottom, even the attic, but mainly there because she wanted to see if Morrison had collected a sample of the blood.

He had. The scrape marks were clearly visible.

Damn it all. But what the hell, he still would have

nothing without her papers. Valerie sat down at her desk and rolled in a new sheet.

Well Gavin, how do you like this little game Morrison is playing with us? Kind of fun, isn't it?

he is the one

What! Him! You've got to be kidding.

why not

Valerie cocked her head, a little smile creeping to her lips. Why not indeed? She wouldn't have to worry about a thing for sure, then. Gavin would be the detective. He would get that blood report back and toss it right in the trash. Any more calls from Steve Whitman and Gavin would tell him sorry, no sign of your sister yet, but I'm absolutely certain Valerie Scott had nothing whatsoever to do with her disappearance. Gavin could probably even invent a witness who had seen Jade at such and such place long after she had left Valerie's. It was perfect, actually. Gavin was a genius. He knew Morrison would be along because of Steve. And Morrison was the one man in Huntington, besides Jonathan, that Valerie knew. She should have guessed.

I suppose you'll have no trouble getting him off my back?

thats the point my love

All right, so I can stop worrying about all that. Where's the damn duchess doll, Gavin? I've looked in every nook and cranny. It's simply vanished.

i dont know but youd better find her

You're telling me! She wants to cut my damn throat with a razor blade! Damn it, I wish I'd burned it when I had the chance. I should have known. Damn that old bitch! She deserved everything I did to her. She did it all to me first.

burn the house

Burn the house? Are you crazy? Where would we live?

morrisons

Of course, Morrison's got a place. Hope it's not too small, but I guess with just the two of us, it doesn't need to be that big anyway. I do like a lot of space, though. And anyway, if we don't like it, we can always get another place we do like with the insurance money. And we'll have your salary and the rest of my inheritance. No need to worry about money at all. I can write while you're at work with no distractions. I've decided to hell with children's books, by the way. I want to write horror.

they say to write what you know

Oh yes, and what I could do is, instead of having to make stuff up, I could just write down what's been going on around here for the last several days, only everyone will think it's fiction.

there you go

Oh Gavin, I'm so happy. And did you hear that about the supposed escapes? They found their way into the prison. I'm so glad to know that, aren't you? Poor hungry things. I wish I could have done something for Vernon. Oh well. I guess I'd better run to the grocery store for those steaks. Until then.

until then my love

Morrison arrived promptly at seven with the wine, a red Chablis. Valerie had gone all out to fix herself up, even rolling her hair and putting on makeup. She had decided to wear the sexiest dress she owned, the form-fitting black dress she had bought for the high school reunion, the one that showed a bit of her cleavage.

Morrison whistled when she opened the door. "Don't you look gorgeous."

He was wearing the same suit he'd had on earlier, but he'd shaved and put on cologne and a fresh shirt. Valerie thought he looked very handsome. Though he was probably getting close to fifty, he still had a nice thick crop of black hair, much the color of her own, except for the gray at the sides, which made him look distinguished. Good build, no gut hanging over his belt. Very nice. Too bad he was there on false pretenses. Not that it really mattered. Gavin would straighten him out soon enough.

They ate the T-bones she had broiled, endive salads, and baked potatoes by candlelight in the kitchen, Morrison making small talk, working to gain her confidence. She offered only nods in return, thinking how the seduction would take place. Why fool around? He certainly wasn't going to tell her he wasn't in the mood. After dinner she would just come right out and ask like she had with Jonathan. This time she *wouldn't* be rejected. He was too intent on getting those papers, and he would stop at nothing to get them.

The moment finally came. Morrison (who insisted she call him by his first name, Alex) poured the last of the wine into their glasses and proposed a toast. "To the beautiful lady who has so graciously favored me with her company tonight. It was a great meal, Valerie, just wonderful. I'm no cook myself. I suppose someday I'll die from junk-food poisoning."

"Not for a long time, I hope." She smiled, raising her glass and clinking it against his. They both returned their glasses to their lips and drank.

Valerie was feeling pretty woozy. She was afraid she might pass out for real, and that could be fatal, with that doll still running around somewhere. But Gavin wouldn't let Grandmother get her. He would protect her.

The moment both their glasses sat empty on the table, she cleared her throat and said boldly, "I think we can probably get to know each other a lot better in the next room, Alex. If you know what I mean. It's been a long time."

Morrison wordlessly took her hand and led her into the dining room. On the bed where Grandmother had died, Valerie lay down, inviting Morrison with her ice-blue eyes. He moved over her and began nuzzling her throat, gently kneading her breasts through the fabric of her dress. Valerie made no sounds, felt no arousal, because she knew he wasn't Gavin yet. He wasn't doing the things that Gavin would do. He was doing the things a detective would do to get what he wanted, so he could put her away for life in an insane asylum.

Then suddenly Morrison grabbed a fistful of her hair and asked tauntingly, "Guess who?"

With effort, Valerie raised her heavy eyelids, her heart thrumming with excitement. "Gavin . . . ? Is it you?"

Morrison smiled. "What do you think, Valerie?"

"I think," she said airily, "that you're teasing me. It is you, isn't it, Gavin?" At last, she thought. Her mind swirled in drunken bliss.

Morrison's smile widened. "Yes, Valerie. It's me,

Gavin. Quite a time we've been having, huh?" He tightened the grip on her hair.

She winced slightly. "Yes, I'd say."

"We kidnapped Tamara, didn't we?"

"Well, I prefer to think of it as rescued."

"And we killed Jade Whitman."

"That lying bitch. She should have suffered more, but I was in a hurry, as you know. I think killing Doug was the most fun, don't you?"

Oh God, Morrison thought. His smile vanished. He rolled away from her and got up, feeling a little sick.

The day before, Jade had called her brother and told him that Valerie was, by her own admission, killing people to "feed" imaginary monsters, and according to some papers Jade had found, Valerie was afterward communicating with her victims on her typewriter. Valerie believed that one of them, Gavin, would take over Jonathan's body if she got him in bed.

After discovering that Jonathan was out of the picture, Morrison had come up with the idea of substituting himself. He'd been a bit skeptical about playing such a charade, having no idea the direction Valerie's lunacy might take, but here she was, spilling her guts because she thought he was Gavin now.

"Yes, killing Doug was a real blast, all right." He wondered if she was talking about Doug Chambers, her old boyfriend. But wasn't he in Savannah?

Looking dazed, Valerie propped herself up on an elbow. "Why . . . what are you doing? What about all those wild things you wrote about? We can do them now. It's just you and me."

"Sure, Valerie. But I'd better have a look at those papers to refresh my memory. Where did you put them?"

Compelled by the alcohol in her system, Valerie lay back down and closed her eyes, patting the space next to her. "Come back to bed, Gavin. You don't need to refresh your memory. You know what I want . . ." Her voice trailed off.

Morrison stared down at her with a mixture of abhorrence and fascination. After a few minutes, he was certain she had fallen asleep. Quietly as possible, he went through the double doors and headed upstairs for Valerie's bedroom.

Valerie's eyes jerked open. How long had she been asleep? She focused on her watch, deciding only ten or fifteen minutes had passed. Where the hell was Gavin?

She was about to call out for him when she heard a scratching noise on the other side of the single door. The duchess. She was in the kitchen.

Slowly, Valerie got up and cautiously inched toward the kitchen door. Holding her breath, she pushed it halfway open and peeked in.

No sign of the doll.

Again she heard the scratching noise. Now it was coming from the bathroom off the kitchen. If the duchess was in there, she was trapped. Valerie hurried across the kitchen floor, shut herself in the bathroom and snapped on the light.

Her mouth gaped as she looked around the tiled room. It was empty. She kicked at the bunched shower curtain even though it was transparent and she could see there was nothing behind it.

A second later she heard a faint scraping sound right behind her. Valerie slowly pivoted, her eyes trailing upward until they met their mirror images on the medicine cabinet.

For a few moments she stood very still, then with a cry of rage flung open the medicine cabinet door.

The duchess was perched on the lower shelf holding a single-edged razor blade in her lap. She hissed at Valerie, showing twin rows of wickedly sharp teeth. "Ready to die, bitch?"

Morrison bolted up from the chair, the papers he'd been reading scattering all over the floor. A second scream pierced the silence, followed by a third.

He bolted for the stairs, wondering what the hell was going on now.

Not finding Valerie in the dining room, he dashed through the side door. In the kitchen he noticed the strip of light under the bathroom door and decided to check there before heading outside.

The first thing his mind registered was the blood. It was squirted all over the tiles and shower curtain. The medicine cabinet door hung ajar, some of its contents spilled into the sink. Valerie lay writhing on the blood-smeared floor. Her throat had been slashed in three places, and there were several cuts on her arms and legs. All of the wounds were flowing profusely.

Morrison watched her for a few seconds, both shocked and puzzled. In her left hand she was holding a single-edged razor blade. Her right hand was clamped to the left hand's wrist in an apparent attempt to restrain it from inflicting more cuts.

"Gavin, help me," Valerie moaned weakly. "She's killing me."

Having read most of the papers in her folder, Morrison quickly came to a decision. He closed the lid on the toilet and sat down.

"Yes, Valerie, and she's doing a damn fine job of it, if you ask me."

WHAT'S WRONG WITH VALERIE?
was only the beginning!

Now the legacy of Valerie Scott's madness
continues as Tamara follows in
Valerie's demented footsteps.

If you enjoyed
WHAT'S WRONG WITH VALERIE?
then get ready for
WHAT'S WRONG WITH TAMARA?

To be published by Pocket Books
in Summer 1992!